GENESIS PRIME

Gary W. Babb

GENESIS PRIME

DOUBLE DRAGON

Prologue
Synopsis of Genesis Logs

Capt. Nick Johns, a wounded and quadriplegic U.S. Marine of the Iraq war, encounters assertive government officials, who, unbelievably, recall him to active duty to serve humanity. Spirited off to Area 51, he meets the president, where he learns Earth will face total destruction from a massive asteroid, but the government had secretly initiated the Genesis Project to save the human race from extinction. Shockingly, the president asks him to volunteer his brain to provide the spark-of-life to the shipboard computer and become the captain of the spaceship, Genesis, for a two hundred year deep-space flight to colonize a new habitable planet called New Earth.

With the unexpected death of the original brain donor, Capt. Johns escalates to the top slot on a carefully screened shortlist of potential donors, all quadriplegic with proven resistance to depression and demonstrated self-sacrificing values. The scientific team of experts and fellow voyagers scramble to make their launch window and hurriedly brief him on the major aspects of the project: the discovery of the asteroid, security of the top-secret project, use of alien technology, Light Wave Drive, location of the target planet and planned astrological route, brain interface and extension, etc.

The briefings were comforting and informative but not actually required. Once he reluctantly agrees, the doctors extract his brain and install it into the core of the human brain cell computer, where his mind extends into the computer, and the Genesis becomes his new body. He remains Capt. Nick Johns, but he also becomes the Genesis. His intellect expands exponentially, and he knows everything...all the scientists' research, background of the project, and all stored knowledge of the human race.

Too soon, the world discovers the imminent doom and plunges into chaos, resulting in total anarchy and global nuclear war. Fortunately, the Genesis launches seconds ahead of an Al Qaeda nuclear attack designed to prevent the salvation of the human race. Genesis rendezvous in orbit with the only other surviving escape vessel, The Hope, a much less sophisticated project developed by the Japanese. The Genesis takes control of the Hope and launches into deep-space towing the Hope with an umbilical attachment, where they witness the asteroid's impact and destruction of Earth.

Nick's intellect mushrooms during the voyage, driving him to the point of insanity. He finds emotional release through a developing friendship and, ultimately, unexpected love between himself and the beautiful Akiko, the director of life support. Capt. Johns devises a plan to escape his cerebral prison and physically be with Akiko by cloning his DNA and, through his heightened intellect, telepathically live through this clone body. Akiko volunteers to host the clone embryo to term, but her body begins to reject the infant, forcing it to be taken early. Unfortunately for her, Akiko refuses to allow the infant to be taken until her body has been severely damaged. The infant, Nick, survives, but

Akiko's body hovers near death and must be placed into cryogenic hibernation, while he works on a way to cure her and bring her back to him.

Genesis reaches Alpha Centauri, the first of six planned jumps in the long journey, to discover an alien race known as The Enlightened. The aliens are far more advanced and will not allow humans to settle. The aliens instantly transport the Genesis forty light years to the second planned hop, Trianguli Australis. From here the Genesis resumes its original journey.

At the young age of three, Katy comes into his life. Katy, the accidental daughter of his doctor and the Genesis' engineer, comes into the control room and begins visiting with Nick's holographic image and wins his heart. With the loneliness of command and the loss of Akiko, he quickly accepts this new friend. Katy and his clone are about the same age and the only children on board. Nick begins living through his cloned body, playing and eventually grows up with Katy. After years of being constantly together, they fall in love and become lovers, yet he still loves Akiko. Both accept this fact.

Nick discovers that Akiko's replacement over life support has virtually destroyed the on board ecosystem she designed and created. In his anger, Nick forgoes his adult and authoritative holographic image and fires the acting director using his cloned physical body, learning a valuable lesson... command is a state of mind, not a physical domination.

One of the Hope's engineers and closet Islam extremist becomes a constant nemesis to Nick's authority and secretly organizes a mutiny. Like the extremists of Earth, he schemes to sabotage what he perceived to be an escape from Allah's destruction of the human race. When the armed terrorists take command of the control room, Nick flares the lights, temporarily blinding them long enough for his team to kill the mutineers.

Through the scientists and doctors, Nick continues to work toward bringing Akiko back to full health. Together they conduct stem cell research and develop an Immortality Gene, which miraculously brings Akiko back to healthy life...an immortal life.

Love always finds a way to survive. The assertive little Katy will not be denied. When Akiko shows signs of reviving, Katy decides to go into cryogenic storage, charging Nick with the task of convincing Akiko to accept a menage a trois. This turns out to be easier than he thought possible, and they eventually become a threesome.

Mid-journey the entire Genesis Project almost collapses in failure when one of Nick's artificial hearts fail. Through quick response of the emergency team, they narrowly avert the disaster, but this launches the team into converting the artificial organs to modular human organs.

Most of the department heads had taken the Immortality Gene (IM). At thirty years old, it became Katy and Nick's turn to take the gene. Unfortunately, of all those that took the IM gene, only the inventor's body, Cdr. Taka, rejected the gene. Katy's body became the second to reject the gene. These two were destined to eventually die of old age...the only ones. Nick and Akiko would not accept losing Katy to old age, while they lived immortal lives. Nick and the scientists develop a plan to slightly modify the DNA and clone Katy and Taka so the altered bodies would accept the IM. They also invented a brain interface that would slowly copy their memories and essence into the clones. This effectively creates new versions of the same people. One version dies of old age, while the immortal clones live on with all the memories of their donor.

A black hole is discovered in the last leg of the journey, threatening also to doom the project. The crew applies extraordinary effort to deviate their course to by-pass its gravitational pull. Nick is required to make some hard decisions and sacrifices many sleeping souls in cryogenic storage to save the Genesis, thus alienating himself from the crew. He realizes this is why he was chosen…to command!

They avert the Black Hole and survive, but regrettably, the course modification takes the Genesis beyond its ability to correct and dooms the project to failure. Science having failed to save them, they turn to Divine Intervention and bring the Chaplin out of cryogenics to lead them in this effort. They begin praying and are miraculously transported to their final destination by The Enlightened, leaving the reader to decide if it was Divine or alien intervention.

The story ends with the Genesis and Hope in orbit around Genesis Prime planning the colonization of their new home on Mount Olympus, the home of the Immortals. This, of course, will be the sequel.

CHAPTER 1
(Introduction)

Private Log of Captain Nick Johns

If I have learned anything from my over 300 years of life, it is the absolute certainty that humans cannot be trusted to govern themselves. Humans by their very nature are self-destructive, and given enough time they will destroy themselves. I wish I had known that when President McIntosh had asked me to serve him, humanity, and as he put it: "Hell, Nick I'm asking you to serve the world and keep humanity alive." I'm still mad at him for asking me to commit to serving humanity and keeping it alive. Amazing, since he has been dead for over 270 years; he died along with the rest of humanity when Earth died.

I should have realized this was an impossible task when humanity turned upon itself and destroyed all life on Earth, even before the asteroid exploded the already dead planet. I should have remembered Humanity's history as filled with never ending wars. Hell, I was even a Marine in one of those wars. Who was right, and who was wrong? It doesn't matter; humans look for an excuse to war, and people died. That very fact should have told me that humans are destined to have strife and war. Maybe the radicalized Muslims were right and it was Allah's will that no humans escape destruction. They said the asteroid was sent to destroy the wicked and the Genesis Project was an abomination.

I should have realized this was an impossible task when we had an attempted mutiny on board Genesis en route to our new home on Genesis Prime, and we only had less than 75 people on the awake team. I couldn't even prevent it. Well, I did prevent the mutiny; I killed them. But, the fact that conflict between humans, even with a small population, is inevitable; it's human nature.

I should have realized this was an impossible task when we met the highly evolved aliens, The Enlightened. They tried to tell me that our species couldn't interface with them because of the destructive emotions humans demonstrated such as lust, pride, greed, conceit, vanity, jealousy, covetousness, etc. They transported us 40 light years away from them before we could corrupt their minds. I should have listened more carefully.

I should have realized this was an impossible task when I was assassinated. That certainly surprised me, but I dare say it surprised the plotters and assassins even more to discover that I had a spare body for just such an event.

I really don't want to sound so cynical. Of course there are good humans that control their emotions and are kind, caring, benevolent, and work for the common good of all; but they tend not to defend themselves and become followers, letting others lead. Unfortunately, the bad ones seem to float to the top and influence the sheep followers. I have learned from my mistakes and will never allow this to happen again, and I have the power. Some think of me and refer to me as a god, and many even

11

call me Zeus. Certainly I have many god-like powers, immortality being only one of them.

Me and my staff created the immortality gene (IG) to restore and save Akiko. I would have done anything to save her. We have since injected this IG treatment into the awake team staff and some of the more key personnel necessary for survival on Genesis Prime. I have since decided to provide this option sparingly. Immortality in some could become a burden to my command in later years; immortal years are forever. No, I have decided to bestow immortality only to those loyal to me and have proven themselves dedicated to the common good of all. I certainly don't need any immortal psychopaths or self-centered narcissists to deal with over time.

I believe I am one of the good ones, and I think I have shown this to be the case over and over. As Marine Captain Nick Johns I sacrificed myself to save my men and was rewarded with a life as a quadriplegic; as Captain of the Genesis I saved the lives of all on board numerous times; and I have kept the Genesis Plan and humanity alive. None of this means anything though, because it doesn't really matter if I'm one of the good ones or not; good or bad I carry the responsibility, thanks to the president talking me into assuming the control and salvation of the human race. I committed myself to this task, and now I have no choice. I will save the human race, even from itself, even if I have to kill some of them to do it. I am no longer interested in saving or even trying to work with psychopaths or bearers of evil. No, I am only interested in working with those that promote the common good, and to do that they must serve me...at least follow my instructions and rules.

My children have asked to read my logs. This is why I am reviewing them to see if anything should be skipped, but I have nothing to hide. Most of it is, however, boring, since so many uneventful years are documented; therefore I am skimming over the logs and eliminating much of the useless or redundant entries. The file for publication will be this reduced and rendered version.

Introduction to the Public Genesis Prime Logs

To those of you awakening that went into cryogenics before leaving Earth, an unbelievably lot has happened since we launched, and the good news is that you survived! Some did not, but you did.

As predicted, the Earth was destroyed by an asteroid a few days after launching, and we are the only survivors of Earth. Earth may have died, but we brought all the history and knowledge of the human race with us. This knowledge and history still lives through us.

We were joined in orbit by another escape ship, Hope, from Japan. They came under our protection and authority and are welcome members of our new society.

The biggest shock will be discovering that a minimum of 132 years have passed, and we have arrived at New Earth, which has been renamed Genesis Prime. Let me put 132 years into perspective in this way. Doctor Rossen and Linda Clark, two of the major designers of Genesis, had a child on board ship. This girl, Katherine (Katy), grew to adulthood aboard Genesis, was educated with numerous doctorate degrees, had a full 50 year career organizing and planning the colonization of Genesis Prime, and eventually she died of old age at the advanced age of 123. Does this put 132 years into perspective?

Now before you become confused, there is a Katy now in charge of the colonization on Genesis Prime. She is a complete doppelganger clone of this original Katy, both mind (memories) and body. She was simply too important to our survival on Genesis Prime to lose. Dr. Rossen, Dr. Taka, and myself made this happen.

We launched from Area 51 on July 8, 2015, but only minutes before a terrorist atomic bomb exploded. Minutes before this happened we worried about a last minute worker's revolt, not unlike everyone wanting to get on the last lifeboat of a sinking ship, but we were saved from this by an impromptu address from President McIntosh. After hearing it I vowed to immortalize his last words.

This happened over 132 years ago, but I remember it vividly as if it happened yesterday. President McIntosh stood outside on the ramp of Air Force One and pointed toward the ship for emphasis and said, "Genesis, we who are about to die salute you! You carry with you our future, our hopes and dreams…all that we are and have ever been. We gave you life, and you are our child, and we sacrifice our lives so our child might live. As long as you live we will live in your memory. Like Genesis of the Bible, in the beginning…this is our new beginning. May God bless this new beginning."

"I am not leaving. I will stand with you and defend our child!" He stood tall and erect and full of defiance. The crowd began to cheer, and I cheered with them.

You might also be interested in knowing that we are not alone in the universe. We even used alien technology in the construction of Genesis, and without it we would not have survived the long, arduous voyage. The government kept the knowledge of aliens a secret, but there is obviously no reason to keep this a secret now.

During the long voyage we met another race of highly evolved aliens, The Enlightened. I won't say they were particularly friendly, but they did help us along the way and cut 40 light years off our scheduled trip. They again helped us during the final leg of our trip. Without their assistance we would have surely failed. Some will say it was Divine Intervention, and it may well have been. Either way, we are here now.

If you want to know more about the voyage, a reduced copy of the "Genesis Logs" is available for you to read and study detailing the entire voyage.

As you rejoin the living there are a few things you need to know. The colonization of Genesis Prime will be governed under military control, and I, Admiral Nick Johns, am the supreme authority. I am in command, and you will follow my rules. My second in command is Capt. McCullah, which you may remember as Major General McCullah. All Genesis citizens will fall under a department head (Cdr.). The rest you will learn as we go along.

CHAPTER 2
(Orbital Survey of Genesis Prime)

Genesis Prime Log: 12 Feb 0001

Our last log entry in the Genesis Logs was dated 11 Feb. 2147, but we decided to start a new dating system to completely separate our journey on Genesis from our colonization on Genesis Prime. Since we arrived at our new home planet of Genesis Prime we wanted to start fresh, starting at year 0001. Everything now would be a new experience from this point.

Since so many new faces, awake from cryonics, were at the last staff meeting, I decided to conduct this meeting in a more formal setting. These newly awake would, of course, be the department heads choice picks for their other key positions, but for the most part would have absolutely no idea who I was or most of my key staff and department heads. They had been given my brochure and maybe a little indoctrination from their department head but very little more.

The main staff members were gathered around my dome housing in the open Control Room, where we usually met. The large open upper dome area surrounding the central control area was filled with attendees. For maximum effect I adjusted the entire dome area of Wonder Metal to transparency, allowing a spectacular view of Genesis Prime to provide the backdrop.

There were many gasps when Genesis Prime became visible, filling the view out of the clear dome. Afterwards the audience fell into total awed silence. Genesis Prime was very much like Earth with vast blue oceans, and five large land masses. White clouds floated and swirled on the planet surface in various stages of weather conditions. It was easy to see areas of dense, green, tropical forest along the equator and also some arid deserts on some of the continents. All and all, it was a very impressive display that required few words.

I flared my holographic image to life at twice my normal size. Actually, I did it for effect and enjoyed the reaction. I then waited for the audience to settle and spoke, "Hello ladies and gentlemen. I am Admiral Nick Johns commanding this successful expedition... so far. I am also this young man sitting in the front row." I stood up in my body and waved to the crowd. "In time you will understand, but for now accept it as fact."

"I won't bore you with any details of our long voyage to get here and the hardships. This information is available through numerous sources, and it will be up to you to find them. What we will be concentrating on is what you see out the dome. This is our new home, Genesis Prime, and you are awake because we will be landing soon and you have been chosen for specific functions and tasks by your department heads, which I will introduce shortly."

"I'm sorry for the confined quarters, but Genesis was never designed to support this many awake personal. You won't have to endure the crowding much longer, but I can assure you that it will be even worse once we land, but improving your living conditions is your responsibility to correct. Again, your department heads will assign your job function."

"The red-headed man in the distinguished red blazer in the front row you may remember as Major General McCullah. He was in charge of the Genesis Project on Earth, and since we are here, he did an exceptional job. He is my second in command with the rank of captain. His title is First Officer and speaks with my authority. He is also head of Security and is in charge of keeping you alive." First Officer McCullah stood and also waved at the crowd."

"The lady sitting next to him is Cdr. Katherine Lynn Clark, and she is managing the colonization on Genesis Prime." Katy stood so the crowd could see her. "She coordinates the department heads as it pertains to anything relating to our activities on ground after we land. She is the go-to girl on Genesis Prime and answers only to First Officer McCullah and myself. Cdr. Clark is highly educated and has more doctorate degrees than we have time to list. Suffice to know, she is well educated in many fields and can answer your questions. She has spent over 50 years organizing this colonization plan, which she will soon begin to unfold for you. You would be wise to listen to her and follow her suggestions, instructions and orders."

"Cdr. Akiko Mitsuhara has been in charge of Life Support on board Genesis and has kept us all alive. She will be responsible for food production for our colony, among other responsibilities, which will become obvious as we go along. Take a bow, Akiko." Akiko also stood and waved.

"Cdr. John Rossen, Doc, wears multiple hats and responsibilities, but he will head up the medical facilities, with his assistant from the Hope, Cdr. Takashi Ishiguro. Gentlemen stand up."

"Cdr. Linda Clark is in charge of engineering and construction with assistance from Hiroshi Tsuji of the Hope. This is a big job and will encompass much effort and time. Linda, Hiroshi, stand please."

"Cdr. Hyung Rae Kim is our astronomer and astrophysicist and has the honor of having named Genesis Prime. Humm, since we are already here Kim is out of a job. I guess we may have to get him to help Cdr. Clark." The staff burst out laughing, even Kim and many in the audience that had only a vague idea what I was talking about.

"These officers are department heads and my key staff, and I wanted you to meet them. In the future there will be others as needs dictates. I see Lt. Bill Boland of Engineering, Lt. Naomi Sami of Life Support, and the big man there is SgtMaj Andy Gomez of Security. There are many more you will meet in time." As I introduced them they stood, holding an arm in the air to be noticed.

"Cdr. Katy Clark will present a general overview of the planet and our plans for colonization, but due to the lateness of the cycle I think we better wait until tomorrow. Plus, we have some other tasks to attend to first, namely the assignment of everyone to a department head. I will forfeit the floor and allow each department head to organize you into groups for additional instructions.

The last thing I want to do is welcome you back to the human race, what remains of us. It is up to us to restore the human race and keep alive the dreams and aspirations of all those that lived before us and are now dead."

I let my holographic image vaporize, ending the initial formal introduction and instructions to those newly awaken. I continued to observe the crowd through my visual centers. They looked scared with wide-eyes, but I could hardly blame them. Much had happened since they had gone into cryogenics. Billions of humans and Earth itself were still alive when they went to sleep. Now they awake in a new century with a bunch of strangers and realize that everything had changed. In retrospect these volunteers probably should have received more counseling prior to entering cryogenics. Oh well, it's too late now.

While I continued to observe, each department head went to the podium and read off a list of names, claiming them within their department. They also scheduled a time and place for their group to meet, where they would provide more information and instruction. The larger groups scheduled the control room, which would take several cycles.

The general went first and his list was a short one. First Officer McCullah had always been General or Mac to me in informal communications. Actually, the general had no list at all. He had awakened all one hundred of his Marines and they already knew where they belonged, because he had personally recruited them.

The other department heads had not been so lucky. They, of course, had their recruited staff, but they had been limited because of available chronic chambers, which the bureaucrats had insisted on filling randomly, apparently, since many had no training or purpose During our near catastrophe with the black hole I was forced to forfeit 1150 chambers including the souls occupying them. As unfortunate as it was losing 1150 souls, I screened each occupant's bio and prioritized them, eliminating some of the bureaucratic mistakes. I chose to keep trade skills such as construction workers, brick layers, mechanics, farmers, etc. over politicians, lawyers, the elderly, professionally unemployed, and those that were rich and had obviously bought their way on board. I tried to keep all the skilled labor and those that could contribute to the common good of all in a new colony. So, I guess what I'm saying is that I tried to increase our odds of survival, certainly through the first few years.

Genesis Prime Log: 13 Feb 0001

In our quarters before our next gathering, Akiko and Katy were at odds with each other, which hardly never happens. Katy wanted to orbit a few more days to gather more data about Genesis Prime, but Akiko voiced her concern about feeding this many people.

Akiko said, "We have got to get all these awake people on the surface. Our life support can't handle this many people. We will crash our sewer system, water treatment, oxygen delivery. We are already tapping into our backup oxygen supply. Nick, our whole ecological system will fail, not to mention the amount of food we are going through. We have to find native food and get crops in the ground if we are going to eat next year."

I had to take sides with Akiko on this issue, but I could appreciate Katy's concerns. So, I said, "Two, we have to respect Akiko's concerns. They are serious. But, we can talk to Kim and Linda about launching an observation satellite so you can continue your research." I cheated because I already knew Kim had plans to launch three orbiting satellites. "Will that work?" I guess it worked, since they both gave me a hug and we went off to the early cycle meeting, where Two was scheduled to give a presentation.

I often call Katy Two, especially in private, as do most of the staff that watched her grow up. I still remember the first time I saw her as a fiery little red-head of three years old. She announced her name was Katherine Lynn Clark (Katy). This Katy we call Two is the exact clone of the original in memories and body, thus the nickname Two. She is in essence the same Katy.

Two was by no means nervous with the large group, quite the contrary. She seemed to enjoy the attention and took the podium like she owned it and began, "For all the new attendees, I am Cdr. Katherine Clark, and I manage the colonization on Genesis Prime. After several days of orbiting and studying Genesis Prime by all the department heads, I have consolidated the data and am now ready to give an initial report. I wanted to remain in orbit for a few more day and study the planet in more detail, but Cdr. Mitsuhara informs me that with so many awake we are over stressing the ecosystem, so we must land soon." Two winked at Akiko. "As most of you know, we learned about this planet and its location from retrieved alien files, which obviously were correct. Cdr. Tsuji deciphered more of the files en route. From these files we learned more about Genesis Prime and the aliens. We now know the elusive aliens who visited Earth also visited here, and thanks to the decrypted files we now know why. The aliens were mining ores, apparently rare in the universe, but found in sufficient quantities on Earth and Genesis Prime."

"You may wonder why I am giving you a history lesson when I am supposed to be talking about colonization. Well, these aliens may still be mining Genesis Prime, which makes Genesis Prime a potential hostile planet and significant to our colonization. The second reason may shock you. The aliens relocated humans from Earth, apparently for slave labor to mine these ores."

"So, any significant indigenous life here should be human, which has been confirmed from our orbit observations. We have not identified any other forms of intelligent life that could be alien. This does not mean they are gone, only that we can't detect them. The alien files tell us that the Earth humans were transported here from the 3rd Century BC, and from observation of the planet we see no signs of advanced technology to indicate they have advanced much beyond that time in Earth history. The unanswered questions is 'Why not'? But, due to their apparent lack of advancement, they will most likely be somewhat primitive and frightened of us, which could also pose a potential danger. We don't know what kind of relationship these humans had or may still have with the aliens and in either case would probably consider us the alien invaders on their world. That is the potential danger and reason for the location of our landing and initial colonization site."

"We have identified the native population centers, which are surprisingly few and scattered, and we have chosen an easily defended location distant from these native human populations."

"As you observe Genesis Prime through the dome you can easily identify the five major continents, and if you look toward the center of the three continents now facing us you will see a land mass in the center between them. This is our chosen location to land and colonize."

The land mass was not really large enough to qualify as a continent, more like a large island. I was trying to get some perspective on the size of the Island, and in Earth's perspective it would be approximately the size of Oklahoma without the handle.

Katy moved to the console and hit a few buttons and the outside dome changed from transparent then to an opaque before a large portion became a video monitor, complete with an outside camera view of Genesis Prime. She began zooming in on the island, which slowly began to fill the monitor section. As the zooming continued, the audience could see dense tropical forests covering over half of the southern end, along with steep rugged mountains cutting the island in half east to west. Toward the northern end of the island, the terrain changed to rolling hills and open plains broken up by spatterings of dense forests. The picture enlarged on a section of the northern coastline with tall hills surrounding a large naturally protected harbor being fed by a large river.

Directing attention to the map with a red laser pointer, Katy continued, "According to First Officer McCullah, this natural harbor and surrounding mountains provides a perfect defensible location for our settlement. The harbor can support our future shipping to outlaying colonies, fishing and industrial activities. Here on this tallest rise," she paused, again pointing with the laser, "is where we propose to land the Genesis. We call this Mount Olympus, since if discovered by the indigenous humans we will surely be considered gods." She stopped, smiling, while the laughter exploded.

Before waking the new attendees from sleep I had cautioned the staff not to say anything about the Immortality Gene. Getting the gene was not going to be an automatic entitlement; it was going to have to be earned. Katy had remembered and didn't mention that we had named Mount Olympus, because it would be the home of the immortals.

Katy continued, "From this vantage point, we can defend the settlement spread out on both sides of the mountain below and also the harbor. The ship's laser on the top of Genesis can defend against anything approaching from ground, sea or air."

"In addition to the shipboard laser, we propose to move the second laser to a permanent location, here, adjacent to the Genesis's location."

The laser mounted on the bottom deck would have been useless once the Genesis landed. Linda and the general had come to me with that recommendation, and I readily agreed.

"We also propose to use some of the spare parts we have aboard to build a third nuclear power plant deep inside caves in the mountain. If there are no caves, we will build them. Initially the plan calls for tying into the Genesis' power plant. It is large enough to supply electrical power to a city much larger than we will have for many years. The Genesis has never used more than a tenth of the available potential from one plant, and I might mention that we have two power plants on board Genesis."

"We can thank the aliens for identifying the locations of mineral deposits on the planets. Many are on the larger land masses but accessible for mining. This is where the shipping comes into play. Our harbor is ideal for receiving ore from ships that we will construct. The good news is that there is an abundant supply of minerals on Genesis Prime to make Wonder Metal for much of our construction. Initially, however, much of our construction will be made from stone from quarries here (pointing). Lasers should work well to cut the stone, which we already designed and built en route."

Katy superimposed a layout of the complete settlement over the video on the monitor, complete with docks, buildings of all kinds, defense walls, gates on both sides, fields, factories, utility distribution, etc. There were multiple levels and a complex system of roads, stairs, and railways interconnecting them. Ironically, virtually all roads eventually led to Genesis on Mount Olympus. I could see the vast work in the planning. The buildings were labeled, and I could clearly see military barracks, housing, sewage plant, water treatment plant, refineries, a hospital, a community center, a large cafeteria, motor pool, church and even a cemetery. It was a totally well-thought-out design of a complete operational city. I knew she had thought of everything. I was impressed.

Katy did not go into a question segment and went directly into her closing comments. "I will leave the plan on the monitor so you can study it with your various department heads. We will be landing ASAP, so I suggest you use what time you have available to learn about your new environment while you can. It will be tough on the surface for a while, and I'm talking about tents, MREs, latrines, no electricity, and danger. Be ready to suck it up. The good news is that the climate is tropical, so no freezing."

Before breaking up, Linda asked one final question, "Do you have a name for the island?"

"I was reserving naming it to solicit suggestions," said Katy.

"Good." Linda said, "Might I suggest Atlantis?"

There was no necessity to wait for other suggestions, everyone loved the name.

CHAPTER 3
(Landing on Atlantis)

Genesis Prime Log: 15 Feb 0001

While my body slept in my quarters, my mind followed the activities of Kim and Linda and their teams as they readied the three satellites, loaded them in the shuttle, then deployed them as the Genesis made a complete orbit of Genesis Prime. By early in the cycle they had all been activated, deployed, and checked out and verified long before our scheduled early cycle meeting. They had worked through the late and early cycle to accomplish this, but there would be no sleep for them this cycle.

The deployment was complicated. Kim wanted the satellites in a geostationary orbit, which required precise placement to obtain. The shuttle, powered by magnet drive and gas jets, had to deploy from the Genesis and rise to the verified exact elevation above Genesis Prime required to maintain the stationary orbit, then the satellite was released. The time factor was critical, since they then had to rush to catch up with the Genesis. The longer it took to deploy, the harder they had to work to catch up, but everything went well.

Today we would land, and both of them were required at the controls. I could have accomplished the landing maneuvers myself, but this was their responsibility and privilege. I would only get involved in an emergency, like I had when launching from Earth.

Once my staff had situated themselves in their customary positions I flared my holographic image to life. I chose this method again for the benefit of all the extras also gathered. I'm sure my staff realized this fact and approved of my methods.

When I had everyone's attention I said, "We are at the end of our journey and ready to launch into another. We are approaching our re-entry time window. Is everyone ready to make the landing?" I waited as my staff all acknowledged readiness, including Taka and Hiroshi responding via the intercom from the Hope. "Very well, commence landing."

Kim, Linda, Dr. Rossen, and several technicians swiveled their chairs 180 degrees to face the curved console of instruments and monitors to begin the re-entry for landing. As we passed into the atmosphere the dome monitor switched to camera feeds, and all were able to see the expanding planet surface clearly.

Once we were into the lower atmosphere, Linda coordinated and triggered the magnet release on the Hope to allow it to descend and land under its own power. We could see the flames from Hope's thrusters biting into the air to slow its descent. We had discussed letting the Genesis land the Hope, but decided against it due to the fact that the Hope was attached to the Genesis at a right angle, and we worried that the unbalanced weight might pose a problem to both vessels. In the end we decided not to take a chance. Theirs would be a more difficult landing, since they didn't have gravity drive and maneuverability, but they were prepared.

As we continued our descent, Atlantis soon filled the video image, and it continued to expand. Soon we were hovering stationary above our landing sight, with only feet to go. Katy requested some slight adjustments to position the Genesis centered on the top of the mountain, Mount Olympus. The video image very slowly watched the descent until we all felt a slight jar as we touched down. We felt slightly uneven for a few seconds until the self-leveling landing struts again righted us.

Cdr. Kim announced, "We have landed! Welcome to Genesis Prime!"

Cheers rang out throughout the upper dome and continued for long minutes. It seemed strange to realize that we had finally arrived and the journey was finely over after 132 years, and we had survived. I said to myself, "Damn you Mr. President. Are you satisfied now?"

Dr. Rossen announced, "The outside atmosphere consists of 77% Nitrogen, 22% Oxygen, 1% Argon, .04% Carbon Dioxide, and traces of Neon, Helium, and Methane; in another word, AIR! It's also 78 degrees. We can live in this!"

Cheers rang out again, but they were short lived as we all turned to watch the rumbling, fiery descent of the Hope. Their descent slowed and they settled down to the ground with sighs from all of us. They did not land exactly where they were supposed to but close enough. We would just have to change some of the roads.

Katy took the podium and turned to look at my holograph image and said, "Give us the order, Admiral."

Katy was making this formal, and I wanted to kiss her for it. Then I smiled, knowing that I would later in my body form. I then said, "Disembark and execute Colonization Phase 1. You have control."

Katy winked, then turned to the audience and said, "Okay citizens, you have all been given assignment, and you know what to do. Let's do it!"

They indeed knew what to do and began doing it, moving in unison toward the air-seal elevators. Even though the air checked out perfectly, Dr. Rossen insisted that we maintain the air-lock on all the upper ten levels ... just in case. The bottom two levels housed the heavy equipment and much of the storage, so this wouldn't be much of an inconvenience, except for the delays of the elevators recycling the air.

Those few of us remaining in the Control Room watched the exodus of people and equipment flooding out the bottom ramp. I'm sure the shock of being outside in the open was disconcerting, however there was only a slight pause in the movement. They continued looking around wide-eyed, but they knew their task. They also knew time was short and got to it.

The general disembarked his Marines first, and some deployed in all direction, establishing a defense perimeter around the Genesis, but most could be seen working their way down the slope of the mountain toward the camp site to be planned along the river leading into the bay. No one expected danger, but the plan erred on the side of caution. I wished I was with them.

We then watched as a bulldozer began carving out a zig zag road down to the river. As the dozer carved out a section of the road it was immediately filled with trucks, backhoes, and other equipment. The precession of equipment and people moved slowly down the slope toward the camp that was still bare.

The one good thing is that nightfall would not come. For at least half the year the second sun, although a great distance away, would still fill the night cycle of our sun (Genesis) with enough light to keep working. We were lucky that our landing time was in the peak of the no night cycle. Katy had said since they had full cycle sunshine she would work them till they dropped, at least the first cycle. I guess it would just be Akiko and me tonight.

Genesis Prime Log: 16 Feb 0001

There was no point having a staff meeting today. Most were in the camp seeing to the needs. I had watched the activities throughout the daylight and semi-night cycles, and it looked like an ant hill of activities. The activity had slowed to a virtual stop about an hour ago, but they had accomplished a lot. There now existed a virtual tent city, but many had fallen exhausted in their tent. Katy must be one of them, since she never returned to our quarters, even by early cycle. I did, however, see Linda.

I could see Linda just downhill from the Genesis barking orders to her engineering crew as they slowly raised the umbilical tank used to tie the

Genesis to the Hope. They were placing it on a platform made of Wonder Metal, apparently constructed in place. As I watched, it fell into place vertically on the platform. It was originally constructed as a water tower during construction of the Genesis. My assumption was that she was again going to use it as a water tower for the settlement. It made sense.

Akiko interrupted my thoughts when she said, "Nick, Lt. Sami and I are going to explore to see if we can find food stock."

"Alright, but take a couple of Marines with you or maybe even Mac. The general might like to look around, too." Then after second thought I said, "You want some company?" That sounded like fun, and I wanted to get out of the ship after 132 years.

Dr. Rossen said, "That's not a good idea just yet. I don't really know how far away from your brain dome you can get and still communicate. We will have to do some experimenting first."

Damn, he was right. I'm so used to living through my human body that I hadn't considered that. "OK, Doc. I can wait. Have fun girls."

After the girls left I was alone in the Control Room, and began watching the activities below. The Hope was perched on its rear struts/wings on the flat ground in the middle of the settlement, and I noticed its crew had joined in on some of Katy's projects and were hard at work. Others of the Hope's crew were working on the larger rocks and boulders, cutting them into building blocks with lasers.

The Hope had not been designed to handle much heavy equipment due to the excessive weight, but they had unloaded what they had and were hard at work moving and stacking the large stone blocks along the staked out fence location following the river. Others proceeded this group with lasers, slicing, filling in, and leveling the granite bedrock for the blocks. It was moving along quite nicely. The fence was going to be very long to encompass the settlement with large gates and sentry towers, so it would take a while.

Genesis Prime Log: 29 Feb 0001

We had our first staff meeting since landing this early cycle, and it was very informative. Of course, I had been following the activities of the crews all 29 hours of the cycles, and indeed, they had accomplished much, especially since the remaining people in cryonics were awakened, processed, and joined the work force.

I saw no real need to switch back to the "Day" standard of Earth. Using the word morning had little meaning, since there wasn't a real night, not at this time of year anyway.

Unfortunately it started out badly when Dr. Rossen said, "I'm sad to report that we had our first fatality last cycle. I lady was clearing brush and was bitten by, I guess, a snake. It looked like a small snake with eight legs. The creature latched on with its teeth and wrapped its body around her arm but did the damage with fanged feet. The fangs sank deep and she was dead in about twenty seconds. It must have hurt like hell, but she didn't have to suffer long. We are burning the brush now so they don't have to reach inside it.

Akiko had been joined by Lt Sami, but Akiko did the talking. Akiko said, "The fields on the southern end of the settlement inside the stone fence have been cleared and cultivated. We will plant them with Earth seeds for our staple crops such as wheat, oats, barley, and the like. Most forms of vegetables will also be planted, but we will have to wait to see if the native soil and its microbes will nourish or kill them. Trees will also be planted. We have also been searching for native equivalent food sources. I'm sure there are some, but we haven't identified them for sure. I wish we could observe some of the indigenous humans to identify what crops they grow and animals they eat. They survived; so should we."

Dr. Rossen said, "We have some almost grown embryos of goats, cows, sheep, hogs, even some horses. Hopefully, they will survive on the native grasses."

"Great!" Akiko said, "We have pens ready for them. We are also about ready to transplant some chickens, turkeys, and other sampling of birds to readied pens.

"Linda, what about your area?" I asked.

"Well, we temporally tied into the Hope for electricity for the camp and, since we don't need to provide night lights, they are handling the load well. The distance from the Genesis to camp poses a problem, but trenching is in progress. We will use a common trench for electrical, communications, water, and sewer. Without the burden of extra people on the Genesis, the ship has reverted back to a self-contained ecosystem, but I have installed the water tower on this upper level to obtain water pressure for the settlement. When the trench is complete we will pump water from the river into the tower."

I asked, "Is the water safe?"

"Doc says it is almost pure H20, even in the bay. We will treat it some, just in case, but we are already using it right out of the river. It's still cold from the mountains, and it tastes good, just like spring water. We think it is cold enough to introduce trout, if it doesn't already have some."

I looked at Akiko and asked, "Does it have trout in it?"

She laughed and said, "You would ask that. I don't know. We haven't checked it out yet, but I guess we will, now."

After a moment of laughter of the staff, Linda continued, "We are almost ready to start on some of the buildings as soon as we have a transportation road to the quarry."

I Interrupted, "Linda, Katy, there is something I have discovered that suggests we take a different direction, at least initially. I might as well bring it up now. Cdr. Kim and I discovered a few days back that there are Grays on Genesis Prime, and we must assume they will be hostile toward us. Grays are what the aliens were referred to back at Area 51."

At the mention of Grays and hostile the general sat straight up in his chair. He said nothing but gave me his full attention. "Sorry you guys, especially you Mac, but all of you were so busy and there was nothing you could do. I tell you now because the settlement is up and running, well, sort of."

"I don't think they are aware of us as of yet, but it is only a matter of time before they do. I think we have some time to prepare. We discovered them while monitoring the human settlements via the satellites. Ironically, the satellite transmissions will be discovered first, probably. They can't know exactly where we are, but they will begin a search and eventually find us. I don't know what to expect from them, but I can't imagine they will like us being here."

"At any rate, we need to take precautions. Instead of opening up the quarry, I want you to start building your buildings inside the granite mountain for safety. Level the earth and start cutting your building blocks from inside. Let's keep our visible footprint as small as possible. Certainly, we want as many structures inside as we can to protect the people. I also want you to concentrate on the placement of the second laser outside of Genesis, like Katy planned, and start your plans to build the nuclear generator inside the mountain as well." All the staff were nodding in total agreement with my instructions.

When I paused the general spoke, "Can you tell me more about the Grays, how many and where?"

"Yeah, I was going to get to that. Kim came to me a couple of cycles ago, concerned about what he had observed at one of the human settlements he had been studying. Together we have continued to observe that one and all of the other settlements we could find."

37

"To answer your first question, there are not many. Each settlement appears to have only one spaceship, and it is a fairly small one. We have only seen four to five Grays at each settlement. They appear to be overseers to mining operations. The humans at each of the six settlements we observed have human taskmasters that seem to report to the Grays, at least that is what it appears."

"Considering the fact that these settlements have apparently been here for thousands of years, there is no evidence of any advanced technology. The only exception is an elaborate stone building or castle where the Grays seem to live. The alien files deciphered indicate that humans were brought from Earth somewhere around the 3rd century, and the humans appear to be living in the same conditions. This is somewhat reminiscent of the Jews as slaves in Egypt before the exodus. All this I find strange, because the Grays obviously have advanced technology, but we see no evidence of any advanced technology being used to speed up the mining operation. There are just too many unanswered questions."

"General, do you think we could send a Marine recon squad to get some intelligence without being discovered, maybe even capture a human straggler to interrogate?"

The general smiled hugely and said, "Yes, I do believe we can. I like that idea.

We broke up the meeting, since everyone was anxious to get started on the changes. Well, all except the general, who stayed to learn more for his planning. I knew he and Kim would be pouring over video images of the settlements for hours.

Genesis Prime Log: 05 March 0001

We decided to limit our staff meeting to once a week, unless there was an emergency. The work was progressing nicely and the meetings were cutting into the staff's production, and since I was observing it all anyway, they were redundant, especially since Akiko and Katy had been returning to our quarters at night. I missed them when they stayed in the settlement, but things were going much more smoothly now. I had teased them, vocally, wondering if it was me or the Control Room coffee they missed more. I got two elbows for my comments.

Genesis Prime Log: 08 March 0001

The Marine reconnaissance mission left today without the general, much to his displeasure. I had to order him to stay, explaining that he was too valuable to risk. He wanted to argue, but I just looked at him and asked, "How many generals have you seen lead a combat recon mission? I know you're immortal, but you can still be killed." He relented, reluctantly.

SgtMaj Gomez led a six-man squad south to the closest continent and the closet human settlement. It still seemed strange to me, but the general had chosen extremely well. He picked highly educated and motivated Marines, and most of his company consisted of officers filling the enlisted slots. They were also trained well and would follow SgtMaj Gomez's orders to the letter. Then again, SgtMaj

Gomez was himself intimating, and not just his large size. He had a dominant and assertive demeanor that forced compliance to his will.

I liked SgtMaj Gomez ever since the mutiny en route. The lone survivor of the mutineers had accidentally got his neck broken when they led him out of the Control Room, according to the SgtMaj. I found it funny at the time how he reported the incident, and I like him since. He was my kind of Marine. SgtMaj was also one the general chose to take the Immortality Gene, so it would be hard to kill the man. He was 46 years old but looked to be 35 ... forever 35.

Lt. Boland of engineering volunteered to fly them in one of the three shuttle craft and remain hidden, while the squad gathered their intel. The general, Kim and I would continuously monitor via the satellite feed, should they be discovered or get into trouble. I figured in worse case I could launch Genesis and go to their aid if they got in trouble.

Genesis Prime Log: 09 March 0001

I was getting a little stir crazy being inside, while everyone else was able to enjoy our new home. When Doc responded to my summons I said, "How can we test the range of my mental communications between my dome and this body?" With all my intellect, I couldn't estimate it myself. Actually, being such an unexplored science, there wasn't any research to draw from.

Doc said, "I knew you would be asking, and I don't have an answer. But, I'm tempted to say there aren't any limits. Telepathy is not like other forms of communication. We don't know how it works, just that obviously it does, since you are using it to control your body. I guess we will have to test it."

That's what I wanted to hear and said, "Well, let's get started!" That's exactly what we did. We went for a walk. At least if I passed out Doc could drag me back. We left Mac and Kim to monitor the recon mission and walked out the loading hatch, and I had my first taste of Genesis Prime. Everything was different. The air felt thicker, native smells assaulted my nose, the temperature was different, the wind pushed against my face, and the bright sun bore down on me. It had been 132 years since I had experienced these things, or even thought of it.

All these sensations bombarded me and caused a moment of panic, but the worst of all was the feeling of the vast openness. I searched my archives and found the phobia (Agoraphobia) the fear of open spaces. Even my long exposure in the open translucent dome in the vastness of space hadn't prepared me for this. Luckily, however, these senses quickly passed.

Doc looked at me strangely, but I give him a big smile and kept walking. We walked down the road, which I noticed had been surfaced with slabs of cut granite. Linda had managed to do this half the way down the mountain, apparently from the excavation of the cave for the laser, which I saw was complete. The laser sat atop the mountain in its shiny new Wonder Metal, retractable, swivel housing.

Linda saw us and waved. I guess she was curious, so she started toward us with a big smile and snuggled up against Doc to walk with us on down the road. She didn't say anything, knowing I wasn't missing a thing.

I sent a telepathic message to Akiko, "Where are you love? I'm coming down the mountain."

She answered immediately, "Great! I see you now. Is everything OK?"

"It is fantastic!" I've never understood why or how the two of us could communicate telepathically, but it has certainly been a blessing. I think this form of communication is what attracted us to each other initially. I mean I was nothing but a disembodied brain at the time. I have since stopped trying to figure it out, just accept it. She is the only person I have ever been able to communicate telepathically with, and I have tried. I tried with Katy, but nothing ever happened. Katy has her own way to communicating with me, and I like that too.

By the time we reached the bottom of the road, both Akiko and Katy met us. They were happy to see me out of the ship and exploring their handy work, and it was in fact exceptional. But, I was actually having too much fun to think of work, strange for me. I walked through the massive gate and stood, watching the river flowing by with my own eyes. A sudden thought hit me and I quickly turned and asked Akiko, "Well, are there any trout in the river?"

They all bellowed out in laughter. Then Akiki said, "Yes there are, at least a close enough facsimile. We are even eating them. I vowed to myself to come back another day and go fishing.

Doc said, "I think this is enough for one day, Nick."

"I think you are right. This all seems so strange to me, and I think I'm disrupting work." I had noticed that most all the people around had stopped work and were staring at me. Katy and Akiko embraced me and gently pushed me back toward the road. What a wonderful cycle.

CHAPTER 4
(New Recruit)

Genesis Prime Log: 11 March 0001

Maybe I made a mistake this cycle. Just possibly I did.

The Marine recon squad returned with a human captive. Well, it was almost human. The dark complected man was of medium but strong build. Even though obviously human, he was wild looking with long and unkept, black hair plastered to the sides of his face. He wore filthy leather buckskins and no shoes. Obviously he didn't want to come with the Marines, since he was tied and dragged into the Control Room kicking and screaming. He even tried to bite SgtMaj Gomez. Andy didn't hurt him, but he did subdue him and held him down on the deck.

I figured I needed an edge to get the frightened human to calm himself and try to communicate. So, I flared my holographic image to life. That's when I saw I made my mistake. The captive human turned completely white and tore away from Andy to fall prostrate on the floor in front of me. He started muttering and talking, most of which I didn't understand. About every fifth word was very clear, and that word was "Zeus"! I continued to listen to his words, and I slowly began to register some of them. In my archives were every known Earth language, and his language began to coincide some with an ancient dialect of Greek. His language was still considerably different from my archived file but barely recognizable. I spoke to him in this dialect telling him to "Rise Up", which he immediately did. He was still tied, but he was able to sit up on his legs and immediately began bowing to me and chanting "Zeus, Zeus, Zeus".

I was wondering why he was calling me Zeus, then I suddenly understood. The humans were taken from the 3rd century BC during the height of worshiping Olympian gods, and for whatever reason, they haven't seemed to evolve socially since then. This human must belong to a religious sect that still worships Zeus. My mistake may be irreversible. He thinks I am Zeus.

I began trying to tell him I'm not Zeus, but I was quickly interrupted by the general saying, "Admiral, he obviously thinks you are Zeus, and I think you better let him believe that you are, for the time being anyway. SgtMaj said he has been a wild man all the time during his capture and transport back. Now he is somewhat passive, at least he quit fighting and is listening to you."

"Very well. Humm, well I can't decipher enough of his language to communicate with him. Doc, can we use the META unit to teach him English?"

We had invented what we now call, META (memory educational transfer apparatus) to transfer memories. This is what we developed and used to transfer the memories of the original Katy into her clone when the original Katy's body rejected the Immortality Gene. Katy's body eventually died of old age, while her memories, her essence, lived on in Katy 2. The transfer worked. Maybe it would work now.

Doc looked toward the dome roof in deep thought for a few seconds before looking at me. He said, "Well, I learned Japanese from Taka in this way, but we had the common working knowledge of English. A language is learned by experience through the senses and in action in pictures and emotions. We can transfer this information, and we know information transmitted directly to the hippocampus in our brains through the META is immediately stored in permanent memory and bypasses the short term memory. This expedites the process of learning. Also, it apparently does not go into conscious thought for rational analysis in the receiving brain, which means the transfer process is much quicker."

"To answer your question, yes, we can use the META to teach him English if, and it's a big if, he will wear the META unit long enough."

"Go ahead and get one in here, and I will see if Zeus can make him wear it."

It only took a few moments for the META to get to the control room, and I got the human's attention and managed to instruct him to sit in one of the chairs in front of me. He seemed eager to comply with my wishes, so Doc helped him to the chair, and at my instruction, Doc untied his hands and feet. I then showed him the META unit, and Doc slipped it on his own head, then I began telling the man I wanted him to wear the unit. I must have gotten the impression to him in my limited ancient Greek, for he looked strangely at me but tolerantly allowed Doc to slip in on his head. Doc proceeded to the console and began working a keyboard. The man's eyes seemed to bug out and he tensed strongly, but he continued to stare at me and didn't remove the unit. I tried to give the man reassuring smiles. This continued for many minutes until SgtMaj Gomez walked by him a little too close for his comfort. Apparently the man still held a major resentment for the SgtMaj from his ordeal and started bellowing out at him in his ancient dialect so fast I didn't follow anything he said. Suddenly, some of the bellowed words started coming out in English, and we clearly heard, "You fucking asshole pile of (unrecognizable) shit! Get away from me, or I'm going to kick your (unrecognizable) ass!" Needless to say everyone present burst out laughing, not the least of which was the SgtMaj. It was even doubly funny, since the man was half the size of the big barrel-chested SgtMaj.

Doc kind of summed it up for all of us when he said, "I believe it's going to work." This of course sent us all into another fit of laughter.

When we started laughing, the man stopped his ranting and looked shocked. He then clearly said, "I don't understand!"

I said, "We are teaching you our language through that device so we can communicate better."

The man fell to his knees again and began bowing and chanting, "Zeus, Zeus."

"No ... no, I'm not Zeus, I'm Admiral Johns," I said.

Emphatically he bellowed, "NO! You are Zeus!"

"Well, I guess I am Zeus. What name are you called?"

"My name is Homer." Then he repeated my name to make sure I know who I am.

"Well, Homer, we need you to sit back and relax so the teaching machine can run its course. Will you do that? We can then talk more."

Genesis Prime Log: 12 March 0001

This has been a busy and informative cycle and it started early. We waited with Homer until the META program finished, completing the tutoring in English. Homer seemed extremely happy with the new knowledge and skill. I suspected that Doc included additional programming on top of the English skill. I guess we will know as time goes on.

After the program was complete Doc removed the META unit. The SgtMaj cautiously approached Homer and said, "Homer, I want to apologize to you for our treatment of you on the trip here, but you are a pretty good scrapper, and we had to seriously restrain you to keep you from hurting us or yourself. I tried to explain to you, but you didn't understand what we were trying to do. Please forgive me."

Homer looked hard and strangely at the SgtMaj for a long minute and said nothing. Finally he spoke, "I know you now. You are Ares, another Olympian. If I had recognized you earlier, I would have done as you wished. Forgive me for fighting with you."

I said, "SgtMaj Gomez, I guess your new name is Ares, the Olympian god of war. I must say, it fits." I was curious and pointed to the general and asked, "And what is his name?"

Homer immediately responded, "Poseidon! And before you ask, I haven't yet recognized the one you call Doc, nor any of the others."

I wanted to go slow with Homer. Hopefully, if he became comfortable with us we might pick up a lot of information. Still, I wanted to be upfront with him and said, "Homer, we mean you no harm, nor your village. We just want to understand your village better and the people. We are new to this world and you can also help us understand it better. When we finish talking we can take you back where we found you. But, for right now I think we can go eat and find you a place to sleep. Are you hungry? Will you go with .. err...Ares and let him get you some food and a bed?"

Homer nodded and followed Andy out. I thought this might be interesting and followed them through my visual centers. I would be watching Homer all evening, just in case.

Genesis Prime Log: 13 March 0001

As we lay talking in our quarter I told Katy and Akiko about Homer. They set up in bed, interested, and I had to tell them all about it. They followed me to the Control Room after breakfast. They had hundreds of questions ready for him, but I think they forgot them soon after we entered.

When Homer saw Katy, Akiko, and Linda come in after me he stared in total awe. Again he fell to his knees and started bowing to the girls. I stopped him in my body form and said, "Homer, you have to stop doing this or we won't be able to talk." Hearing my voice broke his trance, and he jumped up and stared at me. I grasped suddenly that he just realized I was the same person in body that he had talked to in holograph form. "I thought we were passed the prostrating exercise."

He said, "Sorry Zeus, but I have never seen young women before and of such beauty as these three. It is easy to see why these gods are worshipped by my people."

"You believe these three are gods?"

"Oh my, yes." he said, "The red head there," pointing at Linda, "is Hestia. The other red head is without doubt Athena." The darker one is Aphrodite."

"Well, they are all gods to me, too, Homer." I smiled hugely at them, but they continued to stand in shock at being called gods. I continued, "Come on in and let's get this brain picking started."

The general was getting a huge kick out of it and said, "Come on in Hestia, Athena, and Aphrodite. I'm Poseidon by the way, and that," pointing at the SgtMaj, "is Ares." Andy waved.

Katy said, "You said you have never seen young women before. Surely you can't mean that. How are children produced for your village?"

Homer said, "I've heard there are some young women living inside the castle. Our leaders are summoned to breed them but not often. There are no children in our village. Only older women live in the village. They are sent from the castle after they get older. Young men are sent from the castle to replace those killed or dying of old age, but never any young women. I have never seen a child, so they must remain in the castle with the tall ones."

I didn't understand it or why, but that certainly explains why humans haven't populated Genesis Prime, but at the mention of the tall ones my focus changed. I said, "Tell us about the tall ones. How many are there, do they have ships that come and how oven, etc.? Just tell us everything you know about them."

"I'm not sure just how many there are. They seldom come out. Our leaders go to see them and deliver food, but they don't talk about there being many. They speak our language, you know. There are stories among our people that talk about large ships that used to come to pick up materials we mine, but those ships haven't come in several lifetimes of memory. We still mine, and we have a large hill of the material built up, but no one comes to get it. At some point the elders talked about the tall ones saying they were marooned. They have a small round saucer, but it hasn't moved in my memory or anyone else's still living."

There was no doubt in my mind that Doc had transferred additional knowledge via the META to Homer, because he was using words that his life experiences would not have been able to relate to. Doc is a sly one.

Akiko asked, "Homer, what does the village people eat? Can you show me on some pictures I've recorded and you tell me about them?"

"Yes, yes. I would be pleased to help, Aphrodite."

Akiki still looked troubled at her being called Aphrodite, but she didn't correct him. They then began paging through her video log, while he began talking about the pictures of fruit, vegetables,

51

grains, and animals, telling her the good ones, bad ones, dangerous ones. I knew they would be awhile at this, but I had one more question I had to ask.

"Homer, sorry to interrupt, but since you don't have a family, would you like to stay with us? I promise you will meet some young women."

Homer smiled but didn't even look up. He said, "Yes, I would love to live here." He then went back to Akiki's video tablet.

Genesis Prime Log: 15 March 0001

I found Doc in his clinic and asked him to accompany me on another walk in the settlement. I wanted to survey the progress and get out again in the sunlight. Plus, I wanted to test the envelop of distance I could stretch it from my dome. I was beginning to believe that telepathy would not be subject to distance and I would not have a problem.

I asked Homer to come also, and he wasn't hard to find. I knew he would either be in the cafeteria eating or in the Control Room with his coffee cup. He had a real liking for coffee. Sure enough I found him in the cafeteria. When I asked him he quickly agreed.

The first thing I noticed was a completed zigzag road all the way down into the settlement. Linda's crew had evidently already excavated the interior cave for the nuclear generator to have that many slabs for the road. She had been busy. When Doc saw my amazement, he confirmed that Linda had indeed finished the cave. She told me last night.

As we got lower I saw the completed guard towers and massive gates opening to the river and docks, already under construction. They had even started on the planned bridge with "I" beams of Wonder Metal spanning the river. Those beams would definitely handle the weight of anything we might want to put across it. On closer inspection I saw some large complex gearing and realized Linda must have designed some form of drawbridge into it. This settlement was beginning to look like an ancient stone castle of the age of English Knights. They had cut and moved a lot of granite stone blocks, and I wondered how they had moved such massive blocks.

I took a close look at the construction, really for the first time. Engineering had built new equipment for moving the stone using antigravity technology. It was an ingenious application. One man operated the machine with a handheld device. The main machine clamped on to a stone block and lifted it and positioned the stone in place. All along the fence similar machines could be seen at work moving or lifting huge stone blocks. Already the fence was in place everywhere but not to the height of its final level. Damn, these engineers could build an Egyptian pyramid if they wanted to.

As we were walking, I was also talking to Homer. He didn't want to go back home, and we really could use his knowledge of Genesis Prime. I said, "Homer, as you have said, you want to live with us, and we want you. You can be a big help, but everyone needs to pull their own weight. So, I need to assign you to a job. Do you understand?"

Homer said, "Certainly, I understand, and I want to pull my weight, as you said. I'm glad you are bringing this up. I was trying to find a way to ask you to give me a function, but I don't know how to do these things," as he spread his arms wide, "I was a farmer and hunter in my village, but I'm willing to learn new things."

I said, "We don't need you to do these things you see. You have specific knowledge on this planet such as food, plants, animals, dangers, and the like. We also have someone responsible for these things. I want to assign you to this person. Her name is Lt. Naomi Sami. She works for my mate, Akiko. You can help her greatly. I will still need you to come to me when I need you. You can help me, also."

Homer was smiling hugely and said, "Thank you, Zeus. I will be highly pleased to serve you and help this Lt. Sami."

I really wanted Homer's help, but I think I was playing a little cupid also. Homer said he had never seen a young woman. Well, he wasn't going to meet many at the ship. Most were down in the settlement, those that weren't attached already anyway. I actually think it was Akiko that planted the seed. She mentioned that Naomi could use Homer's help, then later in our bed talk she mentioned that Naomi was still unattached. Katy and I both broke out in laughter, knowing Akiko was trying to match Homer and Naomi. If Homer wanted to meet a pretty young woman, Naomi would definitely fill that slot. Naomi was also dark complected like Homer. I'm thinking the cupid arrow would pierce Homer soon.

While I had Homer and Doc both together I said, "Doc, now that Homer is fluent in English can we use the META to teach his dialect of his ancient Greek to others, since they can relate with English?"

"Of course we can, now. Who did you have in mind?"

"Well, me for one, but I will get it as soon as the program exist. I'm thinking maybe Lt. Boland, Mac, and SgtMaj, oh, and Lt. Sami."

Doc gave me a slight private grin at the last comment and said, "I'll get on it right away. In fact I will put Homer and Lt. Sami together for the recording."

Genesis Prime Log: 20 March 0001

I think I took everyone by surprise at this staff meeting. I had invited the full staff for the meeting, including Homer and Lt. Sami. I almost didn't recognize Homer. Apparently Lt. Sami had been working on Homer's personal hygiene over the last five days, and I can't blame her. Homer actually stunk. Today his dirty and stinking buckskins were replaced with the standard blue Genesis jumpsuit, and his normally unruly, long hair was neat and braided. He looked like a different man.

I started the meeting by speaking in the ancient Greek dialect saying, "How many of you understand what I'm saying? Give me a show of hands." I expected the general, Lt. Boland, of course Homer, the SgtMaj, and Lt. Sami, which I had also requested. It was my turn to be surprised when Doc, Linda, Cdr. Kim, Cdr. Taka, Katy, and Akiko also raised their hands, virtually everyone in attendance raised their hands. How had I missed this? With my mind interconnected with the computer, it is rarely that I am surprised, but it felt good to feel the emotion flood through me.

"Your initiative is truly a blessing, and I thank you for it. You're probably wondering why this is important. I'm going to tell you, but first I need to ask First Officer McCullah a question. General, what did President McIntosh make me promise to do?"

At first he seemed confused at the situation, then he began to smile. Mac has always been smart, and he now knew where this was going. Mac said, "President McIntosh asked you to assume the responsibility of the human race and save and preserve humanity."

I sighed and continued, "Yes, this has been my curse through these long years. There have been times I, personally, wanted to give up, but this responsibility haunts me. I accepted this responsibility, my burden to carry. Now let me ask you another question; do you consider Homer and his people human?"

Homer looked scared and set up tall in his chair. The general said, "Yes, of course. His people were brought here by force by the aliens, but they are from Earth and as much human as we are."

I said, "I can tell you already know where I'm going with this and probably the rest of you do also. I think we are required by our charter on life, the very fact that we live, to free and aid these other humans and let them have a chance to a decent life."

"I also think we all agree that the aliens pose little threat to us now, based upon the information

Homer has given us. If they are in fact marooned here and few in number, I don't think we could expect them to attack us. I hope not anyway. Still, we can't underestimate them, especially with their technology. So, it's still good to have the defenses we do."

"Do I have a plan? No, I don't. I just want us to find a way to live up to our responsibility to all of humanity. I just want you all to be thinking about it. Questions?"

They were all silent for many long minutes, but surprisingly, Homer asked the first questions. Homer stood, not knowing the protocol, and asked, "My people are not of this world? We came from the same planet as all of you? We are the same people?"

It was Katy that responded, "Yes, Homer. We had some dealing with the same aliens on Earth but not as personally as you have. There was an alien spaceship crash on Earth, and we learned many things about them. Some of their technology helped us to travel here. We also recovered a computer, which we brought with us. During the voyage we, well Cdr Tsuji and Admiral Johns, deciphered some of the language. This is where we learned that the aliens kidnapped humans from Earth and brought them here. This is also where we learned the location of this planet, which we now call Genesis Prime."

I began chuckling to myself. Yep, Doc had definitely uploaded a vast amount of information to Homer; otherwise, he would never have been able to understand much of what Katy told him. Imagine trying to explain "computer" to someone who lives in a straw and mud hut and hunts with only a bow and arrow. That Doc is a sneaky one for sure.

I also noticed Lt. Sami squeeze Homer's hand as Katy was talking. I couldn't tell if it was a sign of reassurance, friendship, or something more.

The general spoke, "I understand your reasoning about the other settlements, and I agree. It will take some planning, but one thing we should also consider. If we are going to assist them we might as well take all the ore they have mined and put it to use for them and us instead of just leaving it piled up. I'm thinking out loud, but that's what they have been doing, mining, for centuries. They will still need purpose. The aliens aren't using it. I see the beginning of trade."

"We almost have our docks complete, so we should consider building some transport ships."

I said, "Well, that's a good suggestion. All of you consider what has been said this cycle. Let me know, first, if you agree with me. This affect us all, so I don't want to force this decision on you. I want you to agree with me or argue your case. Let's meet again next week and discuss it again."

My girls knew me well and knew something had been bothering me, but they hadn't press me. It was a kind of unspoken rule, to leave work outside our quarters, and I saw the relief in their faces. It hadn't been so serious after all. We exchanged smiles among ourselves.

CHAPTER 5
(The Grays)

Genesis Prime Log: 30 March 0001

I could tell First Officer McCullah was ready at this meeting, and he was anxious to start the discussion. So, I nodded for him to lead off the discussion.

Mac began, "I don't trust the Grays. They have shown that they don't have the best interest of humans as a priority, that they are only interested in their own needs. They have the technology to cause us great harm, so we must not underestimate them. They may be marooned and their technology may be compromised, but we must not rely on this. We have to treat them as hostile and dangerous. Under these conditions we should attack them by surprise and subdue them quickly. But, the problem is that the defenders are most likely humans, and a direct attack means humans will die."

"What I propose is a little more intelligence gathering. I want to take a squad in again as defense and send Homer back into his village to talk to the elders and leaders and bring some of them back so they can see the Genesis and those they apparently may perceive to be the gods they worship. Let us work our magic and convince them we are the good guys. This way the elders can hopefully order the guards to leave the castle. We can then attack and capture or kill the Grays."

I noticed Homer became nervous when his name was mentioned. I said, "Homer, are you willing to go back in?"

Homer hung his head and quietly asked, "Do I have to stay there? I want to live here with you guys and Naomi."

At that, Naomi blushed heavily and her dark face flushed in a shade of red I had never seen on her before, and she actually hid her face in her hands. It was comical, but everyone already knew. They had been working together around the clock. It was enviable that they would pair together. Still, I chose not to comment on this aspect of their relationship. I concentrated on Homer's concern and said, "Of course you don't have to stay in the village. You are a member of our team now, but they know you and will listen to you. We just need you to talk to them and convince the leaders to trust us and come and meet with us. Can you do that? Ares will go with you and bring you back."

Homer liked my comments, smiled, and said, "Yes, yes, I can do this." Homer turned to the now recovered Naomi and they smiled at each other.

I turned back to the general and said, "I like the plan. This way we haven't committed to any course of action, and this could be the simplest way to go. Anyone else have a plan to offer or comments?" After a few moments of silence I continued, "Okay then, I'm assuming that all are in agreement with my intent to save the human settlements. Let's proceed."

Genesis Prime Log: 10 April 0001

Andy radioed ahead that they were flying in, and I called the staff in. We were all waiting, including the Chaplin, Calvin Kline. He had invited himself, but I hadn't excluded him. He was welcome. I think he was going to request a church to be built.

SgtMaj and Homer led a group of five middle-aged and elderly men and one middle-aged woman into the control room. They entered cautiously and definitely intimidated and huddled together. As they made their way toward the center, I, in keeping with my Zeus role, flared my holographic image to life. Homer knew what to expect and quickly held out his arms and stopped them from running, saying, "I told you it was Zeus and the Olympians!"

I spoke in the ancient Greek Dialect, "Welcome to Mount Olympus fellow humans." As expected, that was all I got out before they all fell prone on the floor, but before they could start a chant I spoke again, "Please stand I don't wish you to worship me. I want to talk with you." While they looked back and forth among themselves and cautiously began to stand, I said in English, "SgtMaj, report."

The SgtMaj, recognizing my formal address, stood to attention, saluted, and began, "Well, Sir, the trip and infiltration of the village was uneventful. It did however take several days of steady talking by Homer to convince them to come."

I said, "Do I understand that you also entered the village?"

"Yes, Sir, Homer thought it would be easier to convince them if they saw me, and it was probably good that I did go in. I was able to see things

Homer was unaware of, like spies within the village. Luckily the elders don't trust them either and kept us hidden away so they could learn more about us. We had to stay out of sight and meet the elders in secret. I'm not sure just how much control these elders have over those humans at the castle. There seems to be a group of humans living in the castle that give their allegiance to the Grays. They operate as a military force protecting the castle and personal guards for the Grays and are fiercely loyal. They are poorly armed, swords and spears mostly, but I suspect they became loyal by fear of the Grays."

"At any rate, Homer did a fine job of describing us and our intentions toward them, and they seem to welcome the help."

I said, "Good report SgtMaj. Thanks." I then turned to the elders and spoke to them in their language, "I understand Homer has told you about us and our intentions. Is this true?"

It was the woman that stepped forward. She seemed less intimidated than the others and apparently had been chosen to speak for them. "This is so. We didn't believe Homer, but we wanted to believe. Now, having been in the flying bird machine and seeing this place and the people, we believe. It is hard to believe we are all from a different world, the same world, but it is apparently so. Homer believes it; so do we, now. If you wish to help, we would like that. We don't like the tall ones. They have been cruel to the people. They eat our young."

It was Katy that spoke first, beating me in interrupting the woman elder by only a second. It is probably good that she did, because I would have probably screamed too loudly.

As it was, Katy bellowed, "They do what?"

The woman quickly turned to face Katy and repeated it, "They eat our young! They control all childbearing women within the castle and only allow enough fertile women to supply their food needs and replacement workers. It has always been that way. We never knew there was another way until Homer told us how men and women live together here. That is when we realized just how cruel they had been to us. Yes, we want your help; we pray for it."

Every face in the control room was an ugly mask of pure disgust and hate. The very thought of them eating human children filled me with total rage for the Grays. Surprisingly, it was Calvin Kline that changed my perspective.

Calvin spoke in English, but he obviously had been listening in the ancient dialect. He must have taken a turn at the META as well. He said, "I see the disgust for this heinous act, and I agree it is terrible from our perspective. But, we must also look at it from the Grays' perspective as well. The Gray's aren't human. It isn't cannibalism from their perspective. To the Grays humans are only meat and slave labor. To judge them by our perspective would be like asking a mother cow how she felt about us eating her young. It's the same thing. Of course, we can't allow it to continue now that we know, but we mustn't act on hate. We don't want hate to control our minds or judgment or our action."

I heard him, and to a certain extent he had a point. I knew I wanted to kill them all, but of course the Grays, according to Calvin Kline, would probably wonder why we were killing them and not understand why we hated them so much. They might even think humans were cruel and disgusting for killing them. Yes, I saw his point, but I was still filled with disgust of them and at this point didn't really give a shit what they thought of us.

I calmed myself, reverted back to the villager's language, then said, "General, how do you suggest we proceed?"

He said, "With all due respect to our resident chaplain, I wouldn't have a problem killing them. In my opinion they do not deserve to live. Still, from what I now understand, this human guardian force is the real danger. I believe they will fight to the last man to protect their position and purpose. They know they won't be welcome back in the village, apparently. They have nowhere else to go. We will have to be prepared to take them all out, and once they are out of the way we can deal with the Grays as required. If they surrender and don't fight we can try to capture them alive for interrogation. I'm sure some of the engineers have a few thousands questions they would like to ask."

I noticed Linda and Katy nodding at the general's comment about interrogating the aliens, and Katy, the ever ready professional politician, said, "General, maybe we could give the guardian force a place to go instead of dying. Don't you need more Marines here?"

The general didn't say anything. He just looked at me and shrugged, as if to say, "That's possible."

I had made up my mind and said, "Okay, we are going in in full intimidation mode. We are taking the Genesis. Prepare to launch. General get some of your Marines loaded for an assault on the castle.

Genesis Prime Log: 11 April 0001

Katy and Calvin took the elders to the cafeteria to eat and learn more about the village humans, while the others began organizing the launch. Linda hadn't tied much of anything into the Genesis. The nuclear generator was already installed and operational in the cave. It was just a matter of loading the Marines, closing the hatch, firing off the engines, which didn't require warming up. We began our liftoff two hours after I made the decision using only gravity drive. We took our time but it still only took an hour to reach our destination.

We hovered far off from the castle, but as large as the Genesis is we could be seen for miles and were, judging from all the running villagers. Our rooftop super-laser was deployed, and I was ready for any required action. We hovered long enough to have triggered an attack, and there was none. So, we lowered to the ground and opened the hatch, allowing SgtMaj and his Marines to drive two trucks out. The elders were also with them. The plan was to quickly get closer, drop off the elders in plain sight of the village, then drive closer to the castle and deploy the Marines.

As the trucks were driving, the Genesis rose again and began moving toward the castle, drawing attention away from the trucks. It was my intention to try and intimidate the guard force and hopefully the Grays. If I were them I would have been intimidated. The Genesis was huge and quite impressive.

The Marines had reached their desired location and spread out to reduce the targets. The elders had reached the villagers and could be seen milling with them. It was time to slowly slide the Genesis forward toward the castle. Once we were stationary in front, we just hovered and waited.

After a few moments about twenty of the guards came out and stood on the steps. After a few more minutes one of the more aggressive guards ran forward toward a Marine with his spear poised to throw. At that second I fired the laser and he simply disappeared in a bright bolt of light and smoke.

The SgtMaj stood and addressed them in their language. "I am Ares, and we do not wish to harm you, but if you attack you will be dealt with in the same way. We could destroy all of you, but we want you to join us. If you lay down your weapons and come forward we will take you in and you will become warriors for us. It is your choice to live or die."

If I expected it to be hard, I would have been disappointed. The guards just looked at each other and tossed down their weapons as if they were hot to the touch and came forward. Others inside the castle joined them, also tossing down their weapons as they came. In all about thirty came down the steps and stood in front of the SgtMaj. I didn't hear the order, but the guards kept their hands on their heads and sat down.

The SgtMaj bellowed, "If their remain any guards in the castle when we enter you will be immediately killed. This is your last chance." Three more guards came out and joined the others. "Now all other humans remaining in the castle need to come out." About forty women and fifteen children of various ages came pouring out and were ushered to another location by Marines. "Now we want the aliens, tall ones, or Grays, whatever you call yourselves, to come out. This will be your only chance to live. Come out now!"

We anxiously waited. After a few moments one of the Grays stuck his head out and looked around. Finally he stuck his long arms out and walked out the door. He was quickly followed by five others, three males and two females. Three of the Marines quickly surrounded them and led them to a separate spot and had them sit.

A squad of Marines quickly entered into the castle and began their search, room by room. It was a large castle and it took about thirty minutes for the castle to be checked and cleared. The Marines finally exited and declared the castle clear. All in all the capture of the castle went better than I expected, with only the one causality. I hated to have to kill a human, but by doing so had probably saved the lives of many more.

Kim slowly lowered the Genesis and landed then dropped the bottom hatch. The Marines began escorting the guards and the aliens on board, while the elders and leaders, along with other villagers that had joined them, began mingling with the freed younger women. This was the plan anyway. It would take years to reverse the perverse lifestyle the aliens had inflected upon these humans, but that lifestyle was not within the natural course of human development. I felt that human nature would quickly influence and change them.

Katy had spent much time with the elders en route, and they knew their new role, to help the villagers govern themselves. She knew that if we were successful they would take over the castle and leadership of the village. Katy had also informed them that we would be coming for the minerals and ore they had mined, but we would be giving them trade goods in exchange. Since they had nothing now, we figured metal tools, cloth, and the like would be welcome. Of course we weren't producing any yet, but we knew we would be soon.

I watched and listened through the visual centers as the general immediately took his new recruits into a separate area and began addressing them. They were scared to death in their new surrounding but extremely motivated and interested listeners.

He said, "I am General McCullah. I am in charge of these Marines and more." Waving his hands around at the intimidating Marines facing them. "You are smart; you have agreed to join us instead of being killed, but you must want to be one of us to remain. I will teach each of you to become one of these exceptional fighting warriors. You will be highly trained, skilled, and disciplined. I will also tell you now that not all of you can live up to this level, and I will not keep you if you don't. It is easy to be kicked out of the Marines, because I only keep the best. We will not kill you if you try and don't make it. You will be given other duties. Now, if you want to become a Marine, step forward or leave the ship immediately."

The general knew they had no choice; they were afraid they would be killed if they didn't, but it was important to the general and the new recruits to make the symbolic gesture. Somewhere during the general's address the men seemed to make a change. They had slowly transformed from scared children to proud men, welcoming the new opportunity and challenge in their life. Of course that was the general's intent from the beginning. They all stepped forward and became the general's new recruits. Katy's plan had worked, smart girl.

Immediately after the general's recruits stepped forward, Kim closed the bottom hatch and began our liftoff, which tended to end any meeting with the Grays. I didn't mind, since I was still unsure of what to do with them. They had chosen to live, and I would honor that choice. I figured they could wait for a while and had them escorted to the quickly prepared detention cells (quarters). I would meet with them in tomorrow's cycle.

As we returned and approached Atlantis I noticed that Linda had taken advantage of the absence of the Genesis to level out the landing area and construct a semicircular granite fence around the back side of our landing area. It was quite impressive, but really quite unnecessary, because the back side of the mountain was quite steep. Still it was impressive.

Kim set the Genesis down exactly on target and the general disembarked his new recruits to billet them in the newly finished Marine barracks. I wished I had a camera in there. This should be interesting.

Genesis Prime Log: 12 April 0001

I was not anxious to meet and talk to the Grays. Truth be known, I was not sure if I could control my anger. The full staff hung around waiting, because they didn't want to miss this historic event, but to their credit they said nothing. Finally, I asked the general to bring them in. The staff made room in the front seats for the aliens with a little wiggle room to spare...just in case.

I didn't like them at first sight, especially their apparent leader. He stood about seven and a half feet tall, skinny with long, sinewy legs and arms. He wore metallic looking slip on shoes, shorts and loose hanging shirt, which tended to blend in with his gray skin. Even though he was under heavy Marine guard, he didn't acknowledge them. My holographic image was already alive, and he stared only at me. To be more precise, he stared at my visual center, apparently instantly recognizing the technology in use. The leader stood tall and erect, radiating an air of arrogance. He even walk arrogant. They took the offered front seats and waited.

Since the holograph image provided absolutely no intimidation, I dissolved the image and walked to the podium in my body form. The leader and I locked unblinking eyes on each other for an uncomfortable length of time before I spoke in the ancient dialect, "Can you give me any reason I shouldn't just kill you for feeding on young humans?" I thought I might as well be blunt, since I didn't like him anyway. I also sent a private telepathic message to Akiko, "Move those standing behind the aliens." Akiko immediately understood and silently moved the staff over and out of my line of sight ... laser sight.

The leader stood erect and spoke in perfect English, "I am called Sheen among our superior race. You will call me Respected Leader Sheen. You are human and therefore insignificant. You are a short-lived race that doesn't live long enough to learn anything of use, but your race serves well for our food. Members of our race can live to be a thousand years old, and we have developed great technology, which we might share with you. To do so we will require you to serve our needs." He then waited for my response.

This was the most arrogant asshole I had ever met. I couldn't believe how arrogant he was. I guess that is why I tolerated him to continue. I said, "And what are those needs?"

Respected Leader Sheen continued, "Any need we may desire, but specifically we need your ship to take us to our home planet. We will have to modify it to a more technically advanced drive system suited for ultra-deep space, a plasma drive that transcends many light years instantly."

"Another need: I see you have young women." This last part he said with a sneer on his face. We will need them to produce children for our consumption...."

I had heard enough and that is as far as he got in his instructions, as I sent a laser beam directly through his head, leaving a large, gaping and smoking hole that issued out a sizzling noise throughout the Control Room. Respected Leader Sheen then fell forward to the floor with a thud that could easily be heard in a totally silent Control Room.

I looked at the other aliens, who were in total shock. It appeared that they simply couldn't believe an inferior being such as I would have the audacity to kill one of their superior beings. I said, "Would any of you others like to talk about eating our children?" I think in that moment they all lost their superiority complex, because they were emphatically shaking their heads in the negative. I then barked at the general, "Get these sons of bitches out of my sight before I kill them all. And to the rest of you aliens, when we bring you back for our next discussion I better see more respect and cooperation on your part or you will join your friend in death."

Genesis Prime Log: 16 April 0001

It took me several days to calm down, and I let the damn aliens wait and consider their future fate. I figured they were lucky to still be alive. The biggest surprise to me was that none of my staff, including Calvin Kline, commented to me about my facial adjustment to Respected Leader Sheen. Well, except for the general who gave me a thumbs up. Additionally, later in our quarters Akiko actually chuckled at my reaction to the alien's demands.

Akiko said, "I was so angry at that alien I was ready to shoot him myself. I'm surprised you took his abuse as long as you did."

Katy said, "I agree. Diplomacy wasn't going to work with him."

When the Marines led the five remaining aliens into the Control Room this time, they appeared much different. The stiff pride and arrogance was gone, and their heads hung low. They wouldn't look at me, rather at the floor instead. They were again seated in the front row, and they continued to look at the floor.

I barked, "Do you still have any demands for me?"

One of the other males stood and said, "No, Sir, we have no demands, but we do have some requests, respectfully." I said nothing, so he continued, "We wish to live and, if possible, rejoin our race at some point, and as Leader Sheen poorly suggested to you, we do have great technology we can share with you in return for our lives and a place to live among you." Again I said nothing and he quickly continued as if he might not have another chance. "We are marooned on this planet and have been for hundreds of years. Our supply ships just stopped coming, and we don't know why. We suspect war with another enemy race, of which there are several in this sector of space. Without our supplies our power sources eventually depleted, leaving us helpless and defenseless, as you have noticed."

"I, we wish to apologize to you and the other humans for Leader Sheen's disrespect and arrogance. He was the Leader of all our operations on this planet and another in this system, and quite honestly he was that way with us of his race as well. We do not morn him and hope to start a new relationship with you and your race. You will find us respectful and cooperative in the future."

I considered his words in silence, then said, "You will be given the opportunity to show us you mean what you say, but you will only be given a chance once. If you can win our trust you will be allowed to live and have a life here. You will begin by meeting and being interviewed by our staff to see how you might assist us."

"How many operations do you have here on this planet?

The alien said, "We have five, Sir."

"You and your race must understand that we will not tolerate the treatment that has been given the humans. We will make an end to this treatment and in the other operations on this planet. This can be done peacefully. We will take you to each of them and you will go in alone and give them our instructions. The human guards will stand down and your people will come out into the open to be taken away by us like you were. You will all live together here. Do you understand?"

"Yes, Sir, we understand.

Genesis Prime Log: 18 April 0001

For this meeting I scheduled a full status report from all department heads so everyone would be caught up on our overall status, and I called upon the general to go first.

74

The general took the podium and began, "As you all know, I have twenty-five new Marine recruits. They are adjusting well, but they will not be given any slack. They will be trained to be Marines. SgtMaj Gomez set up a full bootcamp just for them. Initially, their training will not include rifles or pistols. Their status will continue to be guards with swords, spears, and crossbows. We can expect about another one hundred from the other alien operations. Once they are on board we will begin the bootcamp, but right now they have been assigned to Lt. Sami. It is my understanding that Homer has them herding buffalo, or something close, into the open prairie grassland on the other side of the river for food. They found the buffalo a long ways off, so it will take them a while to bring them in. Once trained to fight and defend our castle, these Marines will do double duty as other department may require."

"You might wonder why we need so many Marines. Several reasons come to mind. We are on a new planet and we aren't sure what will happen in the future. The aliens talked about other waring races in this sector of space. Only time will tell, but we want to be prepared for any contingency."

"We have also discovered that native animals here are exceptionally large. The Marines have fired upon some large predators harassing the field workers. From what we have seen, they are large cat looking animals. The closest comparison we could make is a reddish sabertooth tiger. Homer tells us they are extremely dangerous and often drag villagers off in the dim light hours.

We have also noted that there are things in the river that also come out in the dim light. We haven't gotten a good look at them, but they are also big, judging from the size of the wet tracks. As a result, we have started closing the gates in the nonworking hours. It wouldn't do to have one of them wondering around inside the fence. That's all I have for now. Just don't let your people stay out in the open without guards."

Akiko went to the podium, "I'm glad you mentioned the river predators, because I am missing one of my fishermen. That must be what happened to him. We will have to take more precautions. I had heard about the large cats, and once we get the buffalo on our prairie I'm afraid we might attract more of the cats, not to mention the predators that might already be following the herd."

"As far as food supply for the colonists is concerned, we are holding our own. Vegetables are in short supply. We have found some native vegetables and fruit but far too few for the volume required. The fields on the south end inside the fence are growing well, and in this climate we will be able to harvest two crops each year. Still, the fields are not enough, and we are cultivating fields on the other side of the river. As you know the river reduces our growing space on this side, as it cuts through the south end of our mountain. We should be in much better shape once those fields begin to produce."

"We have all but exhausted our food supply we arrived with, but we have an abundant supply of native animals for meat so far, and the river is full of fish. We also now have pigs, goats, lots of chickens and turkeys, and even some cows in pens all inside the fence. It will be some time before they can be added to the menu, however. We need to build up the breeding stock before we dare touch them. The enviro gardens on Genesis are still at full capacity and feeding those remaining on board Genesis and contributing some to the food supply in the colony."

Linda took the podium next, "Katy has the best overall feel for how the colony is coming together. I can just report on those projects I am involved with, which have been many. Let me just say that, from my perspective anyway, the main projects completed by engineering are the nuclear generator, which is now operational, and we are delivering electrical power to all the structures completed to date. The power plant is deep in the mountain and safe. The block fence is complete and enclosing the colony. It stands fifteen feet with a walkway around the inside. We have four guard towers, and two gates, only one has a bridge so far. Within the mountain we have built the main cafeteria, storage facilities, hospital, library and META training center, dormitories for the single people and an apartment complex for those mated. There are not enough, but we have started another complex outside."

"Let's see, the dome for processing our sewage waste is almost complete. Akiko has already begun growing Cdr. Sakata's orange algae as the processing agent to convert sewage into hydrogen fuel. It should be operational before we run out of our supply of gasoline. Hopefully, I can report this project complete at the next meeting."

Katy took the podium next, "Well, I'm happy to report we are all still alive. We have food, water, utilities, housing, defense, and all the necessities of life. We have all worked very hard to accomplish this, and all our people have joined in to do it. I thank those of the Hope for joining our teams and department heads. Hopefully, we can soon reach the point where some of our skilled people can be broken loose to pursue some of the nice to have facilities like flower mills, saw mills, canneries, forges, ore refineries, manufacturing, ship building and shipping, etc.. We still have a long way to go, but our spirits are high and motivation strong."

I asked, "Has politics raised its ugly head yet?"

Katy smiled and said, "No, not really. We have been so busy with necessities everyone is too tired to complain, but I'm sure it's coming. We do have a couple of Congressmen and lawyers beginning to ask questions, but so far I just give them another project to complete and send them off." Laughter rang out at Katy's last comment.

I remember the inventory of the cryogenics souls. Sadly, I had been forced to sacrifice many during the voyage to save all our lives. I had tried to choose wisely, electing to save youth and trade skills over politics, law, elderly, or simply wealth. I felt these skills were useless in a survival and colonization mode. Those Congressmen and attorneys must have also had a secondary trade skill to have survived the final cut.

I asked, "Doc, do you or Taka have anything to add or report?"

Doc stood and walked to the podium, "Taka and I have been establishing the hospital and clinic,

78

Luckily, we have doctors, dentists, and an abundance of nurses and technicians available from our human inventory. The hospital is functional and treating the cuts, breaks, illnesses. We expected new illnesses from this environment and new forms of bacteria, but we haven't encountered anything serious, yet."

"In the library and META training center we installed a Supercomputer we brought from Earth and downloaded as much as we could into it. The training center is up and operational and in constant use teaching skills that can be used here. They come in as a commodities broker and leave as skilled farmers or brick layers. It's working quite well."

"Our research facilities remain on board the Genesis, since our facilities here are exceptional. We have also began growing some of the human embryos. We figured we might as well, since some of the mated women are coming in pregnant. As you will remember, we doctored the water supply on board with birth control to prevent pregnancy, but we forgot about the new water source. Since we will have a new supply of children we figured it was as good a time to hatch some of our backlog."

When Doc set down Calvin Kline injected himself into the presentations. He said, "I know many of you believe religion, faith, and church services are not part of the necessities of life, but I argue that morality is necessary for a stable community. Without morality we are all left to our own ideas of right and wrong, and some choose unwisely. Human nature will send us all off in different directions without being taught what is moral and what is not. I would like to have a facility to do just that...teach the laws of God. I need a church." He then turned to look at me and wait for an answer.

I said, "Calvin, you and I have had this discussion before, and it might surprise you, but I agree with you. We do need a moral compass. What we do not need is eighteen different versions of God's laws in the forms of eighteen separate religions and churches. As I have said before, I believe in God; I just don't believe in religion. I will agree to build you a nice, single church when Katy and Linda deem the schedule can fit it in. You are the chaplain of the Genesis, and that makes you senior in rank among any other pastors. I suggest you find a way to share or combine services, but what I will not do is build eighteen churches."

"Calvin, I need to also warn the Islam brothers through you. I will not, and I repeat ... NOT, tolerate any form of the radical corrupted version of Islam teaching. As you know this entire Genesis project has almost been destroyed twice by these radical teaching and soldiers. As long as any organized religion remains a positive moral compass they are welcome to exist. If any one of them deviates from religious freedom for all and advocates violence, I will destroy them to the root. You know I will do it, too."

Calvin smiled and said, "Thanks Marine grunt."

I laughed at his reference to our past banter and said, "You are welcome underwear salesman." The truth is I liked Calvin Kline; I always have. I met him while I was still in my quadriplegic body the day before they removed my brain and installed it in the Genesis' computer. He even prayed not only for me but with me. Yes, I liked him, and I hated to be so tough with him, but I didn't trust organized religion, and I was afraid of where this might go.

Genesis Prime Log: 21 April 0001

The staff had been grilling and drilling the aliens for days in the interrogations, some of which I had watched and listened to through the visual centers. They were ready to make their report this cycle.

Linda had led the interrogations, since engineering had the most to gain from the aliens, and she led off the report, "We discovered a lot from the Sheree, as they call their race. In fact all their names have the double sounding "ee" in their names, like Spee, Dee, Cree, etc. They seem to be completely open to us now and helpful. They are afraid of us, especially you, but are beginning to trust us."

"Spee is the new spokesman for the group, but the names were hard to keep straight, so we started calling them Two, Three, Four, and Five. Anyway, their home planet is some 300 light years from here, back toward Earth and past, but they have spread out on about five other planets, the two in this system included. We have their coordinates and the Sheree star system map of this galaxy."

"As you may surmise, they do have advanced technology, which includes an advanced star drive. They call it Plasma Bubble Drive, and it sounds similar to what we saw "The Enlightened" use to instantly teleport us the 40 lightyears from their system and again to save us and complete our final leg to Genesis Prime. The Plasma Bubble Drive technology is beyond my ability to understand at this point, but I'm beginning to grasp some of it. The good news is that the drive is projected to surround the ship being teleported, which means it should be adaptable to the Genesis. As you will recall, The Enlightened projected a plasma bubble around us that was used to teleport us."

"I'm also digging into some of their weapons system, and they are quite impressive. I'm pretty sure we can duplicate most of them. Even so, our lasers are still formidable weapons against their technology. They do have one item I am extremely interested in, and that is a Radiation Dome to protect an area from aerial attack. They have them installed on all the castles on Genesis Prime, but all of their technology is currently inoperative. To be so intelligent they are also stupid. Unfortunately, their technology has existed for eons, so long most of their race no longer understand it. They just use it."

"All of their technology uses fuel cells, which is nothing more than a supercharged form of battery. These batteries hold a massive charge that lasts for years, and they don't have a clue how to charge them, and they don't have a power source to do it, even if they wanted to. These fuel cells were charged on their home planet and were part of their incoming supplies, that have stopped coming several hundred years ago. Now, all their fuel cells are depleted."

Linda looked serious for a moment then said, "You know we were very lucky that their fuel cells were depleted or they could have done some serious damage to us when we went after them."

"Yeah, I know." I said, "Linda, I want to know if you can charge the Sheree fuel cells?" I was dying to know ever since she mentioned it.

Linda looked almost offended and said, "Well, yeah! I've been charging batteries since I was in the sixth grade, and these are just big batteries. The only problem is having the power capacity, and we certainly do have that. We have the output of three nuclear power generators. The only problem is rectifying then regulating the current and voltage charge. Somehow we need to build a diode strong enough to hold the charge, but maybe the diode already exists in the fuel cells and will work. The real problem is time. With the amount of charge needed we will probably have to run the generators at 70% for days for each fuel cell. It will take a while to charge them all up." She turned inwards in thought for a moment then said, "We won't have to charge them all up. I can build an AC/DC converter for each unit and run them directly off our power utility line, like any appliance."

I was smiling hugely and said, "Try to get a few of the fuel cells charged up. When you are ready we will go to the other human settlement and free them, but we will also liberate some of the weapons at the castles and take charge of the saucers."

CHAPTER 6
(Freedom)

Genesis Prime Log: 1 May 0001

Early this cycle we launched the Genesis and flew toward the next closest Sheree castle. We didn't plan to land Marines this time. It was the job of the Sheree to go to the castles and tell them all that had transpired and get them to come out and surrender to us. They were also instructed to have the human guards lay down their weapons and either leave or be ready to join our Marines. As with the first village, we assumed that the guard would not be welcome back into their ranks and would readily volunteer to join the ranks of the general's soldiers.

Homer, SgtMaj Gomez, and three Marines, two of which were pretty, young women, would go into the village and let them know what was going on. Linda had suggested that young females would be less intimidating. Besides, the huge Ares (Olympian god of war) would be intimidating enough, and of course that is what Homer would introduce him as. Homer absolutely refused to call any of us by our real names, only the Olympian god names.

We didn't expect any difficulty with the villagers, unless they get too frightened and run off. But, Homer was ready for this, and he liked his new role as advisor to the gods. He had even taken a turn or two at the META center.

We approached the castle slowly and made no threatening moves. We allowed them to see us from way off before settling down outside. Once settled, we opened the bottom hatch to disembark the Sheree and Homer's group. Then we waited.

After about two hours we noticed about twenty guards begin to reluctantly exit the castle. They put down their weapons and began walking toward the Genesis and their new life. I'm sure the general and a few armed Marines would greet them. Following the guards the Sheree we brought came out closely followed by four additional Sheree. They too came toward the Genesis. It was difficult to see how many women and children came out, as they continually milled about with the village elders that came to meet them. Things seemed to have gone well.

Once all were back on board we lifted off again to repeat the whole process at the next castle, which also went according to plan. All the rest went well and uneventful, and we returned to Mount Olympus with an even twenty new Sheree and eighty guards, well newly recruited Marines. The general saved the speech until all were on board.

Homer reported, "I didn't have one bit of trouble with any of the villagers. In fact they came right up to us. They took one look at Ares and heard me speak with the right accent and knew we were gods sent to save them as they have been praying for many years. I told them we would be back in a few days to look in on them. That seemed to make them happy."

I really didn't want to deal with the Sheree right now and had them escorted under Marine guard to their group of quarters, where they were given water and food. We discovered they could eat most everything us humans ate, either that or they were afraid to ask for anything different.

Our next stop was the original castle, where I planned to get the flying saucer. Linda had been successful in charging up a few of the fuel cells we had loaded up from the first castle. We didn't really know what they were at the time. The Marines had just grabbed various items as they swept the castle. Linda had been thankful for those items, and during her interrogations of the Sheree had identified those that could pilot the saucers. As it turned out, Spee was one of the pilots. Lt. Boland and an armed Marine would go with Spee to replace the fuel cell and fly it into the hold on the Genesis. Once that was done we would go back to the other four castles and retrieve theirs.

While that team was retrieving the saucer, Linda wanted to canvass the castle for other engineering treasures only she could identify. Doc wasn't sure that was such a good idea, but the general said he would send Marines with her to do her bidding and protect her from harm. Doc reluctantly agreed.

The villagers saw us coming again and in their exuberance to greet us almost ran under the Genesis. The gravity drive pushed them back as they hit it. Still it was close going to land. Homer ran to the bottom loading ramp as it lowered to see what the excitement was. When he came back to the Control Room he was laughing.

Homer said, "They want to see the Olympian gods, especially Zeus that shoots lightning bolts."

86

I was shocked and said, "I can't shoot lightning bolts!"

"You don't have to. You already have when you fired the laser. Remember?"

Oh crap. That's right. I guess to them that laser blast was a lightning bolt. I'm sure it looked like one. I said, "Very well. Who will they want to see?"

Homer said, "Zeus, Poseidon, Ares, Athena, Aphrodite, Hestia, and Hermes."

Well, let's see, that would be me, the general, SgtMaj, Akiko, Katy, Linda. "Who the hell is Hermes?" I said. Homer pointed to Doc. I laughed and said, "Doc, I guess he remembered your Olympian name."

The others in the Control Room were enjoying our discomfort, especially Taka, and I wondered how he had escaped scrutiny. I asked, "Homer, why us specifically?"

Homer grinned and said, "That's all I have told them about ... so far."

I blurted out, "Taka, you oriental devil, just wait till I tell Homer about Buddha." At that everyone in ear shot burst out laughing, including Taka. All knew I was not disrespecting the Buddhist religion, only reflecting on Taka's abundant belly.

I guess we had no choice, so the seven of us gods were escorted to the ramp by Homer. He began the very elaborate introduction of each one of us, drawing cheers from the crowd at each time a god's name was mentioned. It seemed this went on for hours, but in truth it was about twenty minutes.

Finally, Homer brought the address to a conclusion, then we filed back into the Genesis.

While Homer was obviously enjoying making the introductions, Linda slipped out of sight and joined the away teams. The vehicles gently passed through the crowd to perform their tasks.

We knew part of the plan worked when we saw the flying saucer slowly rise and begin its aerial journey back toward the Genesis. We cheered at the obvious success of that part of the mission. We cheered again two hours later when we saw Linda's truck, heavily loaded with equipment, making its way back.

Once the saucer, truck and personnel were all safely back in the Genesis we launched again to the second castle. All the other castles visited went exactly the same and uneventful, even to and surprisingly the ramp introductions. I didn't expect that, but Homer apparently had relied heavily on the villagers knowing that the Olympian gods had returned to save them from oppression. Yes, we would do that.

Genesis Prime Log: 10 May 0001

Since we returned to Mount Olympus Linda had been scarce. She quickly stored all five saucers and confiscated alien equipment and technology deep in the storage cavern, well protected and guarded. She had hardly come out in days, much to Doc's displeasure. This of course made him grumpy.

The general was elated to have Marine recruits to train, and he was with them constantly. When he was not with them he was with one of his Marines, Lt. Margret McKay. They mated during the long voyage, but he was the general. Everyone knew they were together, but the general continued to maintain his command detachment in public.

Cdr. Kim, Cdr. Taka, and Cdr. Tsuji, were always in their own focused world. I think that was a curse of being a genius, in some anyway. Kim and Tsuji were so intensely focused that they didn't seem interested in sex or having a mate. Their work was everything. I sometimes wondered how Taka managed to find a mate in Ioa Ito, but of course they worked together for over a hundred years.

That leaves my girls, Akiko and Katy. Everyone knew our history, and most department heads were part of it. I fell in love with each in separate lives, Akiko initially, then while she slept for thirty years while we developed a way to save her, I fell in love with Katy. Our love was so great I couldn't pick only one, and their love for me didn't make me choose. We just stayed together. I love them both deeply.

The Immortality Gene was developed to save Akiko, and it did, along with many others. The META device was created to save Katy, and it did. I would have done anything to save them.

Akiko and Katy were also deep into their own projects. They would come back to our quarters late at night, but they were so tired we just cuddled together and slept.

So, I was alone with no one to talk to, and I was feeling sorry for myself. I guess that is why I started talking to the Sheree, and of course Homer would hang around me when Naomi wasn't keeping him busy. During working cycle she too was extremely busy, and I think she was sometimes sending him to me so she could concentrate on her work. I had noticed, however, he always went back to her in the late cycle. So I guess all was well there.

Actually, I think it was Homer that got me started talking to the Sheree. He came to me a couple of cycles back and said, "Do you mind if I take the Sheree out for a while and let them get some fresh air and walk around some? I feel sorry for them being penned up all the time, and I'm curious about them. They can't escape. Where would they go?"

He had a point. The Sheree were marooned on our planet, and we were their only hope of escaping or returning to their home planet, assuming it was still there and there race still alive. After I thought about it and agreed, I said, "Well, Homer, I suppose that would be alright as long as you take a few Marines. Maybe I will even go with you."

The Sheree were surprised to see me enter their area and maybe even a little frightened. They had all heard how I had killed their previous leader. I didn't even remember his name now and didn't want to. He had been such an asshole. Some of them actually recoiled from me but most stood in a respectful manner and waited, their heads slightly hung.

After some uncomfortable silence Spee stepped forward and said, "Was there something you needed from us?"

His tone was respectful with no hint of arrogance. I said, "To be honest with you, we have no idea what to do with you. We don't even know we can trust you." Spee looked nervous, so I continued, "Oh, don't worry, Spee. We are not going to kill you unless you become hostile to us and become a threat. I made a promise to the Sheree and will honor that promise."

Relief flushed across Spee's grey face and he said, "Thank you, Zeus. We will offer no threat to you or your race. We are willing to help in any way possible."

I scrunched my face and waved my hand back and forth at his comment about Zeus. I said, "You know I'm not Zeus, and I know I'm not Zeus. It's the native humans here that insist on believing we are the Olympian gods. I think Homer here started it." When I said this last part I turned to look at Homer, and the little shit was grinning widely at me.

Homer said, "Yes, but they want to believe, and quite honestly they need to believe right now. It will make it much easier to help them start living again."

Hearing that shocked me, and I turned to look at Homer in a new light. There was more to this man than I thought. Suddenly, I realized why. He was in fact a new man, thanks to the META system and influence of Naomi. Homer had spent hours at the META Center learning, only he knew what, but he has obviously become educated. I was still thinking about Homer when Spee interrupted my thoughts, and what he said totally grabbed my attention, like I was hit with a baseball bat.

Spee said, "Yes, we knew you weren't Zeus, but we were willing to call you that if you wished.

We knew, because our race actually knew the Olympian gods. In fact we created them. They were not gods; they were only humans with technology, our technology. In point of fact we brought them to Earth thousands of years ago. The Sheree were the magic behind their popularity until they turned on us. By that time we were few, and they were many and had filled the land. Humans are an ungrateful, greedy, self-centered, and arrogant race and turned on us, like they will one day turn on you and your command. The Olympians called us Titans then and drove us out of Mount Olympus and eventually off of Earth."

My response was highly intelligent. I said, "Huh?" Spee actually laughed. If he had intended to get my attention, he certainly had. I wanted to hear everything. I asked, "You knew Zeus and the Olympian gods?

"Oh, no!" Spee said, "We are long lived but not that long lived, but fathers going back a few generations remembered and passed the story down."

I said, "There are probably several hundred questions I want to ask, but right now I want to know why you haven't brought any of this up with the others that have been interrogating you?"

Spee said, "There are several reasons, but the main reason is: this is the first real chance we've had to talk directly to you." The other Sheree were intensely watching and listening to every word being said, and were nodding in confirmation.

"And why is that so important?"

Spee spoke to his fellow members in their private language for a moment then said, "Please understand this is difficult for us to admit. This is the first time our race has seen technology that we do not understand. This makes us realize that we just may not be the superior race. This is hard for us to accept. You are the technology we are talking about. You radiate intense intelligence, human intelligence and computer intelligence. We don't understand it but sense your essence throughout the ship and feel you watching and listening to us, not just through cameras and such, but as if you are the ship and it is alive with your spirit. This is an obvious and major source of trust for us also. We know you have some intense emotions, we feel them, and you have a strong sense of fairness and justice. With your power and intelligence you easily could and probably should be the god Zeus among your people, but you choose not to rule in this way. We think that maybe you are the exception to the humans our race has known in the past. We believe you can be trusted to be fair and just, and we commit ourselves to your leadership."

I could not believe what just happened. I certainly didn't expect to have this happen. I was just following Homer. I wonder if that little shit set this up. Naw, he would have no way of knowing any of this.

I returned my thoughts back to what Spee had said earlier. I said, "You said you brought humans to Earth. Where did you bring them from and why?"

Spee responded, "We brought them with us from our home planet. Where they previously came from we have no idea. It is not within our memory. They may have always been there. Humans were our workers on our home planet and we brought them to Earth when we colonized to be our workers and servants."

"The Olympian gods, as they were called, were a special, modified breed of humans. They were originally intended to serve us. Our scientists had manipulated their building code so they would be long lived like us. That had always been a disadvantage of humans. Human's short lives were inconvenient to us, because they died too soon, and new ones needed to be trained. Unfortunately, this worked against us and eventually caused our destruction."

"Humans reproduce like rabbits did on earth. Sheree are almost barren. We reproduce so sparingly that the human population exploded around us, along with the long lived one, which other humans called immortals. The raw volume of humans threatened our very existence, and the excessive greed of the immortals forced us to leave Earth. Of course we brought some human workers to serve us here, but not any immortals. In an effort to keep the human population from again exploding and driving us off this planet, our ancestors controlled the childbearing females. This is the main reason, not for food. That came later and not acceptable by many of us. As you have probably ascertained, our previous leader promoted this action. He was not very well liked among us. In fact some of us silently cheered when you killed him. We knew when you didn't kill the rest of us that you were a fair and just leader."

Wow! This was too much to take in all at once. I said, "Thanks for being open and honest with me.

That will go a long way with me, but I will leave you with Homer. He wants to take you outside to walk around some. The Marines will go with you until we determine how we all will move forward. I need to think on all you have said, and we will talk later. Have fun outside."

Genesis Prime Log: 18 May 0001

The staff just finished watching the recording I began of the meeting with the Sheree when our conversation started getting interesting. Actually, this was the fourth time we had watched it in the Control Room. I said, "Well, what do you think?"

The general barked, "I don't believe any of it. Of course, since you killed that arrogant SOB now none of them ever like him, and of course they didn't want to eat human children. They seem to also be telling us that their race tampered with human DNA? Do they really expect us to believe humans originated on their home planet, a planet they want us to take them to? I think they are telling us what we want to hear to manipulate us, pure and simple."

Linda mused, "I wonder why they didn't mention any of this to me? Maybe it is like they said, you are the puzzlement. They do seem to present a believable story, and frankly, I believe them. It certainly explains much of the myth surrounding the Olympian era. Still, Mac's skepticism seems in order."

Doc's comments seemed the most plausible when he said, "They certainly summed you up Nick. They know something about your essence in body and computer, and there is no evidence to have made that assumption. But, they knew without much medical knowledge. That is something I have discovered about them. They have little medical knowledge and in all our discussion they have never mentioned a doctor or medical knowledge. Even when he mentioned altering the building code he said scientist. They seem all technical in electronics. Still, I keep remembering something Linda said about them having technology but never actually knowing how it works. I think she said they were stupid about how things actually work. This is interesting. They apparently are an ancient race and seem to be relying on ancient technology from a long gone era. I think Linda knows more about how their technology works, the actual science, than they do. As she said, they just use it.

Katy said, "Maybe we should just give them enough rope and see if they hang themselves. I mean loosen the controls on them and continue to watch them. Let's see what they do."

Linda said, "Let's take them to their equipment and let me pick their brains on what they know. I'm very interested in knowing more about the Plasma Drive and the Energy Dome. But, like Katy suggested, watch them close."

I thought for a moment and said, "Very well. We can do that, but I think I will continue to interface with them, since it's me they opened up to. Just keep the Marines close, but not too close, Mac."

"Doc, I'm curious. You mentioned that they don't seem to have much medical knowledge. Do you think you and Taka can check them out medically, maybe find out why they don't or can't reproduce? That's assuming they submit to the physical."

Taka cleared his throat to get our attention and said, "Well, I must admit I was curious, too. That is why I took a sample of the dead alien's blood to analyze."

Doc teasingly said, "Why you sneaky bastard! Why didn't I think of that?"

At that comment everyone burst out laughing.

I said, "Well, sneaky bastard what did you find?" The laughter continued.

Taka said, "I've been very busy with the hospital and clinic and haven't had much time to do much. Like I said, I was curious also and did, however, look at their DNA. Their DNA is not all that much different from humans, surprisingly close. It's close enough that they probably have similar organs and functions. Maybe we can discover the fault. It should be interesting anyway."

"Very well." I said, "Is there anything else we need to talk about."

I looked around the Control Room and was surprised to see Homer raise his hand and then stood. "Yes, Homer. What's on your mind?"

Homer tentatively started, "Sir, I've been learning about the Genesis and the Genesis Plan through the META center, and I understand that the Genesis was stocked with hundreds of thousands of embryos. I also understand that the doctors also created artificial uteri during the long voyage. I am wondering if we can help my people out and birth more females for the villages?"

I was in shock, and looking at the faces of the other staff members I could tell they were also. The first shock was learning just how much this once illiterate village hunter had learned, and the second shock came at learning how brilliant his plan was. Naomi even looked at him with her jaw hung open in shock. In all honesty none of us had even thought of this possibility. I recovered quickly and passed the buck. I simply said, "Doc?"

Doc was still a little shocked and said, "In all honestly, I think it is a great idea. I have been thinking. The mated couples in our settlement I fully expect to see many pregnancies soon, so it's not realistic to add other children to their families this soon, where the villages have the older women without children. I think they might welcome having children to raise. Yes, yes, it's a good idea." Doc looked at Taka, and he simply shrugged as if to say, "Why not". "I think we can be operational within a week and be able to birth babies in, well, the standard nine months."

I said, "Very well. Homer, it's your idea, so you get to talk to the villagers and the grandmothers and get everything set up."

Homer was all smiles, and so was I, until Akiko sent a telepathic message to me saying, "Hey hon, I think Katy and I are also ready, and we have stopped taking birth control." I'm not positive, but I think I had to swallow my ass about then. I am also positive that if anyone saw my face at that moment they might have seen me straining to get it back down. Certainly Akiko and Katy saw me, because they were looking directly at me and laughing.

When I went to talk to the Sheree this cycle I made a startling discovery. After I explained about them getting a physical exam, Spee quickly agreed. They would go along with anything that might help them reproduce. Suddenly curiosity overwhelmed me and I said, "Spee, why are you the only one talking? Don't the others have a voice?"

Spee said, "Yes, they have voices, but only a few of us speak English, myself and Dee," pointing at the female Sheree standing beside him.

"We can talk in the ancient Greek language." I said.

Spee shook his head in the negative and said, "It doesn't matter what language we use as long as we have at least one spokesperson. Most of the others don't understand that language either. You will learn in time that most Sheree are not self-centered, jealous, or act independently as humans do. It does happen, as with the leader that is now dead, but it is rare. Mostly we have no ambition beyond supporting our group, and any one of us can be trusted to speak on behalf of the group. Our race tends to congregate in groups with a single spokesman, usually male, but not always. Most here have never been a spokesperson and have not been required to learn a language other than our own since maturity, although our early training included learning a second language in the event it might be required."

I asked, "What languages does your group speak?"

Spee spoke to the others and said, "Of the human languages Dee and myself speak English, five others speak Greek, one speaks Spanish, one speaks Mandarin Chinese, and one speaks Arabic. Some of the group knows other languages, however those are for other alien species."

Hearing that surprised me and I asked, "Do you actually interface with other species?"

Spee said, "We have interfaced with four other sentient races in our past, but only two are in this area of space." Spee spoke with the others again and said, "None of our lives here in this group remember personally dealing with the other two. They are many light years from here on the other side of the galaxy. Some of us remember dealing with two races of sentient beings other than human, both now hostile and dangerous. We learned their language before we went to war and continue to pass down their language, should we ever need to negotiate."

I asked, "When was the last time you met them?"

"Within our lifetime both races came to colonize this world. This was before we depleted our fuel cells, and we were able to fight off one race. The other race we call Gaters in English, and we managed to damage their ship, and they are still here."

I frightened the Sheree when I screamed, "What? They are still here?"

Spee and the others took a step back at my outburst and Spee said, "Yes, Sir. They came in a Plasma Bubble full of water, which we destroyed. They come from a mostly water world and entered our oceans. The race is sentient but not very technical. We had no idea how they managed the Plasma Bubble, but they did, or some other species did it for them. We don't see them often, but they have been known to attack human villages if they are close enough to the water. They kill and eat everyone. This is why we don't have any operations near large bodies of water, now."

"Why didn't you tell us about them? I asked.

Spee said, "Well, Sir, you never asked before, and truthfully we thought you knew, because you built a wall around your city. That was smart."

"I'm asking now. Tell us about them. You called them, Gaters? Why?

Spee had stopped shaking and seemed more calm. He said, "In English on Earth there is an animal that frequents the shores and rivers. Humans called them alligators or sometimes just gaters. That name stuck because this race sort of looks like them. Gaters are large, about our race's height, and reptilian with four legs and a long tail. They are very fast on all four legs, but they can walk and run upright on their larger hind legs when they come out of the water. They have a toothy snout and skin that looks like an alligator. They fight with their snouts, but they also use weapons in their front legs, which have hands with thumbs, so they can grasp swords and spears. They are aggressive, vicious and strong, and they are also very good at throwing rocks accurately. If you haven't met them yet, you will. They will eventually find you and attack, especially with you being close to the water. They will consider this their domain."

Again and of course I recorded this conversation. The staff will want to discuss this latest revelation in detail, but that would have to come later. There was one more decision I had made, so now was as good a time to address it.

I said, "Spee, since Dee speaks English I want her to report to Dr. Rossen. We are going to attempt to learn the Sheree language. We have a device we created for recording and transferring thoughts. I'm positive it will not work on your race, since it was designed for humans. Still, I think we can record it from the human learning your language. Dee will only have to say and explain words and phrases once and it will be recorded into our computer. Once your entire language is there, we can transfer the knowledge to other humans through this META device. My key personnel will then be able to talk to all of you in your own language."

Spee said, "This technology sounds impressive, and we are not easy to impress with technology. It will be as you say. Dee will report to Dr. Rossen and do as requested." Dee seemed startled at the mention of her name and began paying intense attention to our conversation.

Genesis Prime Log: 22 May 0001

My body was still asleep in our quarters, but my holograph image automatically sprang to life along with the dome lights when Doc burst into the Control Room. He looked both annoyed and tickled at the same time.

Doc said, "I wish you would tell me next time you assign me a project."

"Huh?" I said, "What are you talking about?"

"I'm talking about Dee. When I got up early she was standing outside our quarters waiting for me. I have no idea how long she had been there, maybe all night. She told me you had told her to report to me about learning the Sheree language through the META, which by the way is a great idea. I've already assigned a META technician and they are already busy at it."

I started laughing and said, "I meant for her to report to you this cycle. I didn't mean for her to immediately go to you. I figured I would have a chance to talk to you at the staff meeting. Oh well, I will have to be more specific with her next time."

While I was talking to Doc I began nudging Akiko and Katy awake carefully, hoping not to arouse them in any way. It had already been a long night, since they were very serious about getting pregnant. Of late I often think about what the general had once told me about the Immortality Gene, how it kept him at the top of his game in bed. At the time I found it funny, but living with and loving two highly sexual and beautiful women, also recipients of the Immortality Gene, actually became a challenge sometimes. Now I'm anxious for them to get pregnant, maybe we can slow the pace some.

This reminded me of a question I had been wondering about. I said, "Doc, if Akiko gets pregnant, like she wants, do you think she will have problems like she did before? I don't want to lose her again."

Doc smiled and said, "You too? Linda wants to have another child too. But, to answer your question, the odds are very good that she will be fine. Pre-eclampsia is not likely to occur in her again. If it's going to show up it is usually in the first pregnancy, and remember there were other contributing factors involved at that time. Akiko was carrying your clone and none of her DNA contributed to the fetus. This increased the odds of her body rejecting foreign DNA. Another thing to remember is that she had not received small doses of your DNA in the form of sperm to build up any immunity, and at that point you and her had never had sex." He started laughing then and said, "In fact I remember Akiki saying, 'I always thought I would have to have sex in order to get pregnant, but it seems I must have a baby just to have sex.'" I remember how she had everyone laughing with that statement.

Doc continued, "Still, the main reason she will not have a problem is because she has had the IG and is immortal. Simply put, her body will continually repair itself, even if she is attacked by pre-eclampsia again. No, Nick, she will be fine, and you shouldn't worry."

"Here is another thought, though. We didn't have the artificial uteri before, and now we do. Akiko doesn't have to go through the nine months of carrying a fetus nor childbirth."

I laughed out loud before saying, "Doc you know how much trouble we had with her before. You know there is no way she would allow that. She will want to carry her baby to term. The only satisfaction I will have when she tells me, 'You did

this to me,' is to remind her she didn't have to."
We both laughed at that.

Genesis Prime Log: 26 May 0001

I waited for the normal staff meeting cycle to bring up my last conversation with Spee, since Dee already told Doc about learning the Sheree language. I did however caution Akiko and Katy to carefully watch out for workers near the water. They didn't press me for more, since we try to keep work out of our quarters, but they knew there would be more information coming.

I began by showing the recording of the latest conversation with Spee. Several requested seeing it again, and it was just now finishing.

The general quickly asked, "What about the other aliens?"

Katy jumped in and said, "What did he mean when he said, 'They will eventually find us?'"

I quickly held up my hands and said, "Hell, I don't know. You saw the recording. We need to ask Spee. Wait, someone go get Spee. You can ask him."

In a few moments a very uncharacteristically nervous Spee was led into the Control Room by a Marine, and I motioned him to a seat, which he quickly took. I was slowly beginning to understand that the Sheree were uncomfortable being alone and separated from their group, because Spee simply shut down and sat in silence. Apparently the spokesperson of a Sheree group must take strength from the group as a whole, and I wondered if it might just be more of a sharing of minds. It was certainly worth exploring more. At any rate, Spee was intimidated severely.

I said, "It's alright, Spee. You can go back to your group, and we will talk more later. I will come to you. We didn't mean to frighten you, and I apologize."

After Spee left I explained to the staff what I believed was the problem. They all seemed to grasp what I was suggesting, but it was Kim that seemed to put my suggestion into perspective.

Kim said, "The Sheree is an ancient race, and maybe the Sheree species has evolved more than humans. They seem to share more with The Enlightened than humans. The Enlightened shared a common mind and they obviously had Plasma Drive, also suggesting common origins or interface. Maybe this common mind is a sign of being higher evolved."

That was an interesting concept to explore, but we had more pressing business to conduct right now.

Before I could begin, Akiko said, "I think I may have an idea about the Gaters. I have quite a few Bottlenose Dolphin embryos in our cryogenic inventory. I'm thinking we could introduce Dolphins into the river and bay. They are very fast and strong, and they have been known to kill sharks. Maybe they could kill Gaters or at least keep them out of the river. I've even heard tell that, because of the high Dolphin population, there were no sharks in the Mediterranean Ocean. The Dolphin had either killed or ran them out. I don't know if it's true or not, but Dolphin do kill sharks. They ram them at high speed and kill them, and they also launch a coordinated attack in numbers. If we can birth enough to have a mature pod of ten or so they might survive and keep our river and bay clear of the Gaters. This of course assumes they will stay here. I don't think a Gater can catch a Dolphin, since a Dolphin can swim about thirty miles per hour. If this experiment works it could be a long term solution. I guess we might also include some killer whales, but they tend to like the open deeper water better."

Mac said, "I think that is an excellent idea. Still, I think the existence of a hostile and aggressive water based enemy will probably ruin my idea of shipping. Now I'm thinking of a different type of ship, a gravity powered ship, so that the ship won't actually touch or be in the water, maybe hover high above it where it can't be attacked from the water. Now that I think about it, a hover ship could actually cross land to the site of the mines and dock on land. Yep, that would work, and I could still be called Poseidon." At that the room exploded in laughter. After the laughter died down he said, "Can we do that Linda?"

Smiling hugely, Linda said, "Yes, Poseidon, I believe we can." Again the laughter rang out. After a moment she said more seriously, "Honestly, that sounds like a much better idea, and quite frankly it's more efficient and easier to do. I had been planning a form of rail transport, and we may still have to have one, but this would eliminate the immediate need for now."

I said, "Let's get back to the Dolphin for a moment. I'm assuming everyone likes this idea?" I looked around the room and saw a consensus. "Ok then. Let's think about how we are going to proceed and discuss it at the next staff meeting."

CHAPTER 7
(Dolphins)

Genesis Prime Log: 01 June 0001

Lt. Jane Waters joined the staff this cycle. She came in with Akiko, and I knew immediately who she was. In truth, I cheated. I looked her up in the files. She was a marine biologist educated at the University of Miami. Of course she was a PhD like all the other whiz kids, and prior to joining the Genesis team she ran the Saratoga Dolphin Research Program. She was one of Earth's most experienced research scientist and marine biologist specializing in Dolphins. Dr. Waters had been among some of Akiko first choices to fill her allotment of cryogenic slots before the politicians and bureaucrats took over. Oh well, that's another story. In our current situation Dr. Waters had obviously been a great choice.

Lt. Waters, a rank Akiko had assigned her when she came out of cryogenics, was a tall woman, somewhat muscular. I wasn't sure if the muscles were brought with her or earned by the hard work all the newly awake team had endured. She was a very dark black lady with short, black, curly hair, dark eyes, full lips, and a friendly face. She was also quite shapely and pretty. I liked her from the start.

Akiko introduced her to the staff as an expert in Dolphins and could answer all their questions. Akiki immediately turned the podium over to her.

Lt. Waters looked a little startled but recovered quickly. She said, "Cdr. Mitsuhara has briefed me about the potential threat of the, what she called Gaters, and her suggestion to introduce Dolphins into the waterways, and I agree. Dolphins are very social, even with humans, and group in pods of around ten and more if the food supply can support more. They are very smart and communicate among themselves to organize their feeding hunts and for defense. Generally they are gentle and curious, but if threatened they will attack and kill or drive off any threat. A mature Dolphin weighs around a thousand pounds and should be able to defend itself against a Gater, especially with their speed. From what I hear, the Gaters would poise a direct threat to them and would become a natural enemy to them in this environment. As I said earlier, Dolphins are very social, especially with humans, and if we can find the right incentive to them they should remain in contact with humans, meaning here. I do believe they would keep the area clear of the Gaters."

"A little bit about the Dolphins: As I said, they are very smart, probably just under humans. Some say they are smarter than humans. Their brain is actually larger than a human, but that doesn't necessary mean they are smarter. They breath air so they must constantly remain awake to surface for air. If they didn't they would drown. They do sleep, however, but each side of their brain works independently from the other and each side sleeps separately, one side at a time. This is probably why their brain is so large, but don't take me wrong. All evidence suggests that they are self-aware and

110

problem solving smart. On Earth Dolphins were considered the second most intelligent mammal, just under humans."

"Yes, Dolphins are warm blooded mammals and breath air. They also bear their young live and nurse their young for well over a year, and this may surprise you. Dolphins join the ranks of the higher apes as intelligent mammals, other than humans, that have sex for pleasure. I'm not sure if you consider this a sign of intelligence or not." This brought a few chuckles.

Dolphins generate sounds in the form of complex whistles and clicks to communicate with each other and produce a sonar called echolocations to, in essence, see in dark water. This complex sonar system of generating and relieving signals is so efficient a Dolphin can determine size, shape, distance, speed, direction, and even identify their prey or threat. In some cases a Dolphin can generate a signal so strong it can stun and confuse their prey.

"The only potential problem we might have is the extreme purity of our water here on Genesis Prime. Dolphins usually range in ocean or salt water. There are some breeds of Dolphins that prefer fresh water, but they do not necessarily include the most common Dolphin, which is the Bottlenose. I do, however, believe the Dolphins will adapt."

She continued, "Questions?"

I said, "I think we are all in agreement that we should proceed, but how do you suggest we do that?"

Dr. Waters (Jane) said, "The gestation period for a Bottlenose Dolphin is about twelve months, much longer than a human. Within this time period we would need to build a protected bay for them to live in. When I say protected, I mean from the Gaters. Since the Gaters mostly live underwater, we can't allow them to access this Dolphin's cove to attack our defenseless, young Dolphins. The Dolphins would be captive and wouldn't have a chance of survival. We can bar the entrances to keep the Gaters out and the Dolphins in. We will also need some sort of wall or dome to keep the Gaters from walking to the cove to attack the Dolphin."

"The existing river current can be channeled to provide the circulation of the water within the cove to keep the water fresh and clean. The real absolutely necessary requirement is handlers for the baby Dolphins. They will have no mother to teach them. The handlers will have to be there when they are birthed to teach them how to surface to breath, bottle nurse them, but sadly we won't be able to teach them how to communicate. They will have to teach themselves, and maybe us also. No meaningful communication or language between Dolphins and humans has ever been established. Of course, a few words like ball, fetch, etc., and small things have existed, but we know complex communications exist between Dolphins. We just can't understand it ... yet."

I said, "Akiko, where would you like to build this Dolphin cove?"

Akiko took the podium and said, "Thanks Lt. Waters. I'm sure we will have plenty more questions for you as we continue with this project, and I'm sure everyone here would like you to head this project up."

Before she could continue Homer stood and said, "I want to be involved in this project! Thanks to the META Center I have also become a Marine Biologist, and in addition I have watched every episode of Flipper twice at the Library Research facility." At that last comment the room burst out in laughter, much to his embarrassment, but he obviously was serious and held his ground.

Still smiling, Akiko said, "Thanks Homer. I'm sure Dr. Waters will need qualified help with this project. It's still a little early, but I'm sure she would like to talk to you when the time is right."

That seemed to satisfy Homer and he sat back down, but out of curiosity I began researching Homer's activities at the META Center. I was quite surprised to see the volume of entries he had made into the center and even more surprised to see the volume of downloads into his brain. Homer did indeed qualify as a Marine Biologist, among many other professions. This man was highly motivated. His brain must have been starved for knowledge before, and he was not one to have taken education for granted. Others from Earth had partaken in downloads, but it seemed that Earth bound humans, many of them anyway, had considered learning negatively as a chore physiologically associated with years of hard work and time consuming studying. Homer was not inflicted with this negative view. To him learning was an opportunity to be taken advantage of, a gift. Well, good for him.

I also noticed that Homer seemed more sophisticated. I guess education did that to a person. He sat there like he belonged associating with all these geniuses, and indeed he did. He even looked the role with well-kept hair and even a sporty coal black mustache and goatee that blended with his dark Mediterranean complexion. Naomi sat beside him radiating pride in her mate. What a change.

Akiko continued, "We have opened up and cultivated many new fields for crops, many already producing, in the prairie on the other side of the river. After crops are harvested inside the wall I'm thinking we can carve out a section at the southern end of the settlement inside the wall for the nice sized cove. We can also construct a Wonder Metal dome over the cove for further protection. We have a guard tower near this location for protection, and the general increased the Marines on the wall after I lost another fisherman."

I said, "Well, coordinate with the others to see if we have missed anything, and if no one has any objections, let's get it started."

Genesis Prime Log: 10 July 0001

Homer had been taking the Sheree out for short trips into the community for a while now, but he said they felt uncomfortable and didn't go far or want to stay out long. I decided to go with him this cycle.

As we entered the Sheree's area, Spee actually looked pleased to see me. I was a little surprised at his reaction but realized I hadn't been around in a while. I said, "Let's go for a walk Spee. Let's all go for a walk." All the Sheree got up at once, which reinforced my thinking that the group shared some common thought or communication. Since I spoke in English I know the non-English speaking aliens could not have known what I said, other than through Spee's understanding of my words. That confirmed my belief. I would remember to tell the others at the next staff meeting.

We walked out of the ship and down the road. The Sheree seemed calm and comfortable, unlike what Homer had described. I think the difference was my presence and that they had aligned with only me. As we continued down the road I heard Homer and Spee talking, and I was shocked to realize that they were speaking in the Sheree language. I was further shocked to realize that I understood the language. Well, of course I would understand it if it was in the computer, which apparently it was for Homer to have accessed it for download. Apparently Dee's time with Doc and his assistant had been successful in recording the Sheree language.

To test my theory I spoke to the Sheree in their own language saying, "I take it Dee was successful in teaching your language to our computer." I watched the Sheree as I spoke and saw little or no reaction. The only exception was Dee. When I spoke her name she turned to look at me and flashed me a quick uncharacteristic grin. Maybe individual pride does exist in their race. The other Sheree did not react as if they apparently were paying attention to another form of communication. As Spee had once said, in time I would understand their nature better. That I was.

Spee said, "Dee was successful." The technology is impressive.

Spee spoke with no excitement, as if it was no big deal to them, and it wouldn't affect them at all. I guess it wouldn't matter to them one bit, because their internal communication at the thought, reasoning, and emotional level would not be affected. The Sheree were becoming very interesting.

As we neared the settlement we began getting a lot of looks from the busy workers, many of whom haven't seen the Sheree at all. Katy mentioned in a staff meeting that she tried to keep the settlement population informed of all the activities, so I'm sure they knew of the Sheree. They just haven't seen one up close.

I was long overdue bringing the Sheree to Linda's private domain in the mountain where she had been working on the Sheree's secrets of their technology. This was as good a time as any, so we proceeded into the entrance of the storage cave. This was the first time I had actually been inside, and the first thing I noticed there were guards posted. The Marines didn't know what to do. They had obviously been told that no one was to be allowed entrance, but seeing Admiral Johns escorting the aliens they must have figured I outranked all others. They saluted and stood aside, but I was also quite sure they would call the general. I suspected that he would show up soon.

The Marines had apparently also called Linda, because as we headed deeper into the massive cave

Linda and her top assistant, Bill Boland, met us, smiling. When I say massive cave, I do mean massive. I had attended a football game in the Astrodome once, and this felt exactly like that. Once I pasted the initial shock, my attention returned to Linda.

The smiling Linda said, "I see you brought the whole bunch. This is good. Maybe I will finely find out what all this stuff is."

We followed her deeper into the cave. As we went I was admiring the engineering of the cave. At this base level the mountain was almost solid granite and clearly structurally sound, but Linda had added massive columns throughout the cavern as a secondary reinforcement. There was plenty of room to fly the saucers in and out, which she obviously had planned on, because the five saucers were parked in a line along the back wall. Alongside them in an open area she had like equipment separated and stacked, as if in a warehouse, but I saw none of it hooked up.

Linda saw the focus of my stare and said, "No, I haven't activated any of it. I wanted to first make sure what I was turning on and what it would do. Some of the items I identified. It's easy to recognize the guns and some tools, but I still don't know what kind of guns they are or what the tools are used for."

I asked, "Aren't there any user manuals in on their computers?"

She looked sad and said, "We believe so, but we can't read them. I know you deciphered some of their language on the voyage, but this is technical writing and difficult, if not impossible to read."

I had a sudden inspiration and said, "Show me one of the manuals."

When she brought up a manual on the alien computer I leaned down and studied the computer screen for a few seconds. I laughed and said, "I can read it, and you can too once you go to the META Center and get your download of the Sheree Language." I wasn't sure if Dee's teaching of her language included the written version, but when I was able to read it I knew for sure that it did. I also couldn't help but notice that all the Sheree acted surprised and maybe a little upset. Something certainly passed between them, and Dee hung her head. I don't think they intended for her to disclose the written language for just this reason.

Linda was surprised and said, "No shit? I will go this cycle"

I hadn't noticed the general come in and didn't know he was standing behind me until he said, "Linda, you better go when your done here, because I'm going to classify that particular META download. I only want a select few to have this knowledge of alien weapon systems. I'm going to classify others as well. In fact, I'm going to impose some restrictions and approval requirements on all downloads. We can't have too many brainiacs and walking encyclopedias floating around. We already have one to many now." He was smiling when he said it and slapped Homer on the back. Homer just grinned.

I immediately knew why and where he was going. Education was good. It was necessary to get the job done, but over-educated people tended to be more self-centered and aloft, something Spee had warned us about humans. There is only so much room at the top, and I already had my team. The general and I both knew this was going to be a potential future problem, and I welcomed his leadership wisdom.

Linda led the Sheree through her collected bounty asking question after question and pointing at items. At one stack of large round pipes wrapped in tubing, Spee said they were magnetic pulse generators. They came to a stack of what looked like large coffee cans with an even larger funnel sticking out the top, all made out of Wonder Metal. At Linda's point Spee said they were Dome Generators.

That got Linda's interest and she said, "How do they work? What is the technology behind it?"

Spee spoke as if talking to a child saying, "Yes, this is technology. You make it work by turning it on."

Linda's eyes sprang wide open in surprise at the simplistic and patronizing sounding response. But, Spee's expression showed no intent to be sarcastic. To him that apparently was the whole answer. I think Linda in that moment understood that these Sheree had absolutely no idea how the technology was created or scientifically how it worked; it just worked. Either that or they had no intention of telling her. I believe the former to be true.

Linda's eyes reflected her thoughts, which I clearly registered, but she chose to ignore Spee's comment, something I'm not sure I could have done.

They continued down the row of equipment, and Spee continued to identify items such as drills, lasers, torches, and various other tools. One item seemed interesting; it was a type of laser, but it froze water instantly. Apparently it was used to build a temporary bridge over water, but by the general's reaction I knew he saw it as a weapon. I knew he would put it to use as one.

There were five of the next item, which were about the size of a microwave oven with a visual monitor mounted on the top, which must function as monitor and control panel. Linda stopped suddenly in her tracks when Spee called it a Plasma Generator.

Linda said, "Is this all there is to it?"

Spee and the other Sheree looked around the area then said, "For the most part, yes. There is another part about this size." His hands indicated a circular unit about the diameter of a bucket. "That unit connects wirelessly to the main unit and mounts on the outside of your ship. It transmits the plasma bubble around your ship."

That last statement about being attached to our ship spoke volumes and may very well have been an unintentional slip. That slip let me know that the Sheree remained focused on us returning them to their home world, but I didn't let on that I picked up on the statement. In reality, I really didn't blame them. I would want to go home, too.

Linda said, "That's it? That's all there is to it? She knew better than to ask how it worked.

Spee said, "Yes, it's great technology and simple to operate. We can show you."

Once Spee identified all the items, I could tell that Linda was anxious for us to leave so she could get to the META Center and start reading the user manuals. I led the Sheree and Homer back outside. The general stayed with Linda, and I assumed he was also headed to the META Center.

We began our walk back up the road to the Genesis, and I was admiring the engineering and construction work as we went. The wall was totally complete, along with the bridge, watch towers, numerous other buildings inside the wall, and other buildings going up on the other side of the river, which I assumed were the flower mill and ore refineries. Katy had told me that the flower mill was going to use old technology with a huge mill stone powered by a water wheel and river current. She didn't want to be totally reliant on advanced technology.

As we went higher I could see Green fields stretch out for miles, dotted with raised watch towers. I was thinking that those must be to protect the workers from the Saber Tooth cats and in the event of Gater attacks. So far only the fishermen had been attacked, at least we believe it must have been the Gaters.

Far off in the distance toward the forest herds of buffalo could be seen grazing on the waving grasses. We had been lucky indeed to find them and to find them tasty also.

As we approached the Genesis we could see the Dolphin cove was under construction at the southern location Akiko had suggested, and the construction looked to be well ahead of schedule.

Spee noticed the direction of my gaze and said, "The Dolphin in numbers will be able to drive the Gaters away. Early in our species' colonization of Earth we had a similar need to protect against sharks and another water predator, and thanks to the Dolphin that predator became extinct."

"The Dolphin are not native to Earth. We discovered them on a distant water world. They are sentient and highly evolved. They were the dominant species on their planet, and were keenly receptive to colonization and expanding their species on other worlds."

I think it was at that point that I began to realize that the Sheree may also be communicating with me at some sub-level. It could be possible that Homer might have mentioned Dolphins to the Sheree but highly unlikely. I began to believe they had sensed my thoughts to some degree about the Dolphins, and Spee was reacting to my thoughts. Could this be how Spee sensed my connection to the Genesis, and why they seemed to connect with only me? They treated me as one of their own. Certainly they all seemed calmer around me and to accept my leadership. I would talk to Doc about this and get his reaction.

It suddenly hit me what Spee said about the Dolphin, and I'm sure my jaw physically dropped. I said, "How did you know the Dolphin were keenly receptive to being transported to colonize Earth? You communicated with Dolphins? And how did you know we were even planning to use Dolphins against the Gaters?" It just all came busting out at once.

122

Spee actually chuckled. It was the first time I had heard humor expressed in Sheree voice. Spee said, "I believe you are finally beginning to understand us. To answer your last question first, we understand some of your thoughts. You are the only human we have ever been able to communicate with on this level." He thought for a moment and said, "Well, this is not entirely true. We heard you communicate with another in this way, but we only heard it once. It's all very strange to us, but this is why we trust you. You are different. We think in time you will be able to understand our thoughts as well.

My mind was churning. Who could I have been communicating with? The only person I have private telepathic communication is Akiko. Akiko? Could it be her? That could be embarrassing. I said, "Do you read my thoughts?

Spee said, "No. It is not on that level. It is like us. When we put words to thoughts in any language there is a mental interpretation of meaning, which we share. We hear this sometimes from you. Please think on this."

"Now, the first two questions have the same answer. Yes, we communicated with Dolphins. They are very different, but we created a common language that worked somewhat. It is a difficult language, but we have kept it alive." He spoke to the others for a moment, then turned back to me and said, "That language is no longer alive in this group. The Respected Leader kept that knowledge, and he is now dead."

Well, crap. I killed the only one that knew the Dolphin language. Oh well, this is too much to ponder for now, we continued on into the Genesis.

Genesis Prime Log: 25 July 0001

Linda was all smiles at this staff meeting. I knew why, but I let her tell me and announce to the others.

Linda took the podium and said, "As many of you know, I took the Sheree language download on the META unit and since then I have been able to read and understand much of the information stored on the Sheree computers. This also included the user manuals for much of their equipment, technology as they call it. Some of the science behind their technology still escapes me. Maybe it's beyond me, but still, I'm understanding much more of it than I did before. One of the things we have now mastered is the saucer. Back on Earth we had already cracked the secret of the science behind the Gravity Drive, which we used on the Genesis. Now, thanks to the disclosed information, we understand the controls used in the saucers. Yes, we can fly them now. Lt. Boland is our first pilot." Cheers erupted in the Control Room.

"Homer has requested the first charter flight to visit the native villages to check on them and prepare them for the addition of young children. They will be leaving in a few days, so if you want or need to visit the villages, log in with Lt. Boland. There will be a regular schedule to the villages in the future."

"As to the remainder of Sheree inventory, the general has already taken control of the weapons, and if I'm not mistaken, already has them deployed. There are other unknown equipment, but they will be studied in the future."

"The really big item is the Plasma Bubble Drive. I have studied this device intensely, and I am both pleased to tell you I can operate it, but sad to report I don't understand how it works. It is far beyond my science knowledge. The good news is that it is incredibly simple to use, seemingly far too simple. It works on a complex system of star maps. The screen operates as any computer does. You view the maps, scan over to the general location you want to go, expand the maps on the screen, pick the spot you want to go to, then hit enter. Presto you are there. It's almost like a video game except the game is reality. I can't find any scientific basis. It's like homing in on your house on Goggle Earth. You keep expanding your view till you see what you want to see. In the Plasma Drive you would actually BE there. It's as if space (time and distance) is compressed into a computer program to manipulate. To be honest, I'm not sure I will ever be able to understand it, and I doubt the Sheree understand it either."

"I want to install one of the systems on a saucer and try it. At least if it crashes, only a couple of volunteers would perish. I have plenty of volunteers willing to test drive it. I do believe it will work, and truth be known, it doesn't matter if I understand it as long as it works."

I said, "Very well, but I will not allow you to volunteer. No one is expendable, but you are beyond expendable. You can't be replaced. Understood?"

Linda looked dejected, but she reluctantly nodded, but I got a silent "Thank you" from Doc.

I said, "Does the saucer have weapons on board?"

Linda said, "No weapons. It is a simple shuttle and observation craft. Its defense is its speed."

"Should we add weapons to it"

Linda thought for a moment and said, "I don't think we can. The outside structure has a complex spinning arrangement, which could be disrupted. I think the only possible weapon we could use would be focused gravity or use its drive to form a magnetic pulse. That's about it."

"Very well," I said.

Genesis Prime Log: 5 Aug 0001

I had my first test as guardian of the human race this cycle, and my first hard decision. The staff had gathered, had their first cup of coffee, and settled down for the meeting when Katy asked for the podium. I could tell she didn't want to bring up this subject, but she dutifully proceeded.

Katy said, "As all of you know many new departments have, out of necessity, sprang into being. It was expected and a necessary escalation of our growing colony. These departments have begun to organize themselves and conducting their own staff meeting. I attend them, preside over them, and serve as their liaison to what they consider the higher government ... us, and I have been asked to inform you that we are running out of

126

workers. All those professionals chosen from Earth and awakened from hibernation to build the colony became our workers. As we have built and began to operate these facilities many of these previous workers have slowly been absorbed into the functions they were originally chosen for. For example, trained electricians are building and maintaining the electrical grid, dentist are setting up facilities to take care of the colonies' dental needs, chefs cooking, hunters hunting, butchers butchering, and on and on. To put it bluntly, we are running out of workers for the menial tasks such as construction workers, farm and field workers, fishermen, herder, cooks, sanitation, mill and plant, etc. We haven't even began refining ores or manufacturing, and we will need a large number of workers for that. You all get the picture."

"The immediate need for workers cannot be filled until our children grow, and we haven't even started birthing any yet. We are estimating that an influx of additional workers will not be available for many years, so we are faced with a forced industry growth rate reduction or increase of workers."

"Many of the colony's Assembly, as they are calling themselves, are pushing to commandeer the new Marines. They are saying we don't have a threat necessary to justify that many, when they could use them. Don't worry general, I have already said no to that."

The general said, "Let me know who is saying that, and I will be sure to cut protectors for them and we'll see how they like it."

I said, "Do I also assume you have a recommended solution?" I already saw it coming, and honestly I had very mixed emotions about it. And, this was something I didn't want to deal with, but it was inevitable with humans.

Katy said, "Yes, there is a recommended solution. The Assembly wanted me to request permission to recruit workers from the native villages, like the general has done for the Marines."

I said, "yeah, I saw it coming. This reminds me of Earth, in particular the U.S. wanting the Mexicans to come do the work no one else wanted to do and create an underclass to do the menial tasks, while the upper class makes the wealth. I bet your Assembly has already discussed creating money to do business. No, you don't have to answer. That's human nature. Don't get me wrong, capitalism is a decent form of running a vibrant and productive economy, certainly better than communism. Unfortunately, communism is what we have right now. It was necessary to pull together for the good of all, and that's what we did. Capitalism is based upon hard work and risk and deserves its own rewards, but there will be limits. We let it go too far on Earth, but here I will stand in the way of creating an unjust society and a permanent underclass. That will not happen, not here! There will be rules."

"We will continue to operate on a communal good status. We will take care of everyone, including the workers they intend to recruit. They will become a part of our colony. So, you tell the Assembly the villagers that want to come here will be treated as members of this society, be given living quarters, fed in the cafeteria, clothed, all the benefits, have access to all facilities, and they will be given the opportunity for advancement."

"Now, while we are talking about rules, we might as well address this now. We will NOT build a user or welfare society. Everyone works in some capacity at an approved position. Chaplin Kline could read you scripture that says, "Let he that does not work, does not eat." Or something like that. This is probably not a problem right now, because everyone is working hard for our survival; but it will surely come as our population grows."

"I also don't intend to waste resources on prisons, hospitals for the criminally insane, or the like. Anyone diagnosed as a psychopath or antisocial will be exiled from our colony, no exceptions, and the severe cases will be executed. The psychopaths on Earth were responsible for most of the crimes, they filled our prisons, mental hospitals, and far too many among our general population. We don't want them among our colony population. We want a harmonious colony of people that care about the overall good for all. If anyone doesn't fit in this mold and become disruptive, they will be exiled."

"It may be a while before they do, but let them know that when they initiate a court system, I will be the Supreme Court and final say on laws or appeals. They may call me the hanging judge, because I really don't want to get involved and will not be lenient. I think until our population gets much larger I expect the 'Ten Commandments' to be the guidelines for conduct. I mean it covers all the major crimes."

"I guess my answer is 'Yes' with the limits as I have stated. Work through Homer at the village level. I guess he has become our go-to-guy concerning the villages."

My speech pretty much put a damper on the rest of the meeting. I had positioned myself as the bad guy again, but that was my job. Besides, I honestly believed everything I said, and I would not hesitate to enforce it.

The general stayed after the meeting broke up. When the Control Room was clear, he said, "Nice speech, Nick. I'm glad you gave it. I'm even happier to know you believe it. I couldn't agree more, but are you all right? Do you need to talk about it? I'm here if you do.

I said, "Thanks general, but I'm fine. Ask me again when I actually execute someone."

I was happily surprised that Katy was all hugs and kisses during the late cycle, and I was almost positive she didn't like my speech. After all, she would have to be the one to tell the Assembly. I was happy about our rule of not bringing work to our quarters, but as the evening went on I began to believe that there was more to it than just our rule. Katy and Akiko kept giggling and I finally said, "Ok, what's up? Out with it."

Katy cuddled up to me and said, "I'm late."

Stupid me said, "Late for what?" Then after my mind kicked into gear I said, "Oh. No shit?" Sometimes I can be incredibly articulate. I pulled Akiko into our embrace and said, "We're going to have a baby."

Katy and Akiko giggled again, then Akiko said, "Babies."

"Huh? I said, "errr awww ... Katy is going to have twins?"

Again they broke out laughing and Katy said, "No. I'm not having twins, but Akiko is."

Then the reality hit me and my mind swooned. I thought, "Babies? We're going to have lots of babies." Then I began to smile.

Genesis Prime Log: 15 Aug 0001

Homer and Bill Boland were at the staff meeting this cycle. They had just returned from their trip to the five villages, and they were all smiles.

Homer went to the podium and began, "Before I start, I need to let everyone know that Lt. Boland now has a new Olympian name and a Viking name. Through most of the villages, even with his blonde hair, they referred to Bill as Heracles, and that seemed to be a universal reaction." Bill stood and took a bow among the laughter. "It was the last village we visited that they began calling him Thor. I believe Thor was the son of Odin and noted for his blonde hair, large size, and strength, just like Heracles was the son of Zeus. Admiral, is Bill your son?" I knew he was kidding, but I didn't think it was funny and didn't laugh with the others or comment, so Homer continued, "At any rate, the villages are extremely happy about taking children to raise. The elderly women were literally jumping with joy. Now they have a purpose. They are preparing a place to raise them."

"The elders were also pleased to see us visit them. When they saw the saucer they all came running to welcome us. They asked if we wanted them to keep mining the ore, but looking at their needs and scarcity of crops, I told them to concentrate on growing food and providing for the village. This pleased them. Oh, can we give them some metal plows to cultivate the fields? Hopefully they can domesticate some buffalos to pull them."

I was pleased to hear Homer trying to help the villagers, and I said, "Homer, I'm sure we can do that." I looked to Katy who was nodding yes.

Katy jumped up and said, "Homer, I think we can do better than that. We aren't using our tractors and plows right now, since we have already planted. I think we can spare them and a couple of operators to go and lay out and plow and plant their fields."

Homer said, "Thank you Katy. That would be a great help to them."

"The villagers will do anything we ask of them, but we didn't mention bringing them back here as workers, not after the first village. We went first to what I remember as being the smallest village, the third one. They have about a thousand villagers in total. I'm thinking it best to move the entire village. I didn't mention anything to them about that, because I wanted to discuss this with you and the staff first."

I asked, "Katy, can you handle that many?"

"That is a little more than we were expecting, but, yes, we can accommodate that many if we can put them right to work." She said.

"That would be your call, Katy." I said to Homer, "So, I guess your answer is yes. Coordinate with Katy and get it done." A smiling Homer took his seat.

Linda took the podium as it was vacated and said, "I'm pleased to report that a Plasma Bubble has been installed on a saucer and tested. It works, and we are now ready for a more extensive test. We tested the drive in the cave and only moved the saucer a few yards, but it worked exactly as we planned. Any suggestions on where we should go on our maiden voyage?"

"I do." I said, "I've been thinking about our sister planet in this system. Kim, what did you name it?"

Kim said, "We just call it Genesis Two."

"Well, that is as good a name as any," I said. I was thinking that Genesis Two is relatively close enough to come get the saucer if there is trouble. And, I would really like to have a survey done of the planet from orbit to identify the human villages, look for signs that the Sheree might still have charged fuel cells, etc."

Linda said, "I like that idea."

CHAPTER 8
(Genesis Two)

Genesis Prime Log: 25 Aug 0001

The Genesis left early this cycle, heading for village #3. Bill and Homer had immediately visited them after our last staff meeting. To say that the village's reaction had been joyous would be a gross understatement. Homer had given them the schedule and instruction to bring nothing, but when we landed we could clearly see flocks of animals they planned to bring with them. Oh well, the more the merrier. We would have to do a little more cleanup on the engineering level after the trip.

Homer met them immediately after the loading ramp deployed. It looked somewhat like I imagined Noah's Ark would have looked. The villagers began entering leading animals, some of which I did not recognize, and they carried bundles of whatever on their shoulders in spite of their instructions.

After the loading ramp was lifted, Homer brought several of the elders to the Control Room for introductions. I'm sure he just wanted them to see Zeus and the other Olympians. I don't remember their strange names, but I'm not sure they even saw us, they were so intent on watching the liftoff and flight. It was probably the most eventful time in their known history.

The trip was relatively short, and when we again lowered the loading ramp the villagers disembarked at a hurried pace, with Homer leading them out into the colony. Impromptu pens had been hurriedly erected for their animals. Akiko had apparently called ahead to her team. The barracks for the villagers were not complete, but tents used in the original landing had been erected for their housing needs. We could see Homer leading them into their tent city, being greeted by anxious and curious settlement residents. Homer would no doubt spend the rest of the cycle introducing them to the facilities. No doubt he would be busy for several cycles trying to get the new recruits settled and get the right villagers with the right department head. After most of the staff had left to get to their duties, Doc remained. I had been wanting to talk to him anyway, and said, "How long have you been holding back the information about the twins? You could have at least given me some kind of warning."

Doc began laughing and said, "I didn't want to ruin their surprise, and you know my daughter, Katy would have killed me. I take it that it was a surprise?"

"Duh! They also played it up and tricked me, and told me in the most surprising way possible."

Doc said, "Did they tell you Linda and I are going to be parents also? Luckily only a single child, a male. Now we don't have to worry about you seducing this one."

We both laughed at his subtle reference to Katy and her immortal clone, Katy Two, who took Katy's place when she died. I said, "I know everyone thinks I was a dirty old man, but in truth, I was seduced in both cases. I was taken advantage of in both cases. In fact she still takes advantage of me."

Doc said, "Yeah, right. You expect me to believe that?" He was smiling, so I laughed with him.

I said, "Congratulations to you two."

After we quit laughing Doc got serious and said, "I've been meaning to talk to you about the Sheree. I've finished the medical evaluation of them, but it doesn't make a lot of sense. There is no reason they can't reproduce. The females produce eggs, and the males have sperm. The sperm count is very low, but the males do produce sperm. The good news is that I can harvest the eggs and fertilize them with sperm. I can reinsert the fertilized egg in the female's uterus, and it should grow to term. This form of In Vitro Fertilization (IVF) was commonly used on Earth to help couples that had trouble with getting pregnant. The Sheree seem to have all the parts and organs, so it should work."

"I cannot, however, utilize the artificial uterus. I don't know enough about their blood to reproduce it, nor is there any real reason to do it. Unless I am terribly wrong, they can reproduce with help from me. Still, I'm puzzled, though, about why they seem to have so much trouble reproducing."

"Since they relate to you so well, I was wondering if we could talk to them together."

I said, "Of course. Let's ask them to come to the Control Room."

As the Marine made a call, Doc looked at me funny and said, "You want all of them here?"

While we were waiting I explained my suspicion about the Sheree sharing, on some level, a common mind, thoughts, emotions, whatever it was.

He was already deep in thought about what I had said when the Sheree came into the Control Room.

I casually but intentionally spoke in English so Doc could appraise my theory. I said, "Hello Spee, Doc and I have some good news for you and wanted to tell you the results of his medical finding. He tells me he is positive that he can assist the Sheree in reproducing."

The reaction was immediate among all the Sheree. Happiness radiated from all of them and large smiles spread across their faces. I quickly looked at Doc to see if he registered their reaction. I had spoken in English, which only Spee and Dee understood, but all of them instantly understood what I said. In my hypothesis the others understood as soon as Spee processed my spoken word interpretation. Doc looked at me and nodded. He hadn't missed it.

I continued, "Like I said, Doc is sure he can help, but he has questions for you. Are you willing to answer his questions?"

Spee said, "Yes, ask your questions."

Doc said, "There is no real reason Sheree can't reproduce, and I would like to try to figure out the reason. The males produce a low level of sperm, but it should be enough to impregnate a female's egg, which the females seem to produce. Why this isn't happening is the mystery. Please explain your mating habits such as how often a male and female actually mate, how many of the females have actually born babies and how many, do the males and females mate for life, and anything else that may have a bearing on this subject."

Spee spoke with the others in the Sheree language, which I followed. He basically just requested individual answers to the questions posed. Spee then said, "Most of us have had what you humans call sex within the last five years. It is not something we have much urge to do, and when we do it rarely produces babies. We do not permanently mate unless our mating results in a child to raise, and of the nine females here only two have had children. When we have sex and it doesn't result in pregnancy we don't mate."

Doc spoke in Japanese as a private communication to me saying, "It's pretty obvious why they don't procreate. Only one coupling in five years is pretty bad odds to hit the female's fertile window. No wonder they don't have many babies. Well, at least I understand now, and another thing that's obvious. The Sheree don't have a clue about the biology of reproduction."

I responded also in Japanese saying, "I hope this is not a sign of evolving. I don't think I would like only getting the urge for sex once in five years."

Doc went back to English and said, "Spee, I am now positive I can help, but the females will have to go through a procedure in my clinic, the mating males too. So, tell me how many of the females want to be with child?"

Spee spoke to the females and got some emphatic and somewhat loud responses then turned and said, "All of them!"

Doc and I were both surprised, but I said, "It will be so, Spee. Doc will coordinate a schedule with all of you and get it done."

Spee was somewhat emotional when he said, "Thank you very much."

Genesis Prime Log: 02 Sept 0001

I had been anxious for this staff meeting, since the saucer left for Genesis Two. All precautions had been planned for, including extra food, water and oxygen...just in case. Linda had even tried to get me to remove the restriction on her going, but I wouldn't budge. She was simply irreplaceable, so she had to settle for bugging Kim at the telescope as he observed Genesis Two. They had radio communications, but although the distance to Genesis Two was short, relative to Plasma Drive, the distance was sufficient to significantly delay radio signals.

After the launch, well launch was not really the word to use, the sudden disappearance of the saucer, Linda hurried to the Control Room to hover over Kim's shoulders until they verified that the saucer was in orbit. After that was verified she settled down and waited, like the rest of us. They had been gone two cycles without much communication, but they had returned early this cycle and were on their way to the staff meeting, while we anxiously waited.

Bill Boland was the pilot and he took along a Marine volunteer, and Homer insisted on going in case they landed and he was needed to talk to any villagers. Now they entered, smiling, and were greeted by cheers, which quickly died when the team was followed in by three Sheree. This was a surprise to all of us. The team had managed to keep this fact quiet, even from Linda, who was as shocked as the rest of us, and I have no idea how I missed it.

I think they decided that Homer would be the initial spokesman, because he headed to the podium. He was beginning to look like a natural behind the podium, well maybe a little sheepish now. Homer said, "Well, we were successful, as you can see. We identified seven villages. They really only have two major land masses, and the villages are almost on only one land mass. We saw no signs of active technology, so we decided to get closer. Bill's idea of getting closer was to buzz the castles just like the ones here at about a thousand feet. We still saw no reaction so he buzzed them all again at five hundred feet, then we went back and hovered to get a reaction.

"The reaction we finally got was totally unexpected. As we hovered over the first one we came back to, The Sheree came out of the castle without any guards and stood in front waiting on us. I guess they figured we were Sheree also. Anyway, we landed, and they came right up to the saucer. Imagine their surprise when we came out and then began talking to them in their own language. They didn't get scared, so Lt. Boland started laying down the law to them, and telling them how it was going to be. He told them about what happened on Genesis Prime. He even told them about the Respected Leader's death, which they didn't seem to care."

"Well, to our surprise they said they would comply with our rules, and in fact already had, many years ago. After their supply ships stopped coming they released all the young females and children back to the village, even the guards they had. They had resolved to live out their lives in isolation, but once they saw us come they were filled with hope again. They said they wanted to return with us and join with the Sheree here, and here they are."

"If you think that was surprising, what happened next was even more surprising. I, well we, including the Sheree, decided to go talk to the elders of the village. They had gathered and had actually approached the saucer. I walked out and began greeting them, and they looked at me like, 'What the hell are you saying?' They began talking to me in a language I had never heard before. They looked different, too. They were big with blonde hair, but I couldn't understand one word. Then you talk about surprised. Bill began answering them in that strange language. Well, since I didn't understand the conversation, I'll let Bill tell you from here."

Lt. Boland was laughing at Homer's hand waving antics and animation while Homer was talking, but he stepped up to the podium and began, "It really wasn't all that strange. They were speaking Norwegian, a language I have spoken since I was young. My parents and grandparents immigrated to the United States from Norway, and I was born in Michigan and raised speaking Norwegian. My grandparents never even learned English, so if I wanted to communicate I had to speak Norwegian. I couldn't believe they were speaking a language I'm fluent in, and their dialect wasn't that different."

"The villagers were as shocked as I was when I talked to them. Then I felt like you guys must have felt when they fell to the ground and started calling me Thor over and over. I tried to explain I wasn't a god, but they wouldn't hear anything different. Even Renee, oh, the Sheree spokesperson, told me the villagers were devout worshipers of a Germanic religion, and Thor was the focus of it. Anyway, I quit trying."

"It seems that there was no animosity between the Sheree and villagers after the Sheree released the humans several hundred years ago. They have gotten along ever since, and the Sheree have even tried to help them, but as you know, they no longer have technology. And, Sir, there are many humans there. They have thrived and reproduced in their freedom."

"We were able to gather plenty of data on the planet for Cdr. Kim to analyze, but I can tell you a little. It's colder there, and it is mostly water. As Homer reported, there are only two continents, not overly large, and we counted seven villages, which seem well populated. We didn't stop at any of the others, because we didn't have room for more Sheree. I hope we did right in bringing them back with us."

I said, "Excellent report Lt. Boland and Homer. As far as the Sheree are concerned, that was the logical move. I'm sure we can learn more about Genesis Two from them."

Turning to the Sheree I said in their language, "Renee, do you speak English and did you follow our conversation?"

They had been standing together in the back, and when addressed, Renee stepped forward and said in his language, "I'm sorry, Sir, but our group does not speak your language, but we have followed pieces of your conversation."

I understood what he meant; they had received some form of the telepathic meaning, probably from me. I said, "Very well, I will take you to the other Sheree soon and we can talk more." To Akiko I telepathically spoke, "Akiko, I want you to go with me to see the Sheree."

She responded transmitting, "What's up?"

"You will understand soon."

The reaction from the Sheree was immediate, as I suspected there to be. They jerked alert and stared at me then Akiko. I had been thinking about what Spee had said about my telepathic ability. Now seeing the reaction from this group that obviously hadn't spoken with the others, maybe, I was convinced there was more to learn.

I ended the staff meeting and waved the Sheree to follow me, which they immediately did. I led them directly to Spee's group area. As we entered surprise registered briefly on the group, but they quickly recovered. They immediately began talking among themselves. I understood what they were saying, but understood little of the meaning. They were talking numbers, dates, names, which apparently had to do with ancestors. After they completed their conversation, Renee turned to me and said in Sheree, "I'm sorry that I don't speak your English language, but I am now the spokesperson of this combined group. It would be appreciated if we can speak in our language, in which you are obviously fluent."

I had no animosity toward Renee. He had been respectful and had already freed the humans, but there was absolutely no way I was going to let Renee dictate terms to me, I didn't care how nice he did it. I spoke intentionally in English and harshly, "No you are not! I have a history with Spee, and he will continue to be the Sheree I will communicate with. Is that understood, Spee?"

Spee looked back and forth between Renee and me, but I kept staring directly at him for a response and ignored Renee. Finally, Spee said, "Respected Leader Renee is a descendant of a ruling royal lineage and outranks us all. I am not allowed to assume his rightful position as a Respected Leader."

I bellowed, "Who is in charge here?"

"You are Sir." He said.

"Very well, then. I make the rules here, and this is my rule. Is that understood?" I stared unblinking at both of them.

All the Sheree seemed very uneasy and shuffled around, but Renee simply bowed slightly and remained silent as Spee said, "Yes Sir. It will be as you say."

I intended to discuss Akiko's and my telepathy ability, but I was no longer in the mood. I transmitted, "Akiko, we will discuss telepathy another time with the Sheree."

Akiko knew why and responded, "I understand...another time."

As Akiko and I turned to leave we heard a commotion and turned to observe all the Sheree churning in excitement. We waited.

Spee spoke, "How do you do that, speak without speaking? We heard your words in our minds, both of you."

I said more calmly, "To be honest, we have no idea. We were going to ask you. We discovered this ability between us quite by accident. I understand why it happened with me, because I have an artificially enhanced brain, but I can't explain Akiko's telepathic ability."

Renee spoke to Spee, who was about to speak when I interrupted him to say, "Spee, Renee doesn't have to remain silent, none of the Sheree do. He can speak directly to me if he has something to say, any of you can. What I was talking about before is your group's apparent limitations on communicating. If I only have to deal with a single spokesperson, it will be you. That is a restriction your group puts on itself. Now what did you have to say, Renee?"

Renee, said, "Thank you. We understand. I was curious about what happened earlier. You and her communicated with the mind talk, but we didn't understand your words. This time we understand your words. What is the difference?"

I didn't understand at first why, but Akiko did.

Akiko transmitted to me, "Earlier we spoke in Japanese, and they don't understand Japanese. This time we spoke in Sheree, which they all understand." Smiling, she switched to Sheree and transmitted, "Do you understand me now?"

Spee and Renee responded in unison, "Yes."

It was obvious that they had no idea how they understood, and I thought it best to let them discuss it for a while, so I transmitted in Sheree, "Let's give them time to think on the subject. Let's come back in a few days."

The Sheree were nodding in agreement, so we left.

Genesis Prime Log: 12 Sept 0001

I was ready for this staff meeting. It had been awhile since I actually presided over one. I had mostly let the staff choose the direction, but I had some concerns that I wanted to address and some projects I had been thinking about.

I took the podium and began, "There are some projects that need completion and projects needed to be started. Let me just lay them out for you and you can take over. First, we need to make some more trips to Genesis Two in the modified saucer and pick up the rest of the Sheree. From what I understand, all the humans were freed hundreds of years ago, so we don't really have a complaint with the Sheree there. Eventually we will need to make a trip to their home world and take them back, but we need them all. I would also like to deliver them back with a herd of small Sheree children. All the females seem to want children, and I would like to see that we help them. I'll leave that with you, Doc."

"I'm hoping we can establish a friendly relationship with the Sheree' home world. It would be nice to have friends and allies in a lonely galaxy.

"Linda, when we do go to their home world we will need to take the Genesis. Is it fully functional, need any maintenance, or upgrade? If so, let me know what is needed. If you feel comfortable in doing so, we might want to do a reconnaissance flight in the saucer first."

"I've also been thinking about additional defenses. I would like to open up a tunnel completely through the mountain. That would make a perfect escape route if it is ever needed, plus a tunnel opens up the other side of the mountain for colonization. Of course, that would also require a granite wall also."

"And general, while we are talking about defenses I think it would be a great idea to establish a Colony Guard. I think all residence should be trained to defend the colony. Do it like the Israelis, train male and female. What do you think, general?"

The general stood and said, "I think that is an excellent idea, and I agree that all residents should be trained to defend our colony. Still, I must ask why, since we have no real existing threat? Do you know something I don't?"

I knew this would come up, but I expected it to come from the fledgling colony politicians. But, the question needed to be asked, and the question needed to be answered. I said, "Well, we are on a new world and new solar system, we know there are hostile aliens here already, maybe two; and another hostile race once tried to colonize on our planet and there may be others. I just think we should prepare for the worse possible scenario, but the real reason is I have an uneasy gut feeling, a hunch, something is wrong or going to be wrong. You might not understand my explanation, but there you have it."

Doc quickly spoke, "Nick, your mind is integrated into the most advanced computer created by humanity at its prime. If you have a gut feeling, I would tend to trust it, since all that intellect is always awake and analyzing input. I would think that maybe your rational mind hasn't yet identified the focus of your sub-conscious concern. General, I think you should be concerned as well."

The general said, "Of course. I will do what he suggests, and I also trust Admiral's gut feelings."

I continued, "Another thing I have been thinking about. Have you noticed that we are beginning to see darker late cycles? I guess Genesis Prime has circled the sun and is about to come around to the dark side of the second sun. This of course means we will eventually see both suns on one side of the planet. Yep, we will have dark nights for about six months, and you know what that means? Gaters and other predators will probably be coming out at nights. The Sheree tell us they are aggressive, dangerous, and intelligent. That's a bad combination. I interpret this to mean that we can expect to see organized attacks during the dark part of the cycle. Are we ready? Do we need to do anything more for defenses, like night lights, alarms, etc.?"

"Let's talk about these things at the next staff meeting, and Katy, I think we should start including a representative from the colony in our staff meeting. I know you try to keep them informed, but let's give them a direct voice as well. I hate politics and politicians, but I guess they are better than chaos and strife from a hundred separate special interest groups.

Genesis Prime Log: 02 Oct 0001

Akiko took the podium first and announced, "Since Lt. Boland brought the extra 23 Sheree from Genesis Two, we are stressing our ships ecosystem again. We are trying to feed and care for too many, besides, they are not carrying their own weight. We need to get them out into the colony or into their own separate area and find jobs or projects they can do, but I don't know what they can do. They don't look strong enough to do heavy work. I haven't a clue what they can do to help the colony."

I silently transmitted to her in Japanese, "Well, hon, go find out. It will give you a chance to use your telepathy, but hon, keep a trusty Marine with you. I'm not sure I completely trust them, especially with the new ones."

She smiled at me and transmitted, "Good idea. Oh, not about the Marine, about using my telepathy."

I said, "Akiko will investigate the Sheree." I left it at that.

Kim took the podium next and said, "I have completed analyzing the gathered data on Genesis Two, and Mr. Boland and Homer summed up Genesis Two pretty well. As they reported there are only two continents, and they are not really all that large. The planet itself is larger than Genesis Prime, but most of the planet is water, much more so than we are. It has a larger and slower orbit and farther out from the sun. This of course makes the mean temperature lower. That planet definitely has seasons, unlike Genesis Prime. Still it is quite livable, even in the winter, really nice if you like to snow ski."

"In my continued surveying of Genesis Prime I noticed a certain oddity. There appears to be an intelligence made structure underwater near the equator. It's certainly not natural made. It is quite large, but I couldn't tell much more about it, nor if it was ancient or newer. There are no human villages anywhere near it, however. At some point we might want to investigate it further.

Katy was next, "At our last staff meeting we discussed adding a new staff member. I would like to introduce Mr. Pollard to the members. He will be representing the colony inhabitants and their concerns. Mr. Pollard, please stand up so everyone can see you." He stood and turned to greet the members. "Mr. Pollard was elected from the various groups to be their representative."

"The villagers and newcomers to our colony are assimilating quite well and seem to like it. They have all taken a turn at the META center for a download of information Dr. Rossen prepared for them. Knowing him, it was more than the English language program, which was the initial focus. As Doc put it, if they can't speak the language, they can't assimilate. Many mysteriously came out knowing skills they had never heard of before, like ... well you name it. Most of them are already at work all over the compound, in the fields, mills, refineries, everywhere actually. We thought they would assimilate faster if we split them up in the work force. They remain housed together while their barracks and apartments are being completed, so they could remain comfortable being together with their elders. As all know, the villagers are not yet used to a family structure, but that will come."

"SgtMaj Gomez has already begun to cycle select colony grunts, as he puts it, through his boot training camp. I can't say they are happy about it, but they accept the need for it, since we lost another fisherman and almost lost a field worker to one of the giant sabertooth cats. These incidents seemed to accent the need to be prepared. A Marine sentry managed to drop the cat before it got the worker. You know they could probably do some damage with these." As she said that she produced one of the saber teeth. It was as long as her arm from elbow to the tips of her fingers. It was certainly scary enough, and she got several ohs and aws.

"Akiko didn't mention it, so I will. She has opened several other fields for crops, and if I'm not mistaken, they have already been planted. Her department is feeding the Sheree, colonists and the new villagers, and they are managing to stockpile reserves. Akiko asked us to build her a cold storage facility back inside the mountain, which we have completed. It is large and cut into the granite, and she has got it half-filled already. I might also mention that at Lt. Sami's insistence, we waste very little in the cafeteria. Portions are kept small, but they can come back if they want more. What foods that is left over are canned immediately, thanks to Mr. Pollard's operational cannery."

"Yes, the ore refinery is also operational on a small scale, and they are ready for ore to be delivered. We have found some mineral deposits on Atlantis that are being tapped into, but we need more. We don't want to waste manpower on mining, so it's time for Poseidon to rule the seas and deliver the already mined ore from the villages." Katy was already laughing.

I believed the laughter that erupted at Katy's last statement actually embarrassed the general, something rarely seen. At least his face flushed red before his hard face broke out in a huge grin. He interrupted saying, "OK, little miss, it's not too late to bend you over my knee and spank you. I'll take it from here."

It was Katy's turn to blush at the laughter at her expense, but she should know better than to try and best her adopted grandfather. I had to join the laughter, but then I love to see her face flushed.

The general continued, "I was about to report to the staff that our hover ore transport is complete and staffed. We are scheduled to leave for our first pickup next cycle. Linda ... I mean Cdr. Clark, the other one, and Cdr. Tsuji were very helpful. I am happy to hear, however, that the ore refinery is ready for business. I think I can promise you that you will never again hear a complaint about not having enough ore to process."

"Our defenses are improving. You have already heard that the citizens are being trained to fight, alarms and night lights have been installed, but the tunnel is a massive project. It will take a while for that."

As the general was stepping down I said, "General, if you install some cameras and lasers on the fence, maybe I can help from here." He nodded as he took his seat.

Linda was next, and she was still smiling as she took the podium. She said, "Most of what I was to report has already been covered. All I have left to discuss is the reconnaissance mission to the Sheree home world. We've checked and double checked everything and we feel comfortable in scheduling the mission; however, with your permission, I want to send along a few of the Sheree. They can probably tell us what we are seeing when we get there."

I said, "With obvious precautions, I agree, and by that I mean a Marine guard."

Linda continued, "At the last staff meeting you asked about the continued reediness of the Genesis. I want to remind you that I was the principal designer of Genesis, and I spared no detail or expense. The general can vouch for that. He certainly complained enough.

The Genesis is constructed almost entirely of Wonder Metal, and as such is virtually indestructible. It does not wear, and even motor bearings and coil wirings are made of Wonder Metal. Simply put, Genesis will not wear out. Even so, Genesis is stocked with an abundance of spare parts, enough to last for centuries if need be. Now, to answer your question, after landing we went through the Genesis from top to bottom and everything remains in perfect shape. The only limiting factor there ever was, was the human brain cell computer system, which is now self-repairing and immortal. So, everything is in top condition with the Genesis."

Doc was the last to speak, "I'm here to pronounce success with the Sheree reproduction problem. Spee and Dee paired for this experiment, and I was successful In Vitro Fertilization (IVF). I took Dee's egg impregnated it with Spee's sperm and reinserted it into Dee's uterus. Yes, Dee is now pregnant, and they are happy, extremely happy. In fact, out of the twenty-one females, fifteen are now pregnant. The process failed with six of the females. I have no idea why. They want me to try again, and I will try."

With that statement everyone cheered, with the exception of Mr. Pollard. I quickly realized that few below had met any Sheree other than perhaps seeing them. At this point they probably wouldn't care anything about them and would wonder why we do. To be honest I wondered the same thing. I still wasn't sure if I trusted them.

Genesis Prime Log: 08 Oct 0001

After a few days of listening to Akiko's telepathic messages to the Sheree, I finally figured out how to mute her messages. I'm not sure how, but I managed. During this communication break my mind went elsewhere until I heard Akiki say, "Nick, where are you?"

I said, "I'm here hon. What's up?"

She said, "I've been calling you, but you haven't answered. I thought something was wrong."

"The first I heard was when you said Nick..." I then realized Akiko had directed her transmission when she identified her transmission toward me (Nick). She was mastering her telepathic abilities. I explained my theory.

She said, "That's good, huh hon? Can you come to the Sheree area?"

"I'll be right there."

As I was en route to the Sheree area I was amazed to hear telepathic transmissions to Akiko from both Spee and Renee. I wasn't quite sure how I knew who was transmitting, since I detected no actual voice, but I knew, just like I knew it was Akiko. They had certainly made progress. Now I was excited.

As I entered the Sheree area, they saw me, and I was bombarded with an excited jumbled mix of telepathic messages. I said, "Whooa. Slow down. One at a time."

Akiko transmitted in the Sheree language, "Nick, this is fantastic. I've been working with the Sheree. I figured if I could hear your telepathic message and talk back to you, they should be able to, also. I mean they heard our telepathic messages. To me that meant they should be able to transmit also. We have been working on it for days, and they finally figured it out. I couldn't explain it, but being convinced, they kept trying. Now they are all communicating by telepathy."

I said, "Akiko, you have done very well. Don't you think so, Spee?"

Spee said, "Your mate has helped us greatly. We never knew we had this ability, and we are excited and pleased to be under your leadership. We will honor you."

Wooaa! What just happened? I figured I had better find out and said, "What do you mean under my leadership? You do know we are preparing to take your group back to your home planet?"

Renee spoke telepathically, "Sir, we no longer want to return to our home planet. Now that our females are growing children, we want to raise them here. Children are special to our race, since we have so few. Back on our planet they will take our children. No, we will remain and serve you. Still, our race is cautions of humans. We have learned that humans are not to be trusted, but you are a welcome exception. You and all those with you, you call them your staff, are exceptional. Besides, in all honesty, our race is boring. We have had more fun and excitement with you and your group, more than we ever did with our race. Now that we have learned the talking without sound, we have a special bond with you and your mate. We want to stay with you."

You could have pushed me over with a feather I was so shocked. I looked at Akiko for her response. She was no help. She just shrugged. I had to laugh at that reaction, and she joined in. I said, "Do you all feel this way?"

I felt a flood of telepathic "yes" pings bombard my mind. That sure sounded like a unanimous conformation. I said, "Very well." There wasn't much point in saying more.

Renee said, "Thank you." He attempted to say Akiko, but all that came across was an abbreviation, Ako. "Ako explained that we needed to contribute to the colony, and we would like to do that. Let us take on the tunnel through the mountain. We just need access to our tools that are stored in the cave, some power blocks, and some of your block movers. We can build the tunnel, and we would like to move to the other side of the mountain and build our own compound, wall and defenses from the tunnel construction, which we will start from there. We would need some help at first, but we can become self-sufficient eventually."

I transmitted, "That sounds reasonable. Give me a few days to get it started."

Genesis Prime Log: 18 Oct 0001

Akiko and I met with Doc and explained the breakthrough with the telepathy in the Sheree and how we communicated so efficiency. I said, "I still don't understand telepathy, certainly with Akiko. I'm glad we can telepathically communicate, however. I just don't understand how."

Doc said, "Well, if you remember I didn't believe you when you came to me with it originally. I believe it, because I can see it. We know why you have telepathy. Your pineal gland is highly developed in your brain and the brain of your human body. Also, both brains are reinforced by a large section of both brains. That's how your mind can function through your body, but that doesn't explain Akiko. The only thing I could ever come up with was that her brain theta waves must match your brain."

"I don't know what to tell you about this new telepathic ability with the Sheree. I guess I can speculate." At my nod he continued, "We can assume that the Sheree as a race may be more evolved than humans. They seem to be an older race, and we already know that they already possess a weak form of telepathy with the transfer of thoughts among their groups. Maybe their race evolved more than they thought, and it only took

157

Akiko to give them the confidence to take the next step."

"We could also speculate that humans are also evolved and just haven't figured it all out about telepathy. It could be that your telepathic ability triggered Akiko's. Maybe we all have the dormant telepathic ability. After all, humans all have that third-eye pineal gland, although mostly dormant in adults."

"I don't think I could speculate more than that."

After our meeting with Doc, Akiko and I began talking about what he had suggested.

Akiko said, "Maybe it's true that most humans are capable of telepathy. If so, maybe we should start working on Katy. It would be so cool if all three of us could communicate through telepathy. Let's find out."

We both grinned at the obvious possibilities.

CHAPTER 9
(Identifying the Enemy)

Genesis Prime Log: 25 Nov 0001

We gathered outside the Genesis a couple of hundred feet below the cave entrance to the nuclear power plant to watch the Sheree tunnel exit on this side. The Sheree wanted the tunnel to be high, and it made sense, because there would be less tunneling. I had been pleased with the cooperation from all, helping the Sheree get settled on the other side of the mountain and set up for construction. Linda even built a road around the south side of the mountain for equipment delivery and daily food delivery. I was never quite sure if the colonists were just being helpful by delivering food, or if they were afraid to have that many Sheree coming to the cafeteria. Whatever the reason, I was pleased with the corporation.

I had also been surprised at the Sheree's construction abilities. They were very skinny but surprisingly strong. I would never have guessed. Their tools were extremely useful at cutting through solid granite, in fact the tools cut granite like a hot knife slipping through butter, and the cut was smooth as glass. With those tools and Linda's block gravity lifts, the Sheree cut and moved massive amounts of blocks in a short amount of time. I hadn't seen the other side, but I was told that they also built a semi-circle stone wall fence around the small colony of Sheree camping there.

The general said he thought they wanted to surprise me, so he didn't tell me much more. I figured I could wait.

Spee, Dee and Renee and his new mate stood with the gathering, which included almost everyone not working at the moment. It was a large crowd, and the excitement was electric.

Renee had painted an X on the spot they said they would exit. I thought it might be an arrogant show of extreme confidence, certainly far too presumptive to pick the exact spot, because a slight error of measurement could result in a major deviation at this end. We would just have to wait and see.

Just as these thoughts were running through my mind, a smoking blade stabbed through at almost the precise cross of the painted X.

Renee transmitted, "You wonder how I knew so precisely?"

"Yes?"

Renee said, "One of our tools looks through rock. I looked before I came here, so I could impress Linda. Please don't tell her. She is another we wish to impress."

I couldn't help it. I burst out laughing. I glanced over to Linda, but she hadn't noticed my laughter. She was staring in awe. Who knew Sheree had a sense of humor.

Slowly the blade carved out a perfect square and moved on the next one. In a matter of minutes an arched area had been laid out in block. Moments later the upper blocks began to slide back into the cavern. The opening slowly widened until a gaping arch, still rough around the edges, stared back at us.

The Sheree workers then began slicing the rough edges, allowing the corner blocks to fall to the floor and quickly picked up. Standing outside we could only see the blackness of the cavern until one of the workers brought a power line outside to attach it to Linda electrical grid. The cavern blazed to light, illuminating a massive tunnel that seemed to go on and on, so far we couldn't see the end. Spee and Renee led the way inside, and as I entered I saw why. The tunnel slopped down, but the walls of the tunnel looked perfectly straight and aligned and the light seemed to reflect off the smooth walls. All that could be seen within the tunnel were the workers leading the huge blocks away. Even that was impressive, because they were dwarfed by the size of the tunnel.

Spee began our tour by speaking in perfect English and explaining what we were seeing, "The tunnel is just over 1,500 feet long, slightly inclining for drainage and to lower the elevation at the other end, and as you can see, the top of the arch is 20' high and 20' wide, allowing any size equipment to pass through."

I noticed that Linda had nudged herself to the front of the line of visitors. She was still awestruck. I had to laugh. Renee had certainly impressed her, which is hard to do.

As we approached the far end, Spee said, "We have also excavated some rooms off the main tunnel for various purposes. We will build more at your end when we build the entrance."

The two rooms were far more than just rooms, they were the size of basketball courts. We exited out of the tunnel on to a flat platform with a road

161

leading down into the inside of a castle. I had to stare in disbelief. They had built a semicircular castle wall surrounding their castle, and it was at least 25' tall and 5' thick. There was one massive gate in the front at the road. But, the most impressive construction was the castle itself. It was built against the straight slope of the mountain and at least four levels. It wasn't complete, but enough to judge its size and complexity. Guard towers stood at either end of the castle that looked down over the entire complex. I almost looked around for the knights, horses and lances. They took us on a complete tour, but the best part was the initial shock coming out of the tunnel.

Renee had been successful in impressing Linda with their engineering and construction skills for sure.

Genesis Prime Log: 02 Dec 0001

Linda had sent word early this cycle calling for an emergency staff meeting and requested some representatives from the Sheree. For once I had no idea what it was about. Anything aboard the Genesis I would know, so it had to do with something outside the Genesis. I sent a telepathic message to Spee and Renee requesting their presence at the meeting.

As the staff began filtering in I noticed that most of the females were showing their pregnancy, even Naomi. I also noticed that Akiko, due to her petite size and the fact that she was carrying twins, was becoming somewhat round. As Homer and Naomi came passed I said, "Congratulation." There had not been an announcement of their pregnancy or even officially of their mating, but everyone knew, and she was becoming obvious.

Homer blushed, smiled, and said, "Thanks, it was my pleasure."

We both chuckled and Naomi elbowed Homer in the side. That made us chuckle again.

Homer said, "When are you going to announce the names of your twins?"

I looked at Akiko and said, "We haven't named them yet."

Homer said, "That's crazy. They have already been named in ancient history and have been worshiped for centuries." He looked at what must have been blank stares on our faces and blurted out, "Apollo and Artemis!"

"Oh", was all I could say.

When the general came up to me I said, "Hi general. Are you about to tell me Margaret is pregnant?"

His face remained a statue for a long minute, but a huge grin split his face and he said, "How did you know? We haven't told anyone yet."

I said, "I didn't really. I just figured since all the other women in the colony were getting pregnant, Margaret wouldn't want to be left out. Besides, knowing you, exposure wouldn't be a problem." He laughed out loud.

As we began to take our customary seats I noticed the Sheree enter and stand in the back. I had wondered how many would come, since they drew comfort and strength in group size. It was just Spee, Dee, Renee and his mate. Renee must have understood my thought and pinged "Bee." I nodded my thanks.

The timing was perfect, because just as we were taking our seats Linda and her group entered. Linda was first, and she was a picture of seriousness. Following her was Lt Boland, two Marines, and then came three Sheree, which was strange because only two had gone on the reconnaissance mission to the Sheree home world, Markee. I sat up straight in my chair along with everyone else, knowing something important was about to unfold.

Linda took the podium and said, "As most of you know we sent a mission to Markee to survey the situation there, since the Sheree outposts have been marooned for several hundred years. We didn't know if they still existed or not. We also wanted to know if humans still existed on that planet. Well, we found the answers, but we are not going to like them. I have been briefed, but I'm going to let Lt. Boland give you the details, since he was pilot on the mission there."

Lt. Boland went to the podium and began, "Our arrival in Markee space was shocking. We didn't know what to expect, but what we found was unexpected. The first thing we saw was a polluted and dying planet. The Sheree couldn't believe it, and swore that Sheree would not let that happen. So, we cautiously orbited the planet and saw an abundance of life. Lights of cities, roads, factories bellowing out smoke and pollutants, filling the atmosphere with smoke and haze. It was horrible. We even witnessed a war in progress. We hardly saw signs of any advanced technology. They seem to be in the early industrial age, but there were a lot of people. When I say people, I mean humans. We went to where the Sheree center of government and science used to be and observed. There was only humans and military guards. We figured they were guarding something, so we continued to observe from a building rooftop where we landed under cover of night. Eventually, we saw three of the guards taking a Sheree in chains out of the main castle. We saw that they were taking him to another building that was some distance from the main building. We made a quick decision to try and capture the Sheree so we could find out more intelligence. The Marines and the Sheree took off, while I remained in the saucer ... just in case."

"They intercepted the group and held them at gunpoint, while they tried to talk to them. The Marines said the guards didn't respond to any language they tried, including Sheree. They said the humans were wild and charged them with swords, and they had to shoot them. The Sheree freed the captive and as soon as they were back to the ship, we took off back home. We just got back and haven't had time to talk much with the captive."

I said, "Thank you Lt. Boland. Good report." I noticed the Sheree talking together in the back, so I said, "Spee can you tell me anything about the captive?"

Spee looked uncomfortable and said, "Do you mind if Renee speaks for this group at this time?"

"That's fine." I said, "Renee?"

Renee came forward to the podium bringing the Sheree captive with him and spoke in the Sheree language, "It is my distinct honor to introduce

165

Rumbee. This honorable Sheree is of our race's scientific class. This enlightened class designs and builds our technology and are respected among our race. This Sheree class tends to be more demanding, and I request your understanding."

I said, "I'm assuming you have explained what happened to the Respected Leader?"

Renee bowed slightly and said, "I have done that, Sir."

I said, "Rumbee, you may proceed and tell us the situation on Markee."

"Thank you Admiral Johns." He said in perfect English, "What Renee said about our class being somewhat arrogant is based upon ancient traditions, but being in human captivity for two hundred years has drained that out of us. Renee informs me that your branch of the human race and you in particular are different than what I have seen. We had hoped for that, and I hope this is correct, because the human race I have seen consists of self-centered, greedy, aggressive psychopaths hardly able to tolerate itself and function."

"I'm sure there are many questions that I will be able to answer for you, so maybe I can anticipate some of them. First, Markee is the original home of both Sheree and humans. Sheree are long lived, while humans are short lived, but humans reproduce at an extremely high rate, while Sheree have barely maintained their numbers. Those of our race remaining thought us almost extinct. I'm happy to hear that we have a community of Sheree here, and thanks to your race we are now reproducing. Thank you for that assistance."

"What happened on Markee is that the humans out bred us and being jealous of our technology eventually killed our race off. A few of us scientist survived because the humans didn't understand our technology or even operate it. They kept us in captivity to operate the technology. There are ten of us remaining alive on Markee that we know of, and I hope you will free them also."

Linda asked, "There are ten Sheree scientists imprisoned on Markee?"

Rombee said, "That is correct, and I would like to free them."

I said, "Let's go back to something you said earlier. You said something about your race had hoped that our branch of the human race would be different. What do you mean by that?"

Rombee responded, "I'm afraid you still don't understand. The original human race is defective. They are not sane. Our race decided to colonize Earth mainly because we saw the inevitable mental decline of the human race and the inevitable destruction of our race. We wanted to save the human race by carefully screening out the psychopaths from the humans we took with us. Unfortunately, enough of psychopath DNA, as you call it, survived in the race, and we were eventually forced to leave Earth. When we came here we brought humans with us and again we tried to screen out the bad ones. We have no idea how that worked out here."

I said, "This is a lot of information to think about. Renee, you and Spee take your new group member back to your area, and we will all talk later."

Genesis Prime Log: 10 Dec 0001

When the alarms went off, screaming through the colony and within the Genesis, I was instantly alert. My central brain in the Control Room immediately sought the source of the alarm through the camera systems outside, and I saw instantly why. The Gaters were storming over the wall climbing over each other's backs as they built their own ladders of bodies, and they were as big and ugly as we had been told. The top ones were launching rocks at their targets. Several of the Marines on guard were already down. I began firing my laser located on the visual centers, killing many, but there were hundreds breaching the walls all over the complex. I announced over the compound's loudspeakers for all civilians to seek shelter in the caves and bring down the cavern gates. There was no need to tell them why, because Gaters were all over the compound. The Marines were pouring out of their complex firing into the open area as they came. I was trying to keep more from coming over the wall, but I couldn't keep up.

We were a month into total darkness in the late cycle, but the colony lights began blazing as soon as the alarms started, but I could see the Gaters were targeting the lights with their rocks, and they were going out. I could see many of the Marines slipping on their night vision goggles, and my cameras were also low light, so I could see in the dark. Kim had made it to the main laser controls and began firing at Gater groups, and someone had manned the other main laser and was firing. I continued to fire my lasers but they began to go out also. Of the five visual centers, three had gone out, camera and laser, but from the other two I noticed how the Gaters were charging them. The bastards were fast and accurate with those damn rocks. The last thing I saw before my last camera went down was the Marines retreating into the cave doors and firing through slots. I hope everyone made it inside.

Breathing heavily, Kim said, "They've stopped coming over the wall, but there are a lot inside."

From the ship cameras I could see many charging up the road. I didn't know where they were headed, probably the power plant to shut off electricity. I couldn't be sure, so I began raising the Genesis' loading ramp. It was then I saw the Sheree pouring out of the tunnel entrance. Many in the front ranks held the long granite cutting knives. Others held crossbows, which they must have made in secret at some point. The general hadn't felt comfortable giving them back their laser rifles, so they obviously improvised. It was then that I realized the tunnel had been totally dark, but the Sheree could obviously see clearly in the near total darkness with those big, black eyes.

As I watched, the Sheree clashed with the Gaters on the access road and tore through them with ease. The males and females, some pregnant, fought together as a solid unit. The knives sliced through the Gaters with extreme ease. I could see cloven Gater bodies falling all over the road. What surprised me most was the Sheree's speed. They dodged rocks, fired their crossbows, and even seemed to match the Gaters strength in hand to hand clashes. If I hadn't seen it, I wouldn't have believed

169

it. The Sheree began driving the Gaters back, and Kim and the mountain laser continued to pick off groups.

Search lights began to come on from the Genesis and the power cave. That had to be Akiko and Katy. Their beams began cutting through the blackness and shinning down, sweeping into the colony. With additional lights and improved view of the colony, the Marines again began firing into the now scattered Gaters, but the Sheree steadily engaged the Gaters as they drove them toward the Marines to be shot. Soon the fighting slowed, then stopped, with only a random shot being fired.

The Marines spread out, searching for surviving Gaters within the compound, while other Marines remounted the wall sentry posts and began firing at the wounded and retreating Gaters. The compound began filling with colonist looking for human survivors and dragging the Gater carcasses toward the gate. Many of the civilians came out and actually embraced the Sheree, who seemed to welcome the attention. One thing was for sure, the Sheree had been totally accepted by the human colony.

I checked the time and was amazed to find that from the launch of the attack through the completion of the battle only twenty minutes had transpired. The attack had been sudden, vicious, and intense; and the strategy was almost successful. Had it not been for the Sheree, it just might have been.

The action had been so intense I was somewhat shocked to notice that my actual body still remained lying in bed. I got dressed and headed out toward the loading ramp in time to meet Katy and Akiko starting out. I noticed they were coming from the direction of the search lights, so I had been correct in that assumption.

Katy said, "We figured you were busy elsewhere, so we left you alone."

I just smiled at my plump ladies, as we continued out. I noticed that Linda and Doc were coming out of the laser cave she had built. They must have immediately run there to activate the other laser. I know Doc was there for support, because Linda was waddling as she walked, even with Doc's help. Still, she smiled and waved to us as they approached.

As we continued down the road we could see the general barking orders and organizing the cleanup. Already a large pile of Gater carcasses was growing by the gate. I would have the dead Gaters dumped into the river as witness to the Gaters of their loss. I also figured the dead Gaters might feed and attract any natural predators they might have.

As we approached the general he came to me and said, "Damn, that was close! How about those Sheree? I never knew they could see in the dark or could fight that well. I guess I better give them back their rifles."

"I lost some good Marines, too, and we learned some improvements to our defense we need to make. Still, we hurt them bad. They won't be back for a while, but I'm betting they will be back."

During the cleanup I saw the Sheree picking up all the Gaters' long swords, apparently for their own use. In other places I saw some Sheree slicing off

171

some of the Gaters tails. When I asked Renee why, he said, "They are good to eat." Yuck.

The losses on our side were substantial, but they could have been much worse. As it turned out only ten Marines died; four civilians; two Sheree, one of which was pregnant; and one immortal, Hiroshi Tsuji, who had been working inside the hope with the hatch open. The Gaters lost almost five hundred and had been beaten off. We were lucky.

Genesis Prime Log: 15 Dec 0001

Everything was getting back to normal by this staff meeting. Unfortunately, our cemetery was growing, so we took some time at the meeting for Calvin Kline to speak for the fallen. He was an elegant speaker, and I missed our talks. I wonder why we stopped talking. I guess it was the demand on everyone's time.

Katy led off the discussion, "I want to thank Admiral Johns for having the insight to insist on changing some of our defenses. Protecting the colonist within the mountain caves saved many lives, and the lights and alarm system save us all. That Gater attack was well planned and forcefully pointed out our weaknesses. I don't think any of us believed it possible to be so lethal with rock throwing. Those projectiles were incredibly accurate and hit with the force of a bullet. They took out the Marine sentries with the first volley, and if the alarms hadn't sounded, they would have overrun the compound and been in the cave before we knew what was happening."

"As a result of the attack, we have come up with some defense changes. Our lighting was a near disaster. The Gaters targeted them and took them out quickly. In the near future, all the compound flood lights will be changed to a Wonder Metal configuration. As you know, Wonder Metal is virtually indestructible. They can pound them with rocks all night and they will remain on."

"We will also install transparent Wonder Metal windows on the guard towers to protect the sentries from another sudden attack of rocks or bullets."

"We also intend to improve the alarm system on our wall and on the Sheree side to give us a quicker warning. Additionally, we will tie the cavern main doors into the alarm system so they will automatically lower, but after that attack, I daresay they will already be closed at night in the future."

"For obvious reason we will escalate our military training of the colonists. All members must be able to fight for their survival in some way. Most colonist were sadly ill prepared to join the battle. Can we assume no one will resist this training?" When she asked, she looked directly at Mr. Pollard, who slightly hung his head, then nodded. "Good."

"Now the last thing to do right now is to increase the height of our perimeter wall to twenty-five feet, like the Sheree side. The Gaters didn't even attack their side. They picked the easiest wall to breech."

At that statement groans echoed through the Control Room, which changed to laughter. They all remembered the massive amount of work that had already gone into the wall and knew how much more it would take to reach twenty-five feet.

Katy continued, "Yeah, I know, I know. It's a lot of work, but our current wall posed little deterrent to the Gaters. They just built a wall of bodies and ran over them. They may still be able to do that, but it will be much harder and take more time and bodies. That will give us the time to engage them."

Spee raised his hand at the back of the gathering and said, "Katy, we will help build the wall taller."

Katy said, "Why thank you Spee. The assistance would be greatly appreciated."

"There may be other improvements as we continue to plan, but these are the most obvious corrections that need to be made." After a moment of thought, she asked, "Spee, do you need anything for defense on your side?"

Spee looked to the other Sheree then said, "The general has provided us with our rifles, and we gathered the Gater swords and spears. We could, however, use some of the lights you spoke of. Other than that we are protected in the dark, because we remain inside the tunnel and protected during the dark time. This is how we were able to get to this side of the tunnel so quickly."

"Well, I'm glad you did. Thanks," Katy said.

I said, "General, do you have anything to add?"

He laughed and said, "No, not at this time. Katy was windy enough for all of us."

Genesis Prime Log: 01 Jan 0002

174

All the inhabitants of the colony gathered in the compound to celebrate our one year anniversary on Genesis Prime, even the Sheree. Homer had been brewing up beer for months, and he was at the kegs filling cups with various blends. He was having a ball. Even the Sheree joined in to sample the beer. I've seen many humans getting tipsy, but you haven't lived until you've seen a Sheree inebriated. I don't think they knew what beer would do to them until it was too late, but Rumbee caught on and stopped the Sheree drinking, sending some back to their quarters. Watching and hearing a Sheree laugh was quite an experience. The general and I were laughing so hard it hurt.

Human nature has always been the same. The men drank, laughed, and told lies, while the women, most of which were very pregnant, gathered together to talk about men and laugh at us. It was heartening to see also the Sheree females mingling with the human females.

Every so often I could hear Akiko laughing and talking with the Sheree females. I know she was making a special effort to make them feel comfortable, and I think she was surprised, as was I, to even hear the Sheree females talk at all. Dee's confidence had blossomed as her baby grew inside her, which helped her express herself more. At one time I heard Dee addressing Akiko as Ako, like Rumbee called her. I found this strange, because Dee spoke perfect English, and I had even heard her say Akiko perfectly. I assumed all the Sheree would now address her as Ako out of respect for Rumbee's apparent speech impediment.

We were pleased to see villagers and colonist mingle together, laughing and joking, as if they had been together all their lives, and the Sheree could be seen throughout the compound talking with various human groups. There would be some headaches in the morning, but all and all, it has been a joyous and happy day, one that we would all remember for a while.

Genesis Prime Log: 15 Feb 0002

For the last few cycles and especially night cycles my girls have been pacing our quarters. They are very pregnant now and can't sleep and look so uncomfortable, and I really feel sorry for them, but of course there is nothing I can do. They look at me like, "You did this to us." I can tell you one thing, though. I never want both of them to be pregnant at the same time again, but I'm not about to remind them that it was their idea to carry the baby to term. One pregnant mate is bad enough in those last few cycles, but two is terrible, and one with twins.

I got out of there for a while and went to see Doc in the ships' medical clinic, but he was busy delivering babies, lots of babies. So I just stood there looking at the babies in the viewing windows, wondering if I knew the parents. There must have been ten babies lined up along the window, with cots for the mothers lined up in the clinic hallway.

The general came up to my side and said, "You too? Margret is chewing my head off." We laughed together. "But I only have one. It must be worse for you."

I looked at him and he was grinning hugely. Affectionately I said, "Kiss my ass!" We both roared laughing until we drew hateful stares from the nurses and mid-wives inside. That's when I noticed that many of the attending women were the elder females from the villager population. That made sense, since they would most likely be the daycare moms. Yeah, just try and stop them. I suspected Doc didn't have to ask them; they just showed up, like they had spearheaded the construction of the Child Care Center and playgrounds.

I wondered if there was this much activity at the colony hospital. In second thought, that's a silly question. There would be much more activity there due to the volume of people in the colony. Taka would certainly be busy, but he had the advantage of having more trained doctors that had been in cryogenics.

Doc rushed by heading to another birthing, but he stopped when he saw us, grinned, and came over and pointed to a baby. He said, "That's mine! Got to go."

Sure enough the baby had red hair the same color as Katy. Well, that shouldn't be a big surprise since they were siblings. I watched Doc headed down the hall and stop by one of the cots and spoke. I recognized Linda lean up and wave. We both gave her the thumbs up before she fell back to her pillows.

I said, "You know general, we could have planned this better, maybe set up a sliding time schedule to get pregnant."

The general said, "Fat chance of that. I think all the women had the same idea at the same time."

That's when I got Akiko's message, "Nick, it's time. We are coming." I said, "Oh, shit, general. I'm about to become a father."

Just as I was running toward our quarters I met them waddling around the corner. Both girls were in obvious pain, but they were smiling. I helped them into the clinic and was quickly ushered back out as the mid-wives took over. They weren't too nice about it either, saying something about they didn't need any anxious father getting in the way. So, I retook my spot at the window and waited.

It was a long wait, and I watched babies being brought out and slipped into baskets, but I couldn't read the writing on the bands, so I didn't know if any of them were mine. When a nurse I recognized came out carrying two babies, I knew they were Akiko's. The nurse brought them to the window so I could see and smiled hugely at me. They just looked like any other babies, but knowing they were mine made me feel wonderful. I had never felt like this before, and I'm sure I was all smiles.

The general smiled and clapped me on the back and said, "Congratulation daddy." That was right before his beeper went off, sending him running.

I continued waiting and smiling until the same nurse came out carrying another bundle. I knew that had to be my Katy's baby. Our family was certainly growing.

The nurse said, "Akiko and Katy are both well, but they will both sleep till tomorrow. You might as well go get some sleep."

I smiled and said, "Thank you." But, I continued to stare at the babies. I couldn't believe how happy I was.

I was allowed to enter by the next day. Births had slowed down, and Doc had disappeared to get some well needed sleep. The nurses brought me to Katy and Akiko laying side by side. They were nursing their babies and smiling up at me. It was precious and these girls meant more to me than life itself. I asked, "Do you have names for them?

Akiko said, "These babies have already been named. Homer named them Apollo and Artemis, and I liked those names."

Katy said, "Homer also named our baby. Meet your son, Perseus."

I laughed out but caught myself and said, "We are going to have a family of Olympian gods."

Genesis Prime Log: 18 Feb 0002

Over the peak of the birthing season, as we began calling it, the colony gained over a hundred new inhabitants, some very loud. I know; I had three of them in our quarters, but they were very healthy and very welcome. Katy and Akiko doted over the infants, and it didn't seem to matter which child needed attention. I often saw Katy nursing one of the twins, and I doubt any of the babies knew exactly which one was its mother, but they knew who their daddy was. He was the one kicked out of bed at night to tend to them.

At today's staff meeting, obviously many were missing, but the smiles were not. Homer had done a good job of filling in for Akiko and Naomi, but it had taken a toll on him. He looked haggard and sleepless.

I saw Mr. Pollard and said, "Please thank everyone involved at the weavers for making so many of the cloth diapers. I'm pleased that you thought ahead. That is something that slipped past most of us. We get in the habit of taking so much for granted, but it's not like we can run to Walmart when we need to. I'm afraid this generation will never see or know what pampers are. By the way, where did you get the cotton?"

Mr. Pollard said, "We brought a great deal with us. It was compressed and packed into just about every open crack and crevice we could find on the Genesis, and we had a great deal of cracks and crevices. We used some of that cotton, but we also have harvested our first crop of cotton fields. We knew we would need plenty of diapers, so we got busy and made sure they were ready. I'm happy to report that we have also sheered our first flock of sheep and are using the wool."

"Very well done, Mr. Pollard. Please give thanks to all involved."

CHAPTER 10
(Invasion)

Genesis Prime Log: 08 Mar 0002

I called for another emergency meeting for early this cycle. In truth, it was Cdr. Kim that excitedly alerted me, and when I saw what the problem was called the meeting for all department heads, including the Sheree.

The staff began hurriedly making their way into the Control Room, some with their babies. Luckily, Akiko and Katy, living aboard the Genesis, were able to leave the babies with Sarah, one of the village mid-wives who had taken a liking to us and had adopted our children as her own grandchildren. We didn't complain, as she doted over our babies. She also doted over Akiko and Katy. Me she just tolerated. The Admiral or Zeus did not intimidate her in the least, and I liked that about her.

Once all were in attendance, I took the podium and said, "Sorry to drag you from your busy schedule, but we seem to have a major crisis brewing. I don't know if it's an imminent threat or not, but you all need to know the situation. Bottom line is that Genesis Prime appears to have been invaded.

As you all know, Kim monitors Genesis Prime with the satellites we launched before we landed. This early cycle he came to me with an observation. He found a large army of human warriors on one of the big continents. We don't know how they got there, but they weren't there last cycle. We searched, but we can't find a spaceship. It doesn't look like they are there to colonize, as they are equipped for war, ill-equipped I might add. They are carrying swords, spears, and some other weapons we can't identify. They are on the move directly toward the village settlement there, but it will take them weeks to get there. If their intent is to attack the village, the villagers don't have a chance. Did I mention that the invading army is over 10,000 warriors?" At that there were gasps.

Rumbee raised his hand and moved forward toward the podium. He said, "May I?"

I said, "Yes, you may."

Rumbee said, "We understand what is happening, and the danger is more grave than you believe."

I said, "Continue. You have the platform."

"As I said, we Sheree understand what is happening, and I in particular. These humans are from Markee. They are looking and coming for you humans and for me. They want you dead and me returned. I was the senior scientist of the Sheree left alive. When you saved me you set us all on a path for war. Don't misunderstand. I thank you for saving me, but it hurt the humans on Markee. As I have said, those humans are defective. They have little intelligence, just raw rage, psychopaths all. They cannot read and kept us alive to operate our equipment, something they cannot do."

"They would have eventually found you and come after you. That is what they had us Sheree doing, searching. They knew we colonized other worlds and had us looking for other Sheree, but we kept giving them false targets and information, but now they know you exist and have taken one of their scientists. You will be considered a threat to them. The Sheree ship you operated must have been seen by them or the humans seen taking me. Whatever the reason, they will seek to recapture me and any other Sheree, and now that they know about you, they will never stop coming."

I interrupted, "How do you know for sure this is them?"

Rumbee said, "I cannot be absolutely positive at this point, but I am 95% sure. We can know for sure by identifying a Sheree with the human army. From what I hear, I feel positive the army came in a Plasma Bubble, and that would require at least one Sheree to operate the equipment and come with it. I think we will be able to find a Sheree with the army."

"If this is so, and I believe it is, you are in more danger than you think. If they have a Plasma Bubble they can transport the army anywhere on the planet that they want to go, even here. The operating Sheree is not on their side. What remains of our race on Markee are being forced by torture to do the human's bidding. Even so, they have obviously transported the army to a place where they could do little immediate harm. The Sheree operator is giving us a chance to prepare, but eventually they will be forced to comply. Do you understand what I'm saying?"

"Yes, I believe I do." I said, "You're saying the Sheree could have just as easily brought the army to our front door, but he/she/they didn't! You're saying that at any time that army or another army could be transported outside our gates, or for that matter, inside our gates. You are also saying that we need to go capture the Sheree operator and Plasma Bubble generator equipment in order to save ourselves. You are saying we need to travel to Markee and free the remainder of the Sheree or we will never be safe. You are saying we should have listened to you before."

Rumbee had most certainly heard about the arrogance of the Respected Leader and his death, and he was trying very hard to not come across arrogant or even demanding. I must say, he did play his cards carefully, but he had an agenda to save all Sheree, and that was easy to see. Still, his agenda seemed to match our needs as well. I could find no fault with his desires.

Rumbee said, "The way you say these things are far blunter than I would say them, but basically, yes. We have great respect for you and the colony. You and your people have already done much for us, and it is appreciated. In essence, Dr. Rossen has saved our race from inevitable extinction by helping us reproduce. Our race has nowhere to go, and this is now our home as well. We want to be part of your world and hope you will allow us to contribute toward our mutual common good."

Rumbee was a smart cookie and articulate and used many of the key trigger words for me like "common good", but he was also correct and had been correct all along. I couldn't see or detect any trickery. I think at this point I decided to include him in our family, but I wasn't about to admit to him that we had ignored his subtle warning.

I said, "Cdr. Rumbee, in the future we will require your and your immediate staff's presence in our staff meeting, and we will seek and request your input. In the future we want you to voice your recommendations more forcefully, so we truly understand your concerns."

With this statement it was understood among the staff what truly happened, and I got more than a few nods of approval, including Rumbee.

"General, please get with Kim and find the Sheree and equipment and put together a plan to capture the Sheree operator and equipment within the invading army. Maybe we can isolate the army on that continent, and since they are hell bent on destroying the village, let's launch a relocation plan to bring them here. Maybe you can take your ore ship." I looked at Mr. Pollard and said, "Can you take them in and put them to work?" Mr. Pollard eagerly nodded to the affirmative. "I think the general may want some of them for Marines, too. We may need them."

"General, get with Cdr. Rumbee and pick his brains and put together a plan to seize the Sheree on Markee and as much of their equipment as we can grab. Let's stop them from being able to launch another army and attack."

Genesis Prime Log: 18 Mar 0002

At the staff meeting this cycle General McCullah was scheduled to give a report on Genesis Prime's mission to liberate the Sheree operator and equipment. The plan Mac and

185

Rombee came up with was brilliant and surprisingly simple.

From observation Kim had finally discovered the Sheree and Plasma Bubble generator under heavy guard toward the rear of the army. The plan was to use two Sheree saucers. One would buzz the front of the army to draw the army and fire power toward the front, while a second saucer would slip up from behind at low level. Once the second saucer centered over the Sheree and equipment, hopefully by surprise, it would deploy and engage its own Plasma generator and teleport a substantial distance to a predetermined location. Marines would be waiting to kill the guards when they appeared. When they presented the plan I quickly approved. It sounded safe and easy.

One thing had been bothering me about Rumbee's previous speech, however. So, after I approved the plan, I addressed him directly, "Rumbee, before when you talked about the Plasma Bubble generator I thought it was a different type of equipment, but basically it is the same equipment as the Plasma Drive. Correct?"

"Yes, Sir. It is one in the same."

"Before you came to us, Spee told us about the Gaters coming in what looked like some form of a Plasma enclosure. Do we have the Sheree to thank for bringing them to Genesis Prime?"

Rumbee actually looked scared, and his agitation spread to those of his staff that were with him, presumably from their mental linking.

Rumbee visibly shook and said, "Sir, yes Sir. We are responsible for bringing them here, but please remember that was hundreds of years ago, long before you came. The Sheree had brought them to Markee for food from a water world. They are quite good to eat. We kept them controlled in a lake close to our central government city. After the humans killed most of us and took control, we couldn't control the Gaters any longer, and they began coming out of the lake and eating humans. The humans knew what we were capable of and demanded we get rid of them. I'm not sure why we didn't send them back to their world or just kill them, but I was not in charge back then. Maybe those remaining didn't remember where that water world was, maybe it had been destroyed, but we all knew where Genesis Prime was located. It could have been that simple. I do not have the answer. All I know is that a Plasma Bubble collected the entire lake and was taken to Genesis Prime along with a Sheree operator and guards. After the bubble released the Gaters, the Sheree was forced to bring the Plasma Bubble back to Markee."

I said, "Don't be frightened, Rumbee. You answered a question for us we have all wondered about, and you told the truth. You won't get in trouble for telling the truth. At least we know where they came from and that they have no outside help for us to worry about."

Rumbee calmed down and flashed me a look of, I can only assume was a combination of relief and possibly respect.

***

"The general did not look happy when he finally headed for the podium. He said, "The mission to collect the Sheree and equipment is complete and was successful. It was, however, very costly. A Sheree saucer has been destroyed along with the Sheree pilot and two Marines. The saucer buzzed the front of the invading army to draw their attention, which it did, unfortunately. Several weapons were discharged from within the army ranks that exploded the saucer. We thought the saucer would have more time, but the weapons were quick, accurate, and deadly. Luckily, the weapons were not trained on us and we succeeded in coming in undetected. We captured our target, along with about ten guards and were gone before they realized we were there. We had five Marines waiting when we appeared, and they dispatched the guards quickly before they could harm the Sheree. That part was successful."

"There was only one Sheree, and once we landed, Rumbee went to her quickly. She stands beside Rumbee. It seems she worked for him on Markee and they have been talking. Maybe he can describe the weapon." The general motioned for Rumbee to come forward.

Rumbee nervously made his way to the podium and said, "Admiral, as the First Officer has said, this Sheree was in my group, and she tells me they have managed to extract the operating procedures for a weapon called an Energy Disrupter. Are you familiar with the tools used to mold what you call Wonder Metal that uses a complex range of frequency and modulation energy to mold the metal?"

"Yes." I said.

"Well, as the tools temporally break down the virtually indestructible Wonder Metal so it can be molded, this weapon is a high energy output device that does the same thing except the energy beam can be directed in a large rifle form. It disrupts the molecular structure of Wonder Metal and any use that it has been put to, which are vast. Firing the weapon at the saucer would disrupt all its functions, and it exploded as a result."

"This Sheree is named Laytee, and I trust her. She tells me that after I was taken the humans were raging mad, even more than usual. So far we had been able to keep its operation secret, but the humans were determined and began torturing some of the group in a horrible fashion, cutting off fingers and toes and eventually even arms and legs. They killed two of our group before they learned the secret, and it is simple enough for them to fire without an operator."

"This is a dangerous weapon and can do serious damage to Wonder Metal craft or anything using this metal, even to the Genesis. The good news is that we can build a shield against an energy weapon, but there are faults in doing so. You can't fire energy weapons out of it either. That means no laser blasts will penetrate out. So we can help give you defense, but we take away our offense."

I was terribly disturbed to learn about a weapon that can destroy Wonder Metal, a substance we had come to believe indestructible. It was also the building block of virtually everything we constructed. To find out that it could so easily be destroyed was unsettling.

Rumbee continued, "Admiral, there is something else we need to consider much more foreboding. There are other weapons in the Sheree arsenal on Markee the humans might force the Sheree to reveal. If they learn these secrets I'm afraid we could be doomed. I strongly suggest that we launch an attack to either free the imprisoned Sheree or kill them to protect these secrets."

"We have an advantage right now, because the Markee humans do not know we have rescued Laytee. She tells me and the general that the Sheree scientists were moved from their prison after I was taken. The place where they were taken is where I was en route to that night when I was captured. They kept us separated from our equipment in fear we would use it against them, but they moved the Sheree into the same building. They are still separated from the equipment and under heavy guard, but they can't know we know where they are. Such that it is, that is our advantage."

I was impressed with Rumbee's presentation. He, for the first time, was being assertive and a contributing member of the staff. His subtle use of "Our" and "We" revealed that he considered he and his Sheree a part of our family and a welcome part. The most revealing was his willingness to kill the captured Sheree to protect this family. Yes, I was impressed with him.

I said, "Cdr. Rumbee, thank you for your perspective on the issue, but I need to ask you if the dome shields stored here are the same shield you are talking about to shield against the Energy Disrupter. What about the Plasma Bubble? Is it also a shield?"

Rumbee said, "Let me talk about the Plasma Bubble first. We really don't know much about the Plasma Bubble or even understand it. We didn't even build them. We purchased them from an ancient race of space travelers many thousands of years ago. We had some rare mineral that they desperately needed for survival. We allowed them to mine the mineral in return for some of their technology and equipment, which included the Plasma Bubble. They didn't share the technology on this equipment, only the equipment. It has, however, continued to operate."

"As far as a shield? We don't know, and we have been afraid to test it. The technology is extremely complex and involves many disciplines of science, known and unknown. When the bubble transcends time and space it immediately dissolves, and we have no control to alter it. So, I would have to say, for these reasons, it is not a shield."

"Now, the Dome Shield is in fact the same as what I describe, but it will need some calibration adjustments to shield against the Energy Disrupter. For the Genesis it will require a unit on the top and another on the bottom, since they provide protection only for a semicircle radius dome. The downside is that it only protects against energy weapons. For example solid projectiles go right through. I hope this helps."

Genesis Prime Log: 21 Mar 0002

I had been kicking over in my head everything Rombee had said, and I was beginning to formulate a plan. For my plan to work I would need Linda

191

and Doc's expertise. I called Linda, Doc, Mac and Rombee for a private conference.

As they arrived I was not surprised to see Laytee, Renee and Spee accompanying Rombee, but they were welcome. Doc and Linda were the last to arrive.

I said, "Thanks for coming. I think you all might enjoy, or at least find it interesting, what I am about to propose. I have a plan for the mission on Markee. I lowered my mental barriers to think this through, and it can work if we can adapt our engineering."

All but the Sheree knew that by removing my mental barriers my mind could work at a much higher level for research and planning by controlling and accessing the ship's computer as an extension of my mind. In truth the barriers were the real invention. I was forced to create the barriers in order to remain sane. Without them my consciousness worked at a dangerously high level, but when I needed the higher function I could remove them. I had done this many times during our journey, and it had saved us numerous times.

"To our Sheree friends I want to tell you that my staff on the Genesis are all brilliant and accomplish in their field of study and science. They are the best of the best our world had to offer. I tell you this because Linda, I mean Dr. Clark, was the design and project engineer for the Genesis, and while we did use much Sheree technology, we also invented our own. Linda and Dr. Rossen designed and built the propulsion drive we used to get here. It is called Light Wave Drive and involves a complex adjustable matrix of individual drive segments incorporated within the Wonder Metal hull. Doc designed the computer program and controlling system to drive the propulsion system. This matrix controls both the Light Wave drive and the Gravity Drive. The reason I'm telling you this will become apparent soon."

My plan in reality is actually simple. We launch the Genesis with the Plasma Drive and settle over on the building where the Sheree are being held. We use the modified Dome Shields to protect us from the Energy Disrupters. We then use the existing ship's hull matrix to project a Gravity Drive shield outward to isolate the Genesis from being attacked from outside its perimeter, while the Marines take out the guards and any within the gravity shield. Once the area within the shield is cleared, we load the Sheree aboard and all the equipment we can find. We should be in and out within an hour."

I could already see Linda and Doc's minds engaging. I said, "Gravity is a physical reality and not a generated energy, independent of natural or artificially generated shields. As such, the gravity force, according to my calculations, should penetrate the Dome Shield without any difficulty. The existing Gravity Drive programming and controls may have to be modified somewhat in order to form and focus the gravity energy to form the shield without launching the Genesis into space. To do that the gravity energy needs to be projected outward to the side and not down. Even so, there would still be some uplift that must be countered from the upper ship hull. I see your brains working, and I think you are way ahead of me. Can do?"

Linda said, "The Gravity Drive was never intended to be used in this manner, but it is certainly possible, even absolutely possible. This assumes Doc. can alter the controlling program to allow us to do this. BTW Nick, this is a brilliant application of Gravity Drive. Used and focused in this way the shield would be impenetrable against physical forces. It would even be difficult to even get close to it, much less penetrate it, and normal gravity would remain inside the shield. Yes, I'm sure this will work. Doc?"

"I'm already writing the program modification in my head. I second Linda's "Yes" and second the brilliance of this use."

I said, "General, what do you think? The rest of the plan is up to your Marines' talent to execute."

"I love it!" He said, "This reduces the odds of engagement drastically. We can operate well under these parameters."

"Very well. Let's all proceed with this plan, but general, as I have said before, you are not to lead the ground troops. I don't want to lose any Marines, but you are irreplaceable, and don't think I missed the fact that you led the last engagement."

The general flashed a huge grin, but said, "Yes Sir, Admiral. I understand."

Still, the grin never left his face, the bastard, but I returned his grin.

"Before we launch I want all systems tested thoroughly, and I mean in actual deployment."

We adjourned the session, and Linda and Doc were understandably anxious to get to their projects. As they rushed out I noticed Rumbee and his group hurriedly rushing after Linda and Doc. They weren't about to miss out on this engineering research and project. I think the Sheree had found new respect for all of us.

Genesis Prime Log: 08 Apr 0002

This was a scheduled staff meeting, hopefully without any emergencies, so I just set back and let Katy lead. It had been a couple of months since the girls had their babies, and both were back to their normal, healthy self-thanks to the Immortality Gene. It also helped to have our nanny, Sarah. She had simply adopted us on her own, but we weren't about to complain. Sarah even moved into the adjacent quarters to be close.

Katy said, "We have made significant progress thanks to the Sheree. The granite wall now stands twenty-five feet tall all the way around our colony and on both sides of the mountain. They started another cave complex for the required granite blocks, which they are now turning into another housing complex for our new village recruits. They are quite skilled at rock work, and even built decorative columns and arches of stonework at the entrances to our cave complexes. I guess we now see where the ancient Greeks got their designs."

"Major General McCullah and Homer took his ore ship and have completely relocated the entire village under threat. Now the invading army will not have anyone to attack. The villagers are extremely happy to be here I might add, and indoctrination has begun. Of course the general immediately recruited about two hundred for

195

Marine training. Mr. Pollard has already assigned most of rest of them jobs."

The Sheree have completed the installation of the dome generators on the Genesis and Mom and Dad, I mean Linda and Doc, oh crap, Cdr. Clark and Cdr. Rossen have completed the redesign for the Gravity Shield. They all report that we are ready for a field trial

"As I understand, the Dolphins are due to birth next month, and their cove is already complete and secure. All we need now are the Dolphins, and Dr. Waters inspects the fetuses every cycle. She says they are ready, but we are giving them a few more weeks to get really healthy. It will improve their chances at life."

Katy was just about finished, but she saw Rumbee in the back raise his hand. She said, "Yes, do you have something to report?"

"Yes I do." Rumbee said, "You mentioned Dolphins earlier. The others tell me that you have been informed that Dolphins were not indigenous to your home world. Dolphins and some other air breathing water mammals were transplanted to Earth during the time of our colonization. Renee tells me that this staff asked about the language we used to communicate with them. The scientists were at one point charged with developing a language. This is because the Dolphin language is impossible to speak through a Sheree or human's vocal cords. It must be created artificially, and it is a difficult language. Renee tells me you asked if this language still exists. Yes it does. I have this knowledge. We also have a Dolphin translator among our equipment on Markee."

When Rumbee admitted he spoke this language or had knowledge of it, I sat straight up in my chair. I said, "Thank you for that information. We will be talking much more about this, and I'm thinking you will be joining our Dolphin team." At that many laughed, including Rumbee.

Cdr. Kim had arrived very late to the staff meeting, something he never does, and had been standing in the back. He looked anxious, but he had not interrupted. I said, "Kim do you have something to report?"

Kim said, "Yes Admiral. I have a location for us to conduct the field trials for the modifications to the Genesis. We have waited too long to attack Markee, and there has been another invasion." The Control Room erupted into chaos with questions, but he just held up his hands for silence. "The second human army appeared on the southernmost continent just hours ago. As with the first army, they are far from the village, and we have time to evacuate the villagers ahead of them. Also, as with the first army, we must steal their Plasma Generator and Sheree operator or they could wind up on Atlantis soon.

I said, "How large is this army?

Kim said, "It's about the same size as the other army but on a different continent.

Genesis Prime Log: 10 Apr 0002

In some ways setting down in the middle of an army was more dangerous than the planned engagement on Markee. On Markee we knew they would fight hard, but we didn't know how many soldiers would be there. Here we knew exactly how many soldiers there were, and they would all be firing on us. Still, we had no choice. It would be better to handicap and isolate them there than wait for them to come to us on Atlantis.

Everyone was as sure as they could be for our safety, so we lifted off our mountain peak and headed for the invading army. The general had the loading dock filled with Marines ready to rush out of the ramp. Kim had located the Sheree and equipment along the rear of the army, like last time. Linda and Doc were at the controls and ready for anything.

We stayed low and sped toward the army from behind and immediately dropped down on the enemy. Doc and Linda were carefully controlling the sudden drop and quickly stopped and settled. At the same time they engaged the gravity shield, which began pushing dirt into a pile at the circular edge of the shield. Those outside the shield were forcefully pushed back, some even flying through the air from the force. We could all see the humans firing weapons from a distance, and we breathed a sigh of relief when we didn't explode. Obviously the Dome Shields held. We felt the loading dock ramp fall.

The Marines began pouring out of the ramp, firing as they went. The general had instructed them to clear the soldiers around the Sheree and anyone carrying one of the disrupter weapons. From the cameras we could see there were about twenty or so humans, but they seemed that they were still in shock from the sudden attack. The Marines overwhelmed them quickly. We then saw

Rumbee run down the ramp toward the frightened Sheree female. She saw Rumbee and ran toward him. They embraced and he quickly led her back into the ship. That embrace was the most emotions I had seen from the Sheree.

The Marines quickly grabbed the Plasma Generator and any of the disrupters they could find and ran back inside. Damn, that had been quick. I doubt if it had been more than ten minutes. After the loading dock clamped shut we speed upward and away.

The attack had been well planned and executed, and we lost no Marines, captured the Sheree and equipment, and even retrieved two of the disrupter weapons. And, the most important part, we didn't get killed. All and all, it was a successful mission, and we passed the field trial.

As Rumbee entered the Control Room, he still had the female Sheree pulled tight against him and a smile on his face. I said, "Rumbee, is this someone special?

His smile still radiated when he said, "Yes. This is Faylee, my mate. We have had a child in the past and remain mated. Thank you Admiral."

"Faylee confirms that the remaining Sheree, six of them, are guarded and kept within the equipment building. They are making it easier for our plan to work."

"That's good." We are going in two cycles."

As we settled back down in our spot on Mount Olympus I could see Akiko, Katy, Sarah, and the babies approaching, along with another nanny, who I assume was carrying Doc and Linda's baby. I wasn't going to take any chances with my family.

If we might explode, my family would be off ship. I presume Doc and Linda felt the same.

Seeing my children I was reminded of a recent conversation with Doc. He told me that all of the immortal's babies were growing at an accelerated rate and would probably grow larger in size as a result. Well, we didn't explode, so, hopefully, I would live to see my large children.

Genesis Prime Log: 12 Apr 0002

After all the worry and precautions we took for the Markee mission, it was almost anticlimactic. Everything went precisely as we planned. There weren't even that many guards within our shield, but the general's Marines took them out quickly. We took them completely by surprised, and the Gravity Shield deployed perfectly as planned. We were in and out within an hour, and we freed the six remain Sheree and recovered all of the equipment within the complex, which seemed to be a lot, more than I expected anyway. They didn't even have time to launch a counterattack.

Instead of immediately going back to Genesis Prime we launched into orbit. Kim intended to survey the entire planet in search of any other Sheree locations or identify any other surprises. I didn't want to return to Markee. It was simply depressing to see the depravity of the human race there.

As we orbited, the general returned to the Control Room all smiles, leading Rumbee, the two Sheree of their group previously liberated, and the other six Sheree. The Sheree appeared to be happy to be reunited. Obviously, Rumbee had already communicated with them, since they seemed comfortable being around us, even happy.

Rumbee came forward and said, "Admiral, on behalf of our group we want to thank you and your staff for all that you have done for us, especially giving us a new chance of life and continuation of our species. We are in your debt and at your command."

I said, "We welcome your contributions to our colony, your colony too."

Rumbee said, "This may not be the best time to ask, but several of the females of this group are anxious to be impregnated with a child. They are eager to meet Dr. Rossen."

I had to laugh. I wasn't sure if they all spoke English, so I spoke in the Sheree language, "Well, there he sits. They can introduce themselves to him at any time, but it will take a little more than just laying hands on them. I'm sure he can and will help, like the others, but let's give it a few days. OK?"

Genesis Prime Log: 15 May 0002

The long awaited cycle had finally arrived to birth the Dolphins. All the facilities were prepared and ready for the baby Dolphins. Dr. Waters had been doting over the developing Dolphins for weeks, and Rumbee had spent as much time as possible with her, and almost constantly since we returned from Markee. Rumbee also had ten of the Sheree indoctrinated to join the babies in the water, especially during the first few hours, teaching them to surface to breath.

The translator retrieved from Markee had been set up, but as he explained, the babies would have no knowledge of their language, since there were no adults to teach them. What he set up instead was a recording of Dolphin sounds. At least they would be introduced to the language complexities. He had also had installed a large video monitor to give them visual reference to objects that corresponded to Dolphin language sounds. He said it would help them learn.

The truck loaded with incubators pulled up to the Dolphin complex and the helpers began unloading them. After the incubators were stacked on the enclosed dock, the helpers began entering the water to retrieve them. One by one the placenta bladders holding the baby Dolphins were emerged in the water and opened. The babies emerged into the water and the helpers, all Sheree, nudged the babies to the surface for their first breath of air. As all ten babies breathed life for the first time, cheers rang out in the complex, echoing off the walls.

I watched from below through the large Wonder Metal observation window. Each of the babies looked to be around four feet long and weigh about forty or fifty pounds. With their first breaths they seemed to awaken and begin flexing their bodies and flippers. The Sheree kept nudging them to the surface to breath, but they seemed to catch on fast and started swimming around their Sheree helper. I realized that the baby Dolphins would be bonding with their individual Sheree. I really hadn't thought about that, but apparently Dr. Waters and the Sheree had. The Sheree it seemed would be spending a lot of time in the water for a while, but I was somewhat surprised to see that the Sheree were quite comfortable in water and could swim well. They used a swimming stroke that also emulated the stroke a mother Dolphin might use, the feet were together as they stroked their legs up and down. The babies followed alongside.

The swimming, breathing, and exploring their bodies continued for several hours until ten nursing utters were lowered into the water just above my head. Each one emitted an individual ID tone, and the Sheree brought their charges to its assigned utter and nudged their baby against the nursing nipple. They caught on immediately and began nursing, returning often to their own tone and utter. Dr. Waters had told us that the babies would probably nurse these utters for about eighteen months, but would start eating some fish at around four months.

The Sheree were surprisingly fast in the water, but the Dolphin babies seemed to enjoy chasing them and soon could easily catch and surpass the Sheree. They even began to playfully taunt the Sheree. After several hours of this play the Sheree were exhausted and exited the water, much to the displeasure of the baby Dolphins, but there was no longer any danger of the Dolphins forgetting to breath. Without the Sheree in the water they discovered each other and began swimming and playing together, but two Sheree would remain on watch, should one of them forget to breath and needed help. This would continue for several days.

The Dolphin would also return to their utter to nurse each time they heard their individual ID tone, and when they wanted to nurse they would always return to their own nipple without being called. Dr. Waters wanted each Dolphin to have its own utter so she could measure the amount of nourishment each one was getting.

Akiko nudged me and said, "Well, we now have Dolphins. Now all we have to do is wait for about ten years."

I said, "Well, it was a long-term solution at best. Besides, we should be here in ten years."

CHAPTER 11
(Paradox)

Genesis Prime Log: 15 June 0002

Kim had kept me informed about the invading armies, and they seemed to be lost. He said they continued to roam over the two continents in search of an enemy. Finding none, they seemed to be migrating toward the coast. He had no idea why, but for now they were no threat to us or the villages. I decided it best to just leave them alone for the time being and see what they would do. The general had already loaded and transported all the mined ore off those two land bodies. Unfortunately, the Markee army had plenty of game to hunt, so they wouldn't starve as I had hoped, but at some point we would have to deal with them. If they found a way to get across the ocean to Atlantis we would have a major battle on our own land. That would not be pretty, but time would tell.

I began to wonder about Genesis Two. What if they had launched an army there. The liberated Sheree had reported that, Markee, being overpopulated, had sent out other armies, but they didn't know where. They had left Markee without a Sheree operator. It stood to reason that Genesis Two would be a likely target, but there were other worlds capable of sustaining human life. The only way to know for sure was to go to Genesis Two and check. If they did happen to go to Genesis Two, and they had humans smart enough to operate the

Sheree equipment, I didn't want them to have access to the Sheree equipment on that planet, especially the saucers and Plasma Bubble technology. So, I made up my mind to take the Genesis there and survey the planet and load all the saucers and equipment for our use.

We were going there this cycle to take these precautions. In fact we just entered orbit around Genesis Two, and Kim was already busy surveying the surface.

It didn't take him long to report that in fact there was an invading army, but it was on the lessor inhabited second continent. Homer had reported that there were seven villages, but only one village was on the second continent.

Kim hung his head and said, "Sadly, we are too late to help those villagers. The village is totally decimated, and the human army has moved on in search of other villages. They will be busy looking, but they won't find another there. The other villages on the other continent look intact, and I don't see any signs of another army.

"Something else, Admiral. We will need to get closer to know for absolute certainty, but I don't see any sign of any Sheree or Plasma Bubble equipment."

"Very well, Kim. We'll descend and begin the equipment retrieval and come back." I said, "Cdr. Rumbee, what are your thoughts on that observation?"

Rumbee said, "With your telescope I'm positive Cdr. Kim would have seen the equipment if it was there, so I believe we can assume it has been hidden or is in use elsewhere. There are no unaccounted for Sheree, so we must assume the Plasma Bubble has a human operator. There were some smarter ones among the humans on Markee but not many. They must all have left in control of a Plasma Bubbles, because the humans began having to use us to control them. That is where they were taking me when I was rescued. We were in prison and unable to know what they were doing."

"We believe this one may have returned to Markee, or maybe even found and visited the other armies here on Genesis Prime to discover how we captured their equipment. If this is so, the human operator will know about us and our tactics, maybe even know our location. If I may advise, we need to destroy these armies before they unite on Genesis Prime."

I said, "Well, that sounds like good advice, but how would you propose we do that and survive the Disrupters?" I looked around and said, "Does anyone have any ideas?"

The general said, "We don't have enough Marines to attack these armies. We are better equipped with weapons, but they have the overwhelming numbers. They would overrun us. I'm thinking we need to find a way to use our laser on them. This laser is an awesome weapon. I don't know what the range is for the Disrupters, but worse case, I think we can use our laser safely from orbit if necessary. We could just set up here and sniper them with short burst, but it would take a while and a lot of energy."

"Kim, Doc." I said, "We might as well get started on that. Can you automate the sniper function so we don't have to target each shot? Oh, and target the Disrupter weapons first."

They both nodded and took off to initiate the program.

Kim turned around at the console and said, "I will go ahead and begin targeting manually until Doc has something up and running."

It wasn't long before we felt a short burst from the laser. Kim was already conserving energy, and it made a lot of sense. A very short laser burst would kill, and anything more would simply be overkill and a waste of energy. Still, it took precious seconds to aim and target, and the army would no doubt be running, requiring anticipation that would slow the shots.

Rumbee went to Doc's side and they began conferring. I had forgotten that Rumbee was a scientist and quite competent as a computer engineer and programmer. After all, Earth had learned modern computers by studying the Sheree computer on board the crashed saucer. Still, as competent as i knew them to be, it would take them awhile to come up with a program.

I said, "Well we know the laser blast will work of a sort, but instead of making Kim's eyes crossed, let's go retrieve the equipment and warn the villagers of the potential attacks. This will give Doc and Rumbee time to complete the targeting and firing programming."

Kim responded, "I vote for that. I've already killed about fifty warriors, but at this rate it will take a long time without the efficiency of a firing program"

We started on the clear continent and systematically went from village to village. Lt. Boland met with each village population explaining what was happening and preparing them for a potential attack, while detachments of Sheree and Marines stripped the equipment from the castles. All together the crew filled two trucks loads and put them into the storage hold, along with six saucers.

The Markee army was comfortably distance from the seventh village, so we went there last. It had been a slaughter, and there were dead everywhere. There were men and children dismembered laying all over the village, but there were no women. They must have taken them with them, and I hated to consider why and their ultimate fate.

It looked like they had been surprised and never had a chance. They never had a chance anyway, but I expected to see dead Markee humans, but I saw none. The brutality exhibited was unthinkable, and there were far too many bodies to bury or even put to rest in a common grave. All we could do was leave it to nature.

Unfortunately, when we went to inspect the castle it was empty of equipment and even the saucer. That was disturbing. I made a mental note to check with the resident Sheree of this village to find out what was in that missing inventory.

The only thing left to do on Genesis Two was to launch to a sufficient and safe altitude above the Markee army and attack. Doc and Rumbee had indicated that they were ready.

When we engaged the targeting and firing program we felt the vibration of the firing throughout the ship. When I was young I watched my mother using a sewing machine to make something, I don't remember what, but the vibration was about the same, also the sound. There was no denying the results. As we watched the telescope monitor hundreds were falling all over the fields below. The speed at which the program controlled the laser was far beyond what could have been done manually. It was too efficient and Kim worried that the laser might become overloaded, so he insisted that it be shut down and cooled every thirty minutes. After four hours the pace of firing had reduced substantially, then it fired sporadically, then none at all. The army was gone, but we decided not to go back and tell the villages. We figured that it was best that they be prepared just in case another army came. That threat wasn't over.

Rumbee came forward and said, "The laser is a formidable weapon, and it is unfortunate that it can't operate through the Dome Shield. So, while you have launched the attack I have been discussing the technology of the laser with Cdr. Clark. We believe we have found a way to correct this problem by slightly adjusting the shield's properties and lowering the frequency of the laser. The combination of both of these adjustments should allow simultaneous operations of both systems. When we get back we will make the adjustments."

I said, "That's fantastic you guys. That will be a great asset."

The general wanted to attack the other two armies on Genesis Prime immediately, but Kim and Linda insisted on giving the overworked laser a complete inspection before stressing it again. Plus, allowing time to make the adjustment on the equipment seemed prudent. So we went back home.

I was looking forward to this staff meeting, but I was also dreading it. For the first time I did not have all the answers to the hypothesis I had been considering, even with all the baffles removed isolating my mind from the overwhelming cognizant abilities of my extended brain. There simply weren't enough answers to all the possibilities. I needed new and fresh ideas and thoughts, thinking out of the box, and these Wiz Kids were the smartest group I had ever known. For this mental exercise I was extremely excited about the process, but the reason for the exercise was disturbing to think about.

Once everyone was seated and ready, I said, "I have an agenda I want to pursue, and I think you all may find this challenging. First, however, I need to ask a few questions. I think I already know the answers, but I need to confirm my beliefs before I can move forward with my mental challenge." I sure had their rapt attention. They loved challenges and have been excellent at meeting them head on; however, this one could become far more personal.

"Cdr. Rumbee, when you first described the Plasma Bubble Drive you said it transcends time and space. I've been considering that, and it's clear to me that the controls must alter time to be able to move from point "A" to point "B" light years apart instantly. As you said, it transcends time and space.

211

The question I have for you is this: Do you know how it works and can you control time separately? Putting it bluntly, can the Plasma Bubble move forward and back in time separate from space?"

Linda sat straight up in her chair, completely attentive in the answer.

Cdr. Rumbee stood for a long moment in concentrated thought and also apparently in private communications with the other Sheree, then said, "It is as you describe. The machine's technology does control time and space, and I do in fact know how it works. I'm not sure I can explain it in terms you can understand, and I have taken an oath never to reveal this information. I took that oath with the Sheree Race, which no longer exists. Those of us left owe our allegiance to those here; therefore, I will tell you the secret as best I can."

"It's based upon actually simple universal laws. In our universe every object, person, thing, has a physical form that consists of that object in reference to a location in space and time.

Once you exist in the universe the object, person, or thing maintains in that time and space. Like your space travel, even at light speed you still exist in that same time and are altering space physically."

"It is relatively simple to alter either of these controlling factors to tell the object where and when to exists. But, when you tamper with time only it becomes extremely dangerous by creating paradoxes. For example: if you go back in time only you run the risk of altering your own past, which could make you cease to exist in that future reality in which you exist. Our race found this out the hard way, and as a result we disabled the machines from being able to alter time independently and vowed to maintain this secret, which I have now broken."

"Now, Admiral, is that what you had already figured out? We Sheree knew we would probably not be able to keep secrets from you, and we knew you would start digging sooner or later. We didn't want to keep secrets from you, but this one was the most important. Now you know, but I caution you to be careful with this knowledge."

I said, "Yes, Cdr. Rumbee, that is what I had suspected. It is also the basis of a paradox I have created for myself, one which I hope all of you here can solve.

"My thoughts are about going back in time and saving the Earth and its seven billion inhabitants from the asteroid that destroys it. We have the ability to alter the trajectory of the asteroid if we go back early enough to alter its course over a longer period of time. The paradox is that if we alter the asteroid's course, it will no longer be a threat to Earth and thus the Genesis Project may never happen. This means we will never launch and in all probability we would cease to exist, because we would have all died of old age. If we don't exist today how would we be able to save Earth? If we change history do we alter the course of history, our version of reality or do we create an alternate parallel reality?"

"This is only one paradox. If there is only one line of reality, we must launch with our original memories or we won't have the same motivations to survive or even be the same people we are today.

The other paradox is what would we do with a duplicate of ourselves and the Genesis. Could we exist at the same time or would one of us cease to exist?"

Linda said, "Damn, Nick! That's one hell of a challenge to hit us with. I'm not sure there is an answer. We risk a lot, too. We could destroy ourselves in the process and still not be able to save Earth. Still, saving seven billion humans might be worth the sacrifice of ourselves, but we can't be assured that it would even work. We would certainly need to think long and hard about this and come up with a fool proof plan."

Rumbee said, "I advise against trying to alter time. To do so becomes very complicated, but if you do plan to proceed, I can answer some of your questions. I can answer your last question, and the answer is 'No'. Objects from parallel timelines and realities cannot occupy the same spot at the same time. One of them will cease to exist. The universe doesn't explode, but only one remains as time continues to flow."

In support of what you plan, it is possible to create alternate realities. We do know that they can be created, because we have inadvertently done so in the past. I might mention that it didn't work out well for us."

General McCullah said, "I like this idea. If we can save Earth we must consider it, but I dare say even these Wiz Kids will need some time to think and plan. Like I said, I like the idea, but let's not rush into it. After all, we have all the time we want if we can control time. Might I suggest we let the seeds grow for a while and get back together later?"

I said, "Yes. That sounds like a plan. When you have thought it through let me know."

Genesis Prime Log: 04 July 0002

How ironic that America's fourth of July celebration was interrupted with real fireworks. Within minutes a Markee army materialized, thankfully, outside our walls and charged. We had waited too long to address the threat. The alarms sounded and Marines quickly came from everywhere and were backed up by the trained militia. Even the Sheree came pouring through the tunnel from their side. The walls were occupied and laser and rifle fire erupted all along the wall. The army came flooding across the bridge and another ice bridge created by the stolen Sheree ice generator at the upper end of the complex. The soldiers were carrying grappling hooks and ropes with the obviously intent to quickly breach the walls. They charged as if berserk with rage, ignoring the death greeting them. The army was falling, but there were so damn many of them. There was little doubt they would overrun the complex eventually by raw numbers.

Kim ran to the console and activated the targeting and firing program, modifying it to focus outside the walls at the main body of the army. Soon the rat-tat-tat of the laser began firing, carving wide gashes in the wall of wild men. I also noticed the second laser, also modified and programmed with the targeting and firing solution, began carving its own corridor in the army. Those on the wall managed to keep the flow of men from breaching the wall, but just barely. Once the lasers went to work the flood of men reduced drastically. Slowly the tide turned and the soldiers began a retreat, but the relentless lasers continued to pursue them across the meadow on the other side of the river.

The attack had been so sudden the draw portion of the bridge was unable to lift the weight of the charging soldiers. I was thankful that the Energy Dome was in place and functioning, because their obvious plan was to take the Genesis down with this first wave. They may have planned a second wave, but that wasn't going to happen. The army couldn't retreat or run far enough to get away from the powerful and deadly, accurate lasers, and they were being decimated. They would all be gone within an hour at this rate.

The Markee human operator or general had planned well, and if we hadn't been as prepared and trained as we were, the plan would have worked. We would have been overrun and killed in mere moments, and if the Disrupter weapons had been fired upon the Genesis from under our dome shield, that might have destroyed the Genesis as well.

Even during the heat of the attack, I was desperately looking for the Plasma Bubble equipment and operator, but the operator must have left immediately after bringing the army. My hopes were to kill the operator and destroy the equipment, but he must have anticipated this.

I was also impressed with the speed and readiness of all our combatants. The Marines I expected to be our first line of defense, but I wasn't expecting the militia to respond so quickly. Sgt. Maj. Gomez had done an excellent job of training them. I even saw Mr. Pollard leading a group of combatants. The Sheree were also impressive. I was surprised to see some very pregnant Sheree females fighting on the walls. Yes, they were committed to us, and I would say a very welcome addition, because they were great fighters, surprisingly fast and strong.

I would have to remember to ask the general if this side would have been able to mobilize as fast to the Sheree side if the army had attacked there. My guess is yes, but I'm sure he would enjoy answering that question.

I shocked myself out of my mental evaluation of the battle and plans when it suddenly struck me that I hadn't fired a single laser shot. I had observed it all through my control room essence, while my physical body sat in our quarters. How could I just sit there while the colony battled for its existence. I quickly noticed that our Nanny, Sarah had complete control of the kids, but I saw no sign of Akiko and Katy. I quickly located them through the visual centers and joined them at the loading ramp. They had weapons and stood guard with the ships Marines and other at the entrance ramp.

They smiled as I approached them.

Katy said, "Is it over?"

I said, "Yeah, it was another close one, but it's over." To accent this the main laser fired one last quick blast.

The dead from the laser blasts were nothing but dust. The laser blast disintegrated the human target, but around the wall there were many dead soldiers from gunfire. Very few made it over the wall, and those that did were dispatched quickly. Our losses were few, but then we had been lucky that there were no workers or sentry Marines in the fields this cycle. There were, however, quite a few wounds from swords or spears.

The cleanup of the enemy dead consisted of dumping them into the river to be swept out to sea for Gater food. We hadn't seen renewed signs of the Gaters, but we all knew they were still there...waiting.

Early in the battle I noticed a serious flaw in our defenses. Our outside wall encompassed the entire colony, including some farm fields and many animal stock pens, a big enough area a sizable army could have materialized within our defense walls. If they had done that we would have lost this battle.

If we had time, this oversight would be corrected. I would have an inner wall constructed closer to the mountain. This would serve as a secondary defense wall, should it become necessary to retreat behind it. The final defense would be the Sheree tunnel. Of course the tunnel would serve either side as an escape, depending upon which side the attack came from.

Genesis Prime Log: 10 July 0002

I knew the general was pissed at me, really pissed, and he had stayed away from me ever since the Markee army attacked. I know he has been busy organizing the clean-up and getting the colony calmed down and back on its feet, but I also know he has been trying to calm himself down. I don't blame him for being pissed; I should have listened to him when he wanted to attack the other two

218

armies. I should have listened to him, but I erred on the side of caution and listened to Kim and Linda after attacking the army on Genesis Two. They wanted to make sure we didn't harm the main laser from the stress. Of course we didn't, and the extra time facilitated the modification that allowed simultaneous use of the laser and the Dome Shield, which saved us from the last attack. Still, we should have launched an attack sooner. My delay had cost us valuable personnel, something we could ill afford to lose. I felt bad and did have an ass chewing coming.

When he finally came to the Control Room I was alone, which I'm sure he planned. He would never chastise me in from of the others, and I respected him for that fact.

The general walked up to me and stood stiff and business like and stared for a long moment, but then he relaxed and said, "Admiral, I was prepared to give you a royal ass chewing, maybe even a good ass kicking, but there really is no need. I know you well enough to see that you are bothered by the obvious mistake in judgment. So, there is nothing to be gained by bringing it up. But, allow me to say, you should listen to me when I tell you something should be done. I remember when I told to kill that S.O.B. Ichabod Crane during our voyage here. Not listening to me then almost got us all killed. Not listening this time almost did the same."

I said, "Yes, general, you are correct. Forgive me, please. I will try and do better, but did you really have to remind me of that idiot Ichabod Crane. My leg still hurts when I think about that bastard shooting me." We both laughed at the memory.

The general said, "You shouldn't complain. He shot me in the stomach, and at least you got to drive his adams apple through his neck. I wish I had had the satisfaction of killing the mutinying bastard."

Between us we agreed to disagree, but I convinced him to voice his objections more strenuous.

Genesis Prime Log: 15 Aug 0002

Cdr. Rumbee, Renee and Spee came to me today, all wearing an uncharacteristic broad grin. I knew something was up and waiting anxiously for the good news. Doc had already reported that he had begun delivering Sheree babies, so I figured this was what made them so happy, but I didn't want to spoil their news.

Rumbee said, "We wanted you to know that Renee and Spee are proud new fathers, among others. We have eight new baby Sheree, two more due, and six more females are pregnant. Already more Sheree babies have been born here than in the last four hundred years. Our race is alive again, thanks to Doc. We are very pleased to be here with you.

I said, "Is your mate also pregnant, Rumbee?

He smiled hugely and said, "Yes, Faylee is with my child, and Doc says it is a female child."

I said, "Well, congratulation, Rumbee. We will soon have a new Princess among the Sheree."

In the blink of an eye Rumbee's smile vanished. "How did you know?"

I said, "I am the Admiral. I know everything." Rumbee didn't laugh with me so I continued, "Don't panic. It wasn't that difficult. I've suspected since they first brought you in. You and your mate are the only Sheree with longer names, and the others almost bowed when they saw you. Renee, who I also believe is of a high rank among your race, seemed overly protective of you. All these things contributed to my suspicions."

Rumbee said, "I thought you might eventually figure it out, but I didn't expect you to be so quick about it. Yes, I am/was the Supreme Ruler of the Sheree on Markee and all the colonies. It is a hereditary title passed down from my father. My mate and I have been hiding among the scientist or we would have been killed long ago. I am, however, a scientist so it wasn't that hard to fool the Markee humans, but you are far more intelligent than they are. I hope you will forgive me for not being forthcoming with you."

I said, "Thank you for telling me, although I already knew. It makes no different with us. You are welcome here among us."

Rumbee's smile returned, even bigger.

Genesis Prime Log: 20 Aug 0002

The Wiz Kids were ready for me today, and most of the staff bowed to Linda as the spokesperson. They figured she was the most knowledgable, and they probably were right. I had noticed she had spent a lot of time in research and discussion with Doc, Kim and Rumbee, even Taka, and it was difficult to get him away from his hospital.

Linda went to the podium and began, "Rumbee has completed the modification to the Plasma Bubble Drive, which we are now calling the Plasma Bubble Time Drive. In truth, the modification hardly took more than flipping a switch inside the machine, but gaining access to the inside was more like a Chinese puzzle. Everything had to be done precisely in order to reach the insides. Taking a long look inside, I still have no idea how it works, and if truth be known, Rumbee doesn't either." She laughed at that, and Rumbee bowed slightly. "We have experimented with the time controls on the modified saucer in the cave, and everything seems to work. At least we moved in time, not much, but enough to know that it works. The controls look simple enough, but I would still feel more comfortable letting one of the experienced Sheree be at the controls. I guess what I'm saying is we are ready to proceed to the next phase, actually going back in time to Earth."

"We are still not comfortable with the plan, because we simply don't know what will happen. We studied the Grandfather Paradox that says if you go back in time and kill your grandfather then you could never be born. That surely is a paradox, but it doesn't make sense, because if you are never born you can't go back and kill your grandfather. In either case we don't plan to kill anyone, in fact we plan to save seven billion people."

"Several of us got together and had a movie night and watched Star Trek and Daja Vu, both present a logical argument that going back and changing something, at worst alters history in some way and creates a separate branch in time with alternate realities, multiple realities. We are all leaning toward this theory."

"If there was only one timeline reality, we are obviously it. Our reality began 140 years ago, and we all agree that it would take a significant alteration in history to change our reality. Yet, saving Earth is a significant occurrence, but following this scenario, if we are able to go back in time and save Earth, then our reality hasn't changed. If our reality had changed we would not be able to go back. So, therefore, if we do alter circumstances we have created an alternate reality from our own. My vote is that we try. The worst thing that could happen is that we fail to save Earth."

I said, "Very well. Is everyone in agreement?" I saw nods from all, including the Sheree, which surprised me. After all, they had nothing to gain, where we would be saving our home world.

"I guess the next thing we need to test is the actual time transfer. I'm thinking that we can send the saucer back in time to Earth on a test run before we launch. I calculate that it will take us a full week of continuous gravity drive pressure on the asteroid to alter its course enough to miss Earth. Kim, check my calculations when you get a chance."

"Who is going on the test run?"

Kim said, "I am. Spee, Renee and I will go."

I said, "Very well, but there is one thing we must accomplish before you go. We need to destroy that last Markee army. We don't want them attacking while we are saving Earth. Right general?"

Smiling, the general said, "That is correct, Admiral."

Genesis Prime Log: 20 Aug 0002

Kim couldn't find the last Markee army where they were last seen but eventually found them on another continent. Damn that Markee operator/general! They were headed directly for the village, one that had not been evacuated. We didn't have much time to save them and went into emergency operation. I had the general dispatch Homer and the ore carrier to evacuate them, and we hope we have enough time.

The Genesis immediately lifted off and headed to intercept the army. Kim had already left in the saucer for Earth, so I or Linda would be operating the laser. The ore carrier arrived first and had settled down near the village, but I could already see the army charging. I could see the villagers running toward the carrier, obviously realizing they were in trouble. I panicked as I realized the ore carrier did not have a dome shield. Oh crap!

Linda had already fired up the laser and it was firing full speed at the incoming army, as I settled down over the carrier. I couldn't land. All I could do was hover over them as low as I could get. The shield began to cover them and the ship, but all the villagers weren't under the shield. The villagers could run through the shield, but I couldn't deploy the gravity barrier until all were under it. By that time the army would also be moving under it, which

I could not allow. They might have disrupters. I said, "Linda concentrate as close as possible, even if some of the villagers get caught. General, deploy your Marines on the loading ramp and target the disrupters."

"Aye aye, Sir." said the general and was already running.

I couldn't wait any longer and deployed the gravity barrier. It slammed to the ground, crushing some villagers and army but stopped the army in its tracks. I had to sacrifice the slow villagers in order to save us all. The laser continued it vibrating assault on those outside, although I began to notice that the laser path left some standing, those without weapons. Well bless Linda's heart. She had figured out how to exclude the villagers. No, it was Doc. I could see him franticly adding to the targeting and firing program. He had seen the dilemma and acted. I could always count on Doc.

The laser began working outward into the army, and they began to run. With it now clear below I lifted the gravity barrier, lifted the loading ramp, and gained some altitude. The remainder of the villagers quickly loaded into the ore carrier. As we pursued the retreating army the carrier lifted off and sped off toward Atlantis.

The army was dwindling from the continuing laser assault, but again I could find no operator/general. He had hidden again with the equipment.

After two hours of following and destroying the army the laser slowed and finally stopped firing. We continued to search but found no new pockets of soldiers, so we returned to Olympus and docked.

I had considered taking the villagers back to their home, but Mr. Pollard had already taken control of the new villagers. It was too late now. He would have them in indoctrination immediately and probably already assigned to a department head. His organization was growing exponentially with all the new recruits, and Mac was not slow in recruiting new Marines. I'm sure he had already given his standard speech and hand-picked many. It seems Sgt. Maj. Gomez would have a permanent job as recruit trainer.

Genesis Prime Log: 21 Aug 0002

It was in the middle of the sleep cycle when Kim burst into the Control Room bellowing. My body was sound asleep, but the lights and my holography image flashed into existence, along with my attention. I knew he was flustered, because he was usually always calm, and since he was traveling in time, he could have adjusted his appearance for any time. He had not accounted for the difference, which was another indication he was disturbed.

Kim bellowed, "Admiral? Admiral?"

I said, "Yes, what's wrong?"

"Everything!" He said, "Everything is wrong."

"Calm down, Kim." I said, "Take a deep breath and just tell me what you saw."

Kim said, "I saw nothing, and I mean nothing that would indicate the Genesis Project ever existed. We went back in time to a couple of weeks before we launched, and there was no Genesis at Area 51, nor any sign that it had ever been there."

Oh crap! I called an immediate, emergency staff meeting, then woke Katy and Akiko even before their communicators buzzed. We quickly dressed and headed for the Control Room. Since we were close, we arrived before most and watched the others filter in in various forms of dress. The last to arrive were Mr. Pollard, Homer, Naomi, and the Sheree, which was understandable, living outside the Genesis.

I took the podium and said, "Kim and Spee came back from the past Earth with some disturbing information. It seems that they saw no signs of the Genesis or any construction, and this was just two weeks before we were scheduled to launch. It seems that something has changed in our timeline reality, and if we go back now and create a new alternate reality by saving Earth, we would probably cease to exist because we wouldn't launch. Following Linda's logic, we won't even be able to go back in time. It's very confusing. Do any of you have any thoughts? Anyone know what is going on?"

Linda said, "This doesn't even make sense. We are here now, so we did launch. We should be able to go back and save Earth. By all rights the Genesis should be built and ready to launch. Why not? Even if we were able to save Earth and create that reality we change our reality. We would cease to exist. Maybe there is only one reality that can't be changed."

Homer began to laugh and said, "Don't you get it? It is as clear as glass to me."

He had everyone's total attention. I said, "Please explain, Homer."

227

"Think about it. If the Genesis is not ready to launch, and we have not gone back in time to alter our timeline, then there is something we haven't done yet in our own past timeline. For the time being forget about the alternate timeline reality."

Doc said, "Maybe what Kim saw was an alternate timeline."

Homer said, "No, you still don't get it. Right now there is only one timeline, ours. An alternate reality would only be created when we alter the asteroid to save Earth. The reason the Genesis doesn't exist is because there is something we must do in your past in our own timeline to alter it. Since you do exist you have already done it. This means we must go back and do it now. This timeline depends on it. If you don't, we will not be able to save Earth, and you will not exist."

It suddenly clicked for me and I said, "Oh crap! Yes, I see what you mean. The reason there is no Genesis is because of the missing action in the past. We exist now because this action was done. So, it stands to reason that we must go back and preform that time altering function."

Taka said, "Wait. This doesn't compute. If there is something we must do in the past from the future how would we be able to go back if that past action wasn't done first? That's one of the paradoxes Linda talks about. If the action wasn't done in the past we wouldn't exist to go back. The timeline wouldn't exist."

Homer said, "Maybe we don't alter the past, but since you exist here and now, someone did or does. Crap, this is confusing."

I said, "Well, if we don't alter the past, who does?"

After several moments of thoughts, all eyes slowly turned to stare at the Sheree.

I said, "Rumbee, you told us that the Sheree dabbled some in time travel but found it too dangerous. I think you mentioned disastrous effects. What effects?"

Rumbee said, "It resulted in another race obtaining and learning our technology ... humans, which we were at war with on Markee. I was not in charge then, so I don't remember many details. I think we issued a warning."

I said, "Could this have been about 150 years ago?"

Rumbee's eyes went wide and he said, "Yes, yes, we warned Earth of the coming asteroid. I remember now. As you know, we continued to watch Earth after we were driven away, and we discovered the asteroid far out in space. There was nothing we could do, nor do I think we would have done anything, even if we could. We didn't trust humans for good reasons. Not like now. But it wasn't time travel then. It was real time. Wait, yes it was. I'm remembering now. One of our scientists had compassion for the humans we transplanted on Earth and wanted to give them a chance to escape Earth. She went back in time and issued an anonymous warning to Earth. She transmitted the warning and coordinates of the asteroid from deep space from the trajectory of the asteroid, knowing that since the transmission came from deep space it would definitely be received and taken seriously, and Earth would find the asteroid. We altered your timeline reality by doing so."

"Our race was angry, because your race used this extra time to learn and use our technology, much of which I see in evidence here. Wonder Metal, advanced computers, Gravity Drive, etc., all of which could have been used against us. It could have been disastrous for our race, but by altering your timeline reality we have actually saved the Sheree race by saving you. This is wonderfully ironic."

I said, "Kim, when did you first know about the asteroid? You probably would have been one of the first to know."

Kim said, "We learned about it in May of 2006. I was an Astrophysicist working at NASA Goddard Space Center, and we were directed to search coordinates provided to us. They never said where they came from, but NASA is full of secrets, so that wasn't so strange. I think others had also looked, but I believe we were the final authority and verification. It was very clear to me that it was on a collision course with Earth, and that was my report to NASA. I didn't hear anything more about my report until I met Major General McCullah about a year later. I was one of the first recruits and shipped off to Area 51."

I said, "Well, we have our target date of around April of 2006. So all we have to do is go back and transmit the coordinates and warning from deep in space."

Taka said, "Now I'm confused. If the Sheree already transmitted the warning why do we now have to go back and do it? Shouldn't the Genesis already be ready?"

Rumbee said, "I think I can answer that. It could be that our Sheree government was so upset with her that they sent someone back in time to prevent her from sending it."

Taka said, "That doesn't make sense. If she didn't send the warning how does our timeline reality even exist. We're back to the paradox of even existing. We can't go back now and correct it."

Homer laughed again and said, "It is not our paradox. It is the Sheree's paradox. Since we do exist, the Sheree will and did go back to send the message, not us. Our timeline won't be affected by who actually does it; it will be the Sheree's alteration."

"Exactly right, Homer." I said

CHAPTER 12
(President McIntosh)

Genesis Prime Log: 05 Sept 0002

At this cycle's staff meeting we were almost back to normal and discussing regular issues, that is after Kim gave his report.

The various department heads reported how the Dolphins were progressing, how the new villagers were assimilating within the colony, the new granite walls were progressing, how the crops were harvested, Wonder Metal production was coming online, etc. Everything seemed to be going well with no real problems at all. Then it was Kim's turn.

Kim went to the podium and said, "I am pleased to report that all is as it should be in the past on Earth. After Spee and I went back in time to April 2006 and transmitted the signal, we then went forward in time to about two weeks before we launched. When we appeared above Area 51 we saw our shining castle, the Genesis, gleaming back at us. So, our timeline reality was and is as it should be."

"Now, if we haven't scared everyone so bad with our tampering in time, we can begin our discussion on saving Earth. I've been thinking about it, and I believe we will create the alternate time reality when we actually alter the trajectory of the asteroid enough to miss Earth. It won't take Earth's ground tracking long to notice the change.

So, we will want to wait until the last moment before we begin to alter the course, and even then the asteroid must just barely miss. This is when we must start to worry about our own time reality altering. The threat must remain, or Earth may no longer be interested in the escape plans. We can't risk funding and construction stoppage, because we can't be sure when our timeline breaks from the alternate one. Once our timeline reality breaks then it won't matter. Our history will experience what we remember, while the alternate reality continues on its own path."

"Linda, what am I forgetting?"

Linda took over and said, "Kim, you covered it well. You have been thinking about it. I agree it is hard to pinpoint the exact timeline split, but there are a few things that must be factored in. For one, we certainly want the split to come a few weeks before we launch so that we maintain our timeline memories of the last days on Earth. Those memories define us. The other factor we must consider is that we will have to alter the asteroid far enough back to affect the alternation. We don't have enough power to make drastic changes. That is why we must start far back on the asteroid's course, one year I'm calculation."

"I agree that the break of timelines will come slow and begin at the time we change the trajectory enough to bypass Earth. That in essence alters history and creates the split."

"You bring up something I hadn't considered, however. There may very well be an overlapping window of time in which Earth itself could alter both timelines in a not very healthy way, like stopping the funding or project. This begins the paradox again and potentially dooms both timelines."

The general stood and went to the podium and said, "The politics and administration of the Genesis Project has always been my function, and I do it very well. Knowing myself as I do, back then I would furiously resist any alteration, and I have the power then to enforce my will. The only person that could stop me would be President McIntosh. He gave me that power, and he could take it away. But, the Genesis Project was his brainstorm, so I don't see him changing his mind."

I said, "At that point the president has his neck stuck way out, but he probably doesn't care since Earth is doomed. What do you think he would do if he found out the asteroid was going to miss, and there would be a day of reckoning for him?

The general said, "Well, he is a politician, and if you put it like that, he would probably go into salvage mode and try to hide everything. He just might close everything down and try to make it disappear."

"There is only one thing we can do. We must bring him here and tell him the truth. Maybe we can use the META and let him see some of our memories of the destruction of Earth. Those memories are very graphic. I think we can persuade him to keep the project on course. Keep in mind that we have his granddaughters to help him believe."

"There is something else we can offer him. Remember, he is a politician. After Earth has been saved, we can go to Earth with proof and praise

President McIntosh as the savior of Earth. We can even provide the video of his final speech. He would become president for life."

Taka blurted out, "Don't forget about Japan's Hope Project. It must also survive."

The general responded, "Yes, Taka, you are correct. That's especially important for the Immortality Gene. The president can wield major influence in that regard."

"Admiral, the best part is that we can talk to the president even if we decide not to try to save Earth. I mean that if we decide it is too difficult to predict results. In that case we would not change anything for us, because the Earth would still die under that scenario."

Mr. Pollard said, "Can I ask maybe a stupid question? How do you plan to snatch the most guarded person on Earth without drawing attention or being seen?"

I figured I would let the general answer that one, since he is good at covert operations planning, and he would be planning this operation. Plus, he was doing a great job planning so far. He had certainly come up with ideas I wouldn't have thought of. It must be his devious mind.

The general said, "That's a good question Mr. Pollard, but I need to ask Rumbee a question before I answer you. Cdr. Rumbee, The Enlightened projected a Plasma Bubble from their vessel that encompassed the Genesis and used it to transport us forty light years away. Can your Plasma Bubble do the same?"

Rumbee said, "It is our technology that The Enlightened used, and yes, our Plasma Bubble can be used the same way."

"Very well," said the general, "I propose we do the same. We will use a Sheree saucer and project the bubble around Air Force One and bring it to our time, and the place will be on the Sheree side of the mountain. With the exception of the president, those on board Air Force One will be kept on board and will only see Sheree. They will think it is an alien intervention or kidnapping. The government will put a gag order on them immediately, even if they believe them. Remember, we will be using time travel, so we will take them back at the same time we took them. Air Force One will never be missed. There may be a report of a UFO sighting from ground radar, but that too will be hushed. The only one that will see the Genesis and us will be the president. We can work our magic on him, then take him back."

The general stood silent with a smug grin. He knew it was a brilliant plan. Everyone else knew it was brilliant, also, including me.

Genesis Prime Log: 10 Sept 0002

We all kicked the general's plan around and around for days, trying to dissect it and improve it; but try as we did, we found no flaws in the plan and no way to improve it. The plan really was brilliant, and we really had nothing to lose. It could only improve our chances of survival, so the general and Kim researched the history activities of the president on Air Force One and picked a time.

Kim and Spee plotted the location and departed. The plan was to suddenly appear above Air Force One and captured it in their projected bubble. Spee would radio the pilot and order them to cut their engines and lower their landing gear. The surprise of the capture and the fact that the engines would quickly overheat would force them to comply. Once they complied they would blink out of existence over the Pacific and reappear outside the Sheree complex firmly resting on the ground.

The plan must have worked to perfection, because I observed Air Force One magically appear. The bubble disappeared and Air Force One was immediately surrounded by a squad of armed Sherees. So far the alien illusion was maintained.

Over a loudspeaker, Spee said in perfect English, "If you do exactly as I tell you no one will be harmed. You are no longer on Earth and you have no choice but to comply. We mean you no harm, but resistance will not be tolerated. We wish to meet with President McIntosh. All of you remain on board your plane. Only the president is allowed to come out. Please do so immediately. If you comply we will restore you to your flight path on Earth."

A hastily constructed staircase was pushed up to the plane door, and the Sheree waited. After a few tense moments the door opened and President McIntosh stood in the doorway and stared. Spee motioned for the president to come down, and a wide-eyed president slowly descended. Rumbee shook his hand and led him toward the Sheree Complex, then through the tunnel, and finally up the road to stop and stare at the Genesis in recognition and realization partially what this was about. Rumbee then led the president up to the Control Room where he finally met the staff.

President McIntosh looked the same as he did when I first met him at Area 51, tall lean, white headed, but the most memorable feature were his piercing blue eyes, that now scanned the faces of the staff and me.

Since the president didn't know me at this point in his history, the general took control and said, "President McIntosh, as you may have guessed, we are the Genesis Project you started, and we are from your future about 150 years. Obviously, your project was successful and we survived the asteroid and destruction of Earth. I know this is all hard to believe, but there are ways we can help you believe with certainly, starting with the introduction of two young ladies that you may recognize. Just think about three years older." With that the general motioned the nanny forward with his two granddaughters. The president would know them as being about eight and ten, but the two girls running toward him screaming "Grandpa" appeared to be eleven and thirteen. Immediate recognition, however, flashed over the president's face as he dropped to his knees to embrace them.

The general allowed there reunion to continue for a while before saying, "Mr. President, I'm sorry, but we don't have a lot of time."

The president said, "Yes, of course." He gave the girls one last hug and kiss as the nanny led them away. He stood, wiped the tears away and said,

"OK, you have my attention. What is this all about?"

The general said, "Well, obviously your Genesis Project was successful. We survived, but we had to witness the painful destruction of Earth from space. This has haunted us ever since. We now have a plan where we can go back in time and save Earth from destruction, but it involves some potentially dangerous alterations of history. If we fail we could not only not save Earth, but we could potentially destroy ourselves in the process. We don't want to get to far into that paradox discussion, because it will just make your head hurt. Please just trust us on this point."

"We can show you some of our memories so you will experience and understand our history. During the voyage we invented what we call a Memory Educational Transfer Apparatus (META). It will save much time and discussion if you will submit to the download. It won't take that much time. Will you accept our gift of memories?"

Homer, unintimidated at all in the presence of the president, said, "Oh, you will love this part. You'll learn everything just like you experienced it yourself. I never get enough of learning from these downloads."

The president looked at Homer and thought in silence, then said, "Yes, do what you think is best for me to learn your plans."

The general said, "Very well Mr. President." He then motioned for Doc to proceed.

Doc led the president to my captain's chair and showed him the apparatus. He applied and fitted the META unit on his head, then went to his console and began tapping keys.

Doc said, "This will take a few minutes Mr. President, so it's best to just relax back in the chair and try not to fight the flow of information. It will make it easier."

The president nodded and visibly relaxed back in the chair, but soon his eyes popped open wide as the memories Doc had prepared began to flow into his consciousness and become his memories. Slowly the expression on his face changed to knowing awareness and resolve.

After the download was complete, the president said, "Damn, I gave a great speech." At that everyone laughed, including the president. He continued, "I can see how Earth's destruction could haunt you. It haunts me now reliving the experience. I understand your plan and will do my part. I will also make sure Japan's leadership will also comply."

"The president look directly at me and said, "Nick, I sense much resentment from your memories for extracting your oath to protect and save the Human Race, and I can truly understand. That promise has cost you much, but I don't apologize. You were the right and possible the only choice for the job. General, you chose well."

The general said, "Yes, Mr. President. I believe he was the right choice, and he has done well. He saved us and the mission many times and may very well save Earth."

The president continued, "I see the absolute necessity to keep this conversation strictly between us and the complicated details of your well thought out plan, and I will comply. The one thing I hope you won't forget to do is come back to Earth and save my ass from the politicians, because it will definitely be hung out." Laughter rang out throughout the Control Room.

I said, "Yes, Sir, we will not leave you hanging."

The president said, "Admiral Johns, you have done well. The wonders you and your team have created are marvelous. I hope at the right time you will share these medical and technological advances with Earth. You have also made some incredible friendships. Again, at the right time and advanced preparation I hope your alien friends will visit me at the White House. That should get the people talking."

"You know, it was smart to let the Sheree only be seen. I have a plane full of correspondents. Of course they will be strong-armed to remain silent, but when it leaks, and it will, the tabloids will be filled with 'President kidnapped by aliens'. That should destroy their credibility."

Thank you all for saving Earth, and I have no doubt you will, but it's time I get back to the plane. The longer I'm away, the harder it will be to explain. Well, that's not true. I'm not going to tell them shit."

The president shook hands all around like a lifelong politician and followed Rumbee out. I watched as they exited the ship, and he stopped to take in the marvels of the colony. The engineering and layout was impressive. After a moment he turned and started talking to Rumbee as they walked into the tunnel and out of our lives again and back into the past 150 years.

Genesis Prime Log: 01 Oct 0002

Akiko asked me to go with her to the Dolphin lake this cycle. She wouldn't tell me why. She just said I would find it interesting. The Dolphins were about five months old now, still not grown but old enough to be very active. Akiko was acting so mysterious that she definitely had piqued my interest.

As we entered into the enclosed training area I knew immediately what she wanted to show me. I was bombarded with telepathic images coming from the Dolphins. I saw images of food fish, balls being tossed, rings being returned, a never ending string of images and emotions. I felt pleasure, hunger, desire mixed with Dolphin toys. It was easy to decipher what they wanted. There was a flood of messages coming from all ten. Akiko spent a lot of time here with the dolphins, but I hadn't been here since their birth. The dolphins were happy to see Akiko, jumping, splashing, and sending her happy messages. I heard Akiko telepathically messaging them back, which seemed to increase their pleasure greatly.

I said telepathically, "When did this start?" When they detected my transmission they went crazy with excitement, jumping, chirping, whistling, and at the same time they bombarded me with telepathic messages. All at once I couldn't follow the individual messages, but the gist was much pleasure at my ability to transmit a message.

Akiko transmitted, "They have always transmitted some, but only recently have they begun to put hole thoughts together. I guess like a child learning to put words together to transfer meaning."

The dolphins were excited yet again to hear us communicating together. One came close and tossed me a ring, messaging me with an image of me, my actual visual image, tossing the ring far out into their bay. I did so, and the dolphin shot into the air and took off after the ring. It was amazing, and I continued to play with them for a while. I enjoyed it, and they seemed to love playing. That lasted until Akiko got into the water with them, then they left me to swoon over her. They rubbed up against her, lifted her, and chattered, clicked, and whistled at her. Akiko would grab hold of fins and two of them at a time would pull her through the water at super-fast speeds. Both the dolphins and Akiko seemed to love the interplay.

We were alone in the enclosed arena or Akiko probably would not have done what she did. Akiko, having an athlete's body, was not well endowed up above, and she seldom wore a bra nor embarrassed easily. She is strikingly beautiful and had simply slipped off her jumper and dove in with the dolphins. I didn't know if I wanted to watch the dolphins or her. I decided I best not join her in the water; we might frighten the young dolphins.

During the late cycle as Akiko, Katy and I lay cuddled, I told Katy what Akiko had done.

Katy laughed and said, "Yep, that's our Akiko. I'm surprised you didn't jump in the water with her; I certainly would have." We all laughed at that.

All in all it was a pleasurable cycle, and I needed the break. It was enjoyable being alone with Akiko. It was fun, and it was exciting to learn about the maturing dolphins.

Genesis Prime Log: 07 Oct 0002

We heard our first hint of trouble at this staff meeting, but it was just a matter of time. Katy had hinted to me during our late cycle family time, but we had a hard rule to not bring work into our personal time.

Katy took her turn at the podium and said, "We are starting to have some problems in the colony, mostly concerning the children. I don't guess it is a big secret anymore about immortality. Some have it but most don't. It have become abundantly obvious with our children. The children of the immortals are growing and maturing at an advanced rate and on average 20 to 30 percent larger. The nannies have had to separate them from the others into their own facilities. The children don't notice or even care, but many of the parents are questioning us about the Immortality Gene. Obviously they want to know about it and getting it, and as I said, its existence can't be disputed any longer.

I said, "Who is asking?"

Mr. Pollard stood and said, "Well, I for one, but I have had many other citizens come to me in my role as governor with inquires and requests. We feel that we are being discriminated against and forced to become second class citizens. There is a lot of talk about the ruling hierarchy of immortal Kings."

Needless to say, I was instantly pissed but somewhat controlled and said, "Mr. Pollard, you have been told and should know that 'The Genesis Project' is not now nor has it ever been a democracy; it is a military oligarchy. I was given this authority by President McIntosh. I am not King, but as the military supreme commander, I am in control, along with my designated department head commanders. This means that you and everyone else serves at my desecration."

"Furthermore, the colony does not have a governor, and if it did, it would be Cdr. Clark. She manages the colony. You have done a good job for her and the colony, and I would hate to see you lose the respect you have earned. I realize that you once served in congress, but that has no bearing here on Genesis Prime. At some point in the future we may consider change, but not for a long while."

"Now, as far as immortality and who gets chosen, you do not get to tell me who gets it. We are still deliberating whether it is a good or bad thing. We developed the Immortality Gene out of necessity during our voyage. We would not be here now had we not, so it was a good thing at the time, but there are disadvantages, which I am not prepared to talk about at this time. If we determine that the benefits are greater than the alternatives, we will provide the IG to others, probably as an incentive for superior contributions to the colony, but not all will get it. That's not going to happen."

Mr. Pollard said, "Admiral, I hear and understand your position, but we have many living in the colony that are from Genesis Prime. Your rules should not apply to them. They should be free to govern themselves and choose a leader to represent them."

I spit out my response, "They are free to accept our rules, or they are free to leave our colony and our protection, as is anyone else. I seriously doubt, however, that unrest among the villagers is coming from them. Remember, these villagers were screened by the Sheree before being transplanted here. Their population will have far fewer self-centered psychopaths. Maybe you should look around for a psychopathic agitator, a manipulator among the population. When you find one, he or she will be invited to leave."

Mr. Pollard was not happy with my speech, but he had the good sense to remain silent. He knew that I knew that he was the manipulator. I would have problems with him at some point. I really don't like politicians, the ultimate psychopaths.

I asked the military Cdr. staff to stay for another meeting. Once the number of members reduced down to my trusted few, all immortals, I began.

I said, "I wasn't expecting political problems this soon. I expected that there would be problems, but I thought it would be years away. I guess bringing the villagers into our fold has exaggerated the problem, but I don't regret it. That blood line has been screened to weed out the self-centered psychopaths, thanks to the Sheree, and to some degree so has the blood line we brought. Unfortunately, they are still among us, and we need to plan for that contingency."

"Linda, I want you to secretly move all the Plasma Bubble Time Drive machines, and the other

Sheree technology as well, into the hold of the Genesis. I want to control them and their access. I want the modified saucer moved into the hold as well. We can't afford to let the time travel technology get out. It is just too dangerous for our continued existence."

"I also want stronger, impenetrable access gates installed on the major sensitive gates like the power plant, laser, storage caves, even the Sheree tunnel. I want to be able to control them from here if necessary"

"Taka, I want you to delegate the hospital to your underlings, and move your family back into the Genesis. I want you and your IG technology kept exclusively within the Genesis. Actually, I want all the immortals living within the Genesis' protection, that includes your immortal Marines too, general. We can build housing and facilities just outside the Genesis."

The general said, "Don't you think this might cause more problems by bringing more attention to the immortals?

I said, "It will, but the difference has already been discovered and noticed. It was inevitable, and will only get worse no matter what we do. It is best to face the problems head-on, and there is more than just one problem. We are looking at it from colonist's point of view, but we must also look at it from the immortal's point of view also. There is and will be resentment from the normals. This puts the immortals in danger from the masses, but the other problem is that the immortals through age, or the lack of it, will begin to feel superior. In time and through generations passing around them they will appear to the normals to actually be superior. We will become a repeat of ancient history and become the Olympian gods. This is also inevitable, but by keeping all the immortals together I'm hoping to minimize the superiority complex for as long as possible."

Rumbee said, "Do we understand that some of you are long lived like Sheree? Is that what you mean by immortal?"

I had actually forgotten that Rumbee, or any of the Sheree for that matter, knew nothing about our experience with the Immortality Gene.

I said, "Yes, Rumbee. Many of us are beyond just long lived. We are immortal in that we do not age at all. In fact we are self-regenerating. Unless we get injured to the point of death, we regenerate. But, we have introduced this gene to only a few of us. We created it, well Taka created it, to save Akiko, but it became necessary for those of us that were awake and required to make our long journey awake."

Rumbee said, "This is good, because we Sheree have worried about surviving in your human colony after you passed. Now we feel far more secure knowing you and these others here will live long. We trust this group, but we don't trust humans in general."

Calvin Kline said, "Admiral, it sounds like you don't trust humans either. You seem to think so little of the human race. There is inherent goodness in the human race."

I said, "I always hope for the best, but I am also realistic. We all desire the goodness of our race, but even in your theology teaching there is evil. Good battles against evil, but evil seems far too prevalent and seems to win the battles. Look what we saw happen on Markee. Evil won, with hardly any goodness left. Look what happened on Earth. The human race destroyed itself even before the asteroid hit. Now it begins here. No, I don't trust the human race to eliminate its own evil."

Calvin Kline said, "Yet, the human race created us and the Genesis Project, and we have done much good. We saved the human race, we saved the Sheree race, we saved the villagers, and we might conceivably save Earth and its seven billion inhabitants. This is not evil; this is good. Maybe this is God's will, and we are God's angels and doing his work."

I laughed and said, "Maybe you are correct, but until our goodness can destroy or control this self-destructive evil, I will continue to be pessimistic. Hell, maybe my plans are God's plans. Did you ever think of that?"

Genesis Prime Log: 10 Nov 0002

Perseus, Apollo and Artemis turned nine months old this cycle, along with most of the other human children. The Sheree built a children's nursery and day care center just down the hill from the Genesis for all the immortal children. Akiko, Katy and my children spent the majority of their time there being supervised by their nanny, Sarah. They were becoming a task for Sarah, since they were already running in different directions and getting into everything. I was thankful, however, that Sarah didn't put up with any nonsense from our kids. When they needed it she wouldn't hesitate to swat one to keep them in line, but she dished out far more hugs and kisses. The kids adored her.

Of course all the children were developing fast and seemed equivalent to children twice their age in size and maturity. I was even more thankful that we separated them from the others because of the these increasing differences

The Day Care Center was always full of happy children and busy nannies, and Akiko, Katy, and I also made it a point to spend as much time as possible with them during this play time. We also noted, happily, that the Sheree were bringing their young children to the center, and, although younger than the human children by several months, they were developing quickly. The Sheree children seemed happy to mingle and play with the human children. I liked the idea of the races intermingling, which boded well for the future relationships. I never really liked the separation of the Sheree from the colony, but the Sheree were just now reestablishing their race and needed and wanted the separation. I'm sure from their past experience that the Sheree weren't comfortable around humans, and I'm sure the villagers weren't comfortable for the same reasons. I was happy that they also realized that our races must be comfortable with each other and chose to let the children mingle.

Akiko and I spent time with the Sheree whenever we could. We both felt at ease with them. I think, well, I know it was the telepathy we shared. We had worked with Katy often to try to break through the telepathic threshold with her, but nothing had happened. As a result, Katy didn't share the comfort of the mingled minds, so she always seemed to have other more pressing things to do. Akiko and I had slipped into an easy flow of minds with the Sheree and them with us. Our minds began communicating on a subliminal level, linking and sharing thoughts, and direct communications with individual minds became easier.

CHAPTER 13
(Altered Reality)

Genesis Prime Log: 01 Dec 0002

The inevitable came this cycle at our normal staff meeting, and I wasn't sure how to present it to the staff. Actually, I personally didn't really know how to deal with it. I was confused, and with my augmented mind, that never happens. I had listened to the department heads addressing all the issues dealing with returning in time to save Earth from the asteroid, but they seemed to have run out of additional problems to solve.

Finally, Linda just blurted out, "Well, Admiral, when do you want to do this?"

I sat in silence for a few uncomfortable moments, then said, "We already have."

It was their turn to sit in silence, looking back and forth at each other.

Linda said, "I don't understand. What do you mean, we already have?"

I said, "Don't feel lonesome. I don't understand either, but apparently we already saved Earth, or once did. At least I have memories and recorded history of us doing so. We also apparently reversed our action and altered our own reality, which is why you have no memory of it happening; because by altering our own reality, it never happened. I don't remember it happening, but I have the actions and memories recorded, so it must have happened. Yes, it's very confusing   ."

According to my internal log, a separate log I began recording when the operation began on November 15, 2014, we launched back in time and began the slow alteration of the asteroid's course. According to the recording, this took a full week to complete."

Dr. Rossen interrupted me, "Wait! Nick, how can there be a recording of activities if they were reversed and it never happened?"

"I've asked myself that a hundred times, but the records exist, and in truth you are the one that insisted we make this record. I must have set myself an alarm in the past to access this specific file on a specific date in our future. I don't remember doing that either. All I know is that an alarm went off in my head telling me to go to this file and access it, and that's exactly what I did. That was three days ago, and I've been in a stupor ever since."

"The only way to explain it, I think, is like this: When the recording was made, that was our reality. It was actually happening in that altered timeline and recorded. When we went back and negated our actions to save Earth we changed the reality back to our original timeline, the one we are in now. Therefore we didn't save Earth, so the alternate timeline disappeared and effectively never happened. That's why we don't remember it, but it was real when we recorded it, and we have the record of the alternate events. I hope that makes sense, because that is the best I can do."

Doc said, "yeah, it kind of makes sense, but like you said, it's confusing."

The General said, "Well, why did we change our minds? I mean in the recorded records."

"I've watched it repeatedly since I became aware of it, and from what I have seen, we changed our minds in retaliation for them killing you and Rumbee and also to save ourselves from destruction."

At that little tidbit of information there were many gasps and expletives of outrage.

The general said, "Maybe we should just watch the recorded record. I want to see how a S.O.B.s killed me."

I said, "That's a good idea."

(Alternate) Genesis Log: 20 July 2015

I chose to start the alternate recording at the day the asteroid actually collided with Earth during our previous reality. This way we could compare and watch the asteroid bypass Earth, meaning we had saved Earth from destruction.

As customary during any operation, the staff was gathered in the Control Room watching. We could see the huge asteroid streaking toward Earth as before, but it quickly became apparent that the asteroid would miss Earth. We anxiously watched the asteroid, Armageddon, streak past Earth, and we all cheered. Since we were still here, the president had obviously kept his word to keep funding and the Genesis Project going and also the Japanese Hope project as well. We had succeeded with our monumental project to save Earth and keep ourselves alive in the process.

254

In the recording I said, "Very well done guys and gals. I think we can go ahead and contact the White House by radio and check in. I'm sure, even though the asteroid missed Earth, they will be experiencing some nasty tides and weather as a result. Traveling at sub-light speed it should take us a couple of days to reach Earth, and the worse of the weather problem should be passed by then."

"Surprisingly, it didn't take long to receive a response to our transmission, but also surprisingly, the response didn't come from the White House. It came from the Joint Chief at the Pentagon."

The response said, "Welcome, Genesis. We have been expecting a transmission from you. We on Earth thank you for your action in altering the course of the asteroid, and the president and the world want to give you credit and honor the Genesis and its crew."

"We want you to land in the Ellipse between the Washington Monument and the White House. You can't miss it."

Kim responded, "Thank you. We should be there in about thirty-six hours."

The general said, "Well, obviously we don't have to save the president. The world already seems to know what we did. That's strange. I would have bet money the president would be in deep shit by now. I wonder what happened."

(Alternate) Genesis Log: 21 July 2015

We were still far out in space, but Kim had found and been monitoring the location of the Ellipse area where they wanted us to land. He said,

"There is plenty of room to land there. We shouldn't have any problems."

Uncharacteristically, Rumbee spoke up, "May I address you and this assembly?"

I said, "Of course you may, Cdr. Rumbee."

He solemnly approached the podium, stood in silence, then said, "I think us Sheree have proved that we stand with you. We respect you and want to be a part of your community. But, we must make a demand on this assembly."

Everyone knew the following would be important, if not profound. Rumbee had everyone's attention.

"We have been completely open about our technology and have held nothing back, especially about time travel. This technology has been protected throughout our existence, until now. You have it now, but we can't allow you to share it with others, certainly not humans. We do not trust most humans, for good reason. We can't allow you to share it with Earth humans. We can't even allow you to bring this technology within reach of them. This means that we don't want you to land the Genesis on Earth. I know for certainty they will try to take it if they know we have it, which obviously they do. You gave this knowledge to the president when you downloaded your history through the META unit. Even if he did not share the information, the others will know due to the fact that we came back in time and saved them. I'm thinking that the president shared this information or it was forced from him, but trust me when I tell you they know."

"Time travel is extremely dangerous to all of us. This technology must be controlled. Please hear me and comply with our wishes."

I said, "Yes, Cdr. Rumbee. I'm not totally in agreement, but we will honor your demands. We will remain in orbit and not land. We will launch an Earth delegation in one of the saucers, and land it in the Ellipse. Who should we send? Any volunteers?"

The general said, "I am the most logical one to represent the Genesis Project, since you must remain on board. They all know me, and I can deal with them one-on-one. The Joint Chiefs don't scare me, and the president respects me. I should go.

Rumbee said, "I will also go. You will want a Sheree, as you promised the president you would provide to validate the story. As I have said, I don't trust them, so I can't be tricked. Oh, we will be sure to take a saucer that hasn't been modified for time travel."

(Alternate) Genesis Log: 21 July 2015

As we approached Earth and settled into orbit above Washington DC, Kim reported that military personnel, equipment, and even tanks had been positioned around the Ellipse landing area. None of us were overly concerned, thinking crowd control for our protection could be expected.

We depressurized the hold and opened the outside ramp, allowing the saucer to exit and begin its decent toward D.C.. The saucer continued its approach toward the landing area.

Kim suddenly said, "I wouldn't suppose military being use is not that unusual for crowd control for our landing, but after Rumbee's voiced distrust I notice something else unusual. The tanks and weapons are all faced inward. Like I said, I probably wouldn't have noticed that before, but if the military is only used for crowd control, why aren't they facing the crowd? I don't even see a crowd"

It clicked for me and I bellowed, "Abort! Abort! Call them back. It's a trick."

The saucer had almost landed but abruptly stopped in mid-air and shot back up. The saucer never had a chance. Missiles shot toward it from every angle, and the saucer exploded in a fiery display, littering the landing area with debris. The general and Rumbee died instantly.

Almost simultaneously messages rang out from Earth through our communication center, "You were ordered to land the Genesis, not a landing craft. We have multiple lasers targeted on the Genesis. You will comply immediately with our orders or you will be destroyed."

Unbidden, Kim screamed back at them, "Why are you doing this? We just saved your sorry asses."

Surprisingly, they responded. "Just comply with our orders, and you will not be harmed. We mean you no personal harm, but your technology is far too dangerous. We, Earth, must control it. You will not be allowed to leave with it. Land immediately!"

I said, "They tracked and watched us approach Earth in gravity drive. They will think that is how

258

we will leave. Linda, take us back to the future and home in the instantaneous method, but take us back before we left to alter the asteroid. That is the only way we can save the general and Rumbee. Earth just killed itself...again."

"When we return home none of us will remember it, because it never happened. The general and Rumbee will be there, because they didn't die. And, Earth will still be dead, because we didn't save it.

Doc said, "I don't like the thought that we did all this, Earth did all this, and we won't remember. I don't want to forget that Earth, our own people, betrayed us. I don't want to worry anymore about trying to save Earth. Can't we establish a record of these exploits and review them later?"

"I believe we can," I said.

Genesis Prime Log: 01 Dec 0002 (Continued)

I said, "Well, Doc, I believe we can blame you for this record. It was your bright idea." Even though all were at high tension, everyone got a good chuckle out of my statement.

Doc said, "I guess you are right, but I still think we should know what happened. I certainly won't bother worrying about saving Earth anymore."

The general blurted out, "I can't believe those sorry sons a bitches killed me, but I'm kind of happy I don't remember my death or the pain. Doc, thanks for having the foresight to record it. If my death would have been a one-on-one fight, I might have wanted to go back in time again, just to kick his butt." At that laughter rang out again, partly because everyone knew it to be true.

At least I was feeling better about the situation, mostly because they had experienced what I had, and the secret that had been haunting me was now out. I guess I just felt relieved that it was over.

It was Akiko that snapped us all back to reality when she said, "You know I'm sorry that our mission didn't work out, but are we just going to let a bunch of military and political psychopaths ruin it for all the Earth's inhabitants? Isn't that what we have been talking about in our own world, not letting self-centered narcissist run us into a self-destruction direction? surely there are humans worth saving that could be saved."

"I was so very proud that we, the Genesis, were able to save the Japanese Hope Project. They are good people, well most were, and have contributed much to the general welfare of all of us. I can't help but believe there are others back then on Earth that are worthy of being saved. This failed project of saving Earth has just got me in the mood to save something or someone."

I know Akiko had not forgotten about Ichabod Crane and his group of mutineers that almost succeed in destroying us, and I was positive she would never forget about Sakata who had also almost destroyed her ecosystem on the Genesis when she was in cryogenics, but still she had a valid point about other good people worthy of being saved. By her way of thinking there were many more good people, but the real concern would be if we the will and ability to survive until we weeded out the undesirables. We could certainly believe this would be the case.

I had analyzed the disaster created by the black hole during our journey many times. I had been forced to sacrifice 1,150 souls from cryogenics in order to save us, which was tragic, but in a morbid view, I had been able to heavily screen the inventory of humans to sacrifice many undesirables. As a result, the Genesis arrived on Genesis Prime with the best of the best. Like I said, it was a morbid view, but the colony was better off for it. Now Akiko was suggesting that we go through this all again. She has a great and caring heart, and I owed it to her to consider her wishes.

When she mentioned the Japanese Hope project I immediately thought of the other escape projects I discovered on Earth before we launched. My searching at that time had found and located the location of the Hope Project, which led to our making contact with them and eventually led to our rendezvous in space. But they weren't the only ones.

The French had a well advanced escape project, which had a good chance of being successful. Unfortunately, however, they had been discovered and destroyed by radical Islamic factions of the French population just days before we launched. The Germans and Russians had a joint plan, and the Chinese had also started one. Neither had progressed very far and had absolutely no chance of survival, which is why I didn't investigate them further at that time. We were out of time and almost didn't make it ourselves.

Now, due to the Time Bubble, we had unlimited time, so it might be worthwhile to take another look, especially the French project.

Genesis Prime Log: 10 Dec 0002

This staff meeting was focused upon security. I had asked the staff to report on our various threat risks, which seemed to be many. We had been attacked by two sources, and they have not gone away.

Kim took the podium first and said, "I have continued to monitor Genesis Prime through our satellite network, and I have not seen any additional reappearance of the Markee armies. The remaining villages are still safe. I haven't, however, been able to check on Genesis Two. I might suggest that we send the saucer there to re-evaluate the situation. They may have launched something there, but I sort of doubt it. The three times we have engaged them they were soundly defeated. Still, we know Markee still has at least one Plasma Bubble, and they could attack again at any time. They are overpopulated and apparently have an abundance of human armies to throw at us. We know that Markee is a dying planet. In order to survive they must colonize somewhere."

Rumbee said, "The Markee humans do not colonize. They are not sane or rational. They attack and destroy, and they hate both the Sheree and you humans that protect us. They will not give up their focus on us. Trust me. They will attack again. They want to recapture the Sheree and take what you have, that being our and your technology, food and stores. That human race, the Markee, doesn't raise crops, only consume and destroy. If for no other reason, they must come for food stores."

The general stood and said, "I don't like just waiting on them to attack. When we do that they control when and where. That gives them the advantage. If we must war with them it is better to be the aggressor, then we control when and where the battles occur."

"We must do one of two things. We must utterly destroy them or destroy their ability to attack by destroying their remaining technology. They keep hiding their Plasma Bubble, but if we can find it and capture or destroy it then we destroy their ability to war with us. If we can't we must destroy them."

I said, "Linda, can we send Lt. Boland back to Genesis Two to check on the villages' status? As to the recommendation of Major General McCullah, I agree. I bow to his judgement. Let's come up with a plan and discuss it at our next staff meeting"

"What do we know about the Gaters? Are they still a threat?"

Surprisingly, it was Akiko that responded first, saying, "I believe they are a threat. Actually, I know they are a threat, because we continue to lose fishermen. No one has actually seen a Gater take a fisherman, but I don't believe they just fall in the river without help. We hurt the Gaters badly, but they demonstrated a great deal of hate toward us during their attack. I believe they are just waiting for the right opportunity to attack again."

Katy said, "I agree with Akiko. We can't forget about the Gaters. We have raised the height of the security wall and made other defensive precautions, but I also believe they will try again to destroy us. We must be ready and vigilant."

I said, "Cdr. Rumbee, we were told by Spee, I believe, that in the past two races landed on Genesis Prime. One of those being the Gaters, but we haven't heard anything about the other alien race that the Sheree drove away. What can you tell us about the other group of aliens? Could they be a danger to us?"

Rumbee looked shocked and turned to Renee and Spee, exchanging thoughts at super speed. It was so fast I couldn't really follow their exchange. Rumbee, still looking surprised, said, "This planet was visited by the Moor. This must have happened after the fall of the Sheree on Markee, because I was unaware of their visit here. Sadly this is bad news. The Moor inhabit a planet many light years from here, but they have occupied other planets. They are an aggressive and conquering race. They love fighting. If they visited here, they will be back in force. They don't send a single ship to colonize; they send many to conquer and occupy a planet. This must have been a scout ship seeking target planets to colonize, and I don't have to tell you that Genesis Prime is a prime planet for that. You can bet they are on their way.

Fortunately, however, they do not possess Plasma Bubble Drive. They do have advanced technology in energy propulsion and can achieve multiple light speeds, but it will take them years to travel any distance. According to Spee it has been close to 200 years since they were here, meaning they are probably overdue and could show up anytime."

I said, "Tell us about the Moor and their technology."

Rumbee said, "They are air breathers like us, which is why they are probably attracted to Genesis Prime. Moor are brown fur covered and run in packs. They walk upright on thick short legs, but they run on all fours. At full height they are about this height." He placed his hand at about five feet. "They have a thick chest and arms and are extremely strong and fast. Their face resembles what you call a gorilla with double fangs top and bottom. One of the most deceptive features is the tail. It is long, thick, very agile and functions as their primary weapon. They impale their victim with a hooked barb on the end of the tail and hold the victim in place while they tear it apart with their front claws, but they seldom resort to hand to hand fighting. Mostly they use laser rifles."

"The Moor typically fight from the air and on ground. They are not overly technical, but their war craft do fire lasers somewhat like yours, except they are not nearly as powerful. They are, however, quite effective as a weapon. The Moors don't have Wonder Metal technology nor disrupter or shields, at least they didn't in the past. Their attacks usually involve multiple smaller craft deployed from a larger main ship supporting ground troops. The attack ships are not as agile as a saucer, but they are fast."

I said, "Linda, I suggest we devise defenses against these attacks. Consider arming the saucers so we can engage the Moor's attack vessels, and get with the Sheree to see how we can defend against lasers. Since the Moor are overdue, I suggest you get right on it. It may be some time before they come, but it would be prudent to be ready for them when they do."

Genesis Prime Log: 25 Dec 0002

This cycle marked our second Christmas on Genesis Prime, and Calvin Kline insisted on making it a Colony holiday. His newly constructed church had been completed, and he had been busy preaching the gospel to all his newly converted villagers and the predominantly Catholic Earth colonists.

Calvin Kline, whom I always called the underwear salesman because of his name, had come to me some months back complaining that many of the villagers openly still worshiped many of the Olympian gods. He said it had even increased since many villagers believed some of us were in fact those same gods of ancient times. As I have told him many times in the past, I don't believe in organized religions and don't encourage it. Still, I don't want them thinking we are Olympian gods, so I agreed to be seen attending church. He held me to my promise, and Akiko, Katy, and myself decided to attend the Christmas service with Mac and Lt. Mckay, who had been regular attenders. Even Homer and Naomi had begun to attend.

As we walked toward the new church on this Christmas cycle, I was extremely surprised when Rumbee and about ten of the Sharee joined us. I really didn't know if they were new converts or just wanted to support the colony and socialize. They, after all, had built the beautiful church, so why not? Certainly, Calvin was jubilant to see all of us enter his cathedral.

I was focused upon Calvin's pleased reaction to our presence, and I was feeling pleased myself to be here. It reminded me of my childhood attending church with my mom, dad, and sister. Those were good times before they died in that terrible car accident. That's why I joined the Marines and made them my new family.

I was deep in thought and missed the initial reaction from portions of the congregation. By the time I realized what was going on it was too late. I saw a group roughly pushing through the crowd shouting, "Abomination!" and others shouting, "He has the audacity to bring the alien abominations with him." Others saying, "Kill them. Don't desecrate our holy place." The group was loud as they charged me. I was shocked and hardly had time to even try to defend myself. I managed to push Akiko and Katy away from me, since I seemed to be the focus of their attack. I heard gun shots and felt a thud to my chest and burning heat, then I felt nothing. I was nothing.

My consciousness exploded to life in my holographic image back in the Control Room. I tried to reach out to my body but found nothing. I panicked and scared everyone in the Control Room with my screaming. My permanent Marine guards snapped to attention and ran to my image. I began barking orders, "Send Marines to the church and protect Akiko, Katy, the other staff and also the

Sheree! Hurry!" Instant alarms sounded, and I could hear the Marines barking orders.

I began cycling through outside cameras trying to see the church, but I could not find an angle or direction to see the church through any of the cameras. All I could do was wait.

Dr. Rossen burst into the Control Room saying, "What happened?"

I quickly said, "I'm not sure. I was attacked in the church, and I'm worried about the others. I can't find my body, so I can't monitor."

Doc said, "I understand."

I heard him speaking to his medical staff telling them to dispatch an emergency team to the church. He then grabbed one of the Marines as he was headed out and told him to have a Marine detachment protect his team at the church.

I was back to just waiting. I had grown so accustomed to living through my body and now, being limited back within my Control Room essence, made me feel like a prisoner to it. I had been living through my bodies, two bodies, for almost 130 years, and had forgotten how confining it was living solely through my Control Room extended brain. But, waiting was all I could do.

I don't think the mob were targeting Akiko or Katy, but I couldn't help worrying about them. If anything happened to them I'm not sure I could keep my sanity. I saw them as I pushed them away from me, and didn't see any movement toward them. Still, with a mob you could never know. Anything could happen. So I waited.

I finally saw the make-shift ambulance speeding up the hill. Finally, I would know something. As I watched through the lower deck as an anxious Doc exited, and I was immediately relieved as Akiko and Katy followed him out. They were crying and looking back into the truck. Several Marines pulled a litter out and I, my body anyway, was on it. I didn't have time to see much as they rushed me to the medical clinic, but I didn't see any movement from my body.

Once my body was transferred to an examining table and uncovered, I saw my poor body. There were two bloody holes in my chest, but what got my attention was the bloody hole in my forehead. When Doc turned my head I could see a gaping hole in the back of my head. My body was obviously dead ... really dead.

Doc said the obvious, "Nick, your body is dead."

I noticed that Akiko and Katy were still crying, and I wanted to comfort them. If they would have thought about it they would realize that I just lived through my body, but my essence was still alive. I don't know why I hadn't thought about it before, but I could speak mentally with Akiko. I guess I was too shocked to think about it before.

I spoke mentally, "Akiko, I'm still alive. Don't be upset. Tell Katy."

Akiko instantly responded, "Oh my God! In the excitement I forgot. I love you so much. We thought we lost you."

Akiko said, "Katy, Katy. OMG Katy. Nick is still alive. We forgot that he is in the Control Room. He spoke to me telepathically." Katy hugged her ... hard.

Katy spoke telepathically, "Nick, talk to me. Tell me you're alive."

I was shocked to hear Katy transmit her words telepathically. It must have been the pure emotions of the moment or intense desire to speak that allowed her to make that final connection in her brain. Akiko and I had thought it possible. There was no reason she couldn't, but we had been unsuccessful in teaching her so far. But, the connection had now been made, and Akiko spun to her in surprise.

I transmitted, "Katy, my Katy. Yes, I am alive. We can hear you. Now we will be even closer, all of us. Both of you come to me in the Control Room, please."

They were there in moments. When they saw my holographic image smiling at them they grinned hugely, knowing I was alive. They tried hugging my image, but their arms passed right through. In frustration, they hugged each other.

I said, "What happened? The last thing I remember is pushing you two aside, then the searing pain took me."

"Katy said, "It happened so fast and we fell to the side when you pushed us. It didn't last long, and all I saw was Mac grabbing at the gun. He took a shot in leg, but he will be alright. He took control of the situation and wouldn't leave. It was the villagers that save us all. When they saw what they did to you they jumped the attackers and pulled them to the floor. By then Marines were everywhere. I think the Sheree killed one of the attackers before the Marines came to protect us. The Marines cleared the area for Doc's team, and they hauled you out. You were obviously dead, and we sort of lost it until just moments ago. Mac can probably provide more information."

Concerned, Akiko said, "Nick, what does it mean, with your body dead? What happens now?"

I hadn't really thought about the future yet, but it became clear, and I said, "Well, nothing really. Remember that I have another body in cryogenics. It is the original body that Akiko gave birth to. The body that died grew up with Katy 2." I saw the recognition register in their eyes. I will continue to live through that original body. There will be no difference. Both bodies are/were the same physical age with the Immortality Gene."

Doc, having just walked in, said, "I think we will get Taka to start you another body. The way you attract danger, you may need several spare bodies."

At that we all laughed. Crying one moment and laughing the next. It's nice to have a happen ending.

Genesis Prime Log: 30 Dec 0002

I have had several cycles to think about what had happened, and it seemed the more I thought about it, the madder I got. I saw the faces of all those that attacked me, and I studied them. I saw the pure hate and repulsion in those faces. In all the excitement and confusion none were captured. They all got away in the crowd and probably thought they got away with it completely, but I knew them all, especially the face of Mr. Pollard. He was the one that shot me. I replayed the memory and video over and over in my mind. Yes, I knew them all. Mr. Pollard was the leader and direct supervisor of all the other attackers. It was quite apparent that he had been influencing many, poisoning those around him for his own purpose. I just wasn't quite sure what that purpose was, but for sure it was personal gain, as only a psychopath would conceive. Maybe he wanted to assassinate me to get me out of the way so he could take over the colony. Only a total narcissist would dare to believe the staff would ever allow him to do so. My gut had been correct, never trust a politician. I knew there would be a day of reckoning for him, and I would deliver the verdict and punishment personally.

Doc had thawed out my spare body and my mind was already reaching into it, filling it with life. It was easy to connect and take over the body, like nothing had happened. Unfortunately, it took a couple of days for my body to recover from hibernation, which required me to remain in Doc's clinic under supervision. At least I had a body again, but the worst part was not being able to sleep cuddled between my two loves. But, they spent as much time with me as possible, so it wasn't unbearable.

The first thing I did when Doc released me was go visit the general. Doc refused to put us together, knowing we would talk business, especially after my assassination, and he would have been correct.

Mac was all smiles when I entered and said, "Well, Admiral, how does it feel to be dead?"

"It fucking hurt! That's how it felt." I responded."

"Now tell me what happened, since I didn't see much of it."

The general said, "Well, as you know, it happened very fast, and I couldn't believe it was happening until too late. I saw that ass hole, Pollard, pull a gun and start shooting at you. I yanked the gun away but too late. He managed to shoot me in the leg, but thanks to the IG I'm almost healed. I think Doc was keeping me in here only until you were ready. He knew I would go kill someone. I think the time was well spent, because I do have a plan."

"I, of course, knew you had another body in cold storage. There are a few others that also knew, but not that many, just some of those awake during the voyage. None of those people would say anything, so I suggest we keep it a secret for a while. This will give us the advantage in trying to find out who all was involved."

"The most surprising reaction was from the villagers. They attacked the mob and ran them off, all but one. Rumbee pulled one guy off you and killed him outright with his bare hands. He and the other Sheree were really pissed when they saw what happened to you. I mean it was abundantly obvious that you were dead. Hell, your brains were blown out the back of your head."

I said, "I'm glad I missed that part. I like your plan by the way. As the second in charge, call an emergency staff meeting, and I will remain quiet and hidden until then."

Genesis Prime Log: 05 Jan 0003

I watched through the cameras and kept my body hidden as all the staff members had entered and took their seats. I could not convince Akiko and Katy to attend. They did not trust themselves at the meeting. All knew why this staff meeting was called, and the tension throughout the Control Room was so thick it could almost be cut with a knife.

The general went to the podium and began, "We know why we are all here, and I want to open the floor for anyone to voice ideas."

As expected, Mr. Pollard rose and said, "It is unfortunate that the Admiral is dead, but we must now quickly reorganize our government to fill this absence. As the elected president of the colony and the majority of colonists, I will naturally assume overall leadership of the colony, the Genesis, the combined armies, and the Sheree community." At that statement the Sheree actually bellowed their outrage, but the general just smiled, as Mr. Pollard was just digging his grave even more.

At the Sheree's outburst Mr. Pollard held up his hands for silence and continued. "Nothing will change. Mr. Rumbee you will remain in control of the Sheree community. The only change will be whom you report to. The Admiral is dead, and he will be greatly missed, but I will attempt to support you as he would have."

"Major General McCullah, as second in command of the Genesis, will assume leadership of the Genesis. You and Mr. Rumbee will be part of my staff and a significant part of my command. Together we will keep our colony strong and functioning efficiently."

274

I had heard enough crap from this asshole. Mr. Pollard had made his move and stated his position. He had committed. Now it was time for me to make my move.

As I entered I said, "Mr. Pollard, aren't you a little premature in your attempt to take over?

The look on his face was worth the facade. I swear his eyes actually bugged out, and his jaw almost hit the floor. It was comical to watch. Best of all, he was speechless, and for a politician, that is a death sentence. How ironic, since that is what was about to befall him.

The worst part about the facade was allowing the Sheree to believe I was dead. Their shock was even more pronounced, and they too were speechless.

I said, "Cdr. Rumbee, as you can see, I am NOT dead. I will explain later. Now, Mr. Pollard. I find it difficult to believe that you could actually try to take over after personally killing me. Only a psychopath could even believe that possible. Hell, if I were truly dead at your hands, you would already be dead. My staff would have already ripped you apart. As it was, I had to keep the general away from you, and he still would love to have that honor. I have to disappoint him, however, because I intend to do that personally."

Mr. Pollard finally recovered and found his voice again. He said, "I am a United States Senator, and I am also the elected president of the colony. I have official standing."

I interrupted him, "No! You have nothing. The United States no longer exists. As far as your elected position, I never authorized or sanctioned it.

I am now and always have been in total control of this military campaign and colonization effort. You have no standing. Even if you ever did, which you didn't, you forfeited it all when you became a manipulator and murderer. No, you are finished."

To the others present I said, "Someone haul this piece of shit out of here. Let's reconvene this meeting in front of the church."

By the time our procession made it to the church, word had spread and a large crowd had gathered. Apparently many in the crowd were gathered to receive word from their new leader about the change, because I saw all those I was looking for among the crowd. They were certainly in for a surprise in that regard.

Somewhere during the walk down the hill the general had handed me a .45 caliber military pistol and holster, which I strapped on. When he handed it to me he informed me that from now on it was a part of my uniform, and he left little room to argue. So, as we approached, I was fully armed, but it was quite unnecessary. I was surrounded by Marines.

Total silence filled the space around me. This floating cloud of silence fell heavily on all close enough to see me. The reaction was profound and varied. All were in shock at seeing me alive. Many stood in frozen silence, some of the crowd showed primal fear, and the villagers present fell to their knees and humbled themselves as I passed.

As we passed through the crowd and I recognized one of the mob that attacked me, I pointed them out. A Marine would pull him out and bring him along. I found all ten of them, although two tried to run and were tackled by a Marine.

When we reached the top of the walkway leading into the church I turned and stared at the crowd, letting them get a very good look at me. I didn't want there to be any doubt that it was me, Admiral Nick Johns, standing there ... very much alive.

I said very loudly, "These men attacked me in this church, and this man," pointing to Mr. Pollard, "Shot me three times and killed me. I am the victim of his crime. I am the witness of his crime. I am also the judge of his crime, and I find him guilty!"

At that point I drew my .45 and shot a very surprised Mr. Pollard right between the eyes. The single shot could be heard echoing throughout the colony in the absolute silence.

I broke the silence and said, "General, now interrogate his accomplices here with these witnesses and do with them as you wish." I then walked off back toward the Genesis through an ever widening corridor of open space, and I never looked back.

***

I was waiting in the Control Room with Akiko and Katy as the staff began to filter back in from the church. It had been almost two hours.

The general was laughing when he entered and said, "Nick, I wish you could have seen what happened after you left. All I had to do was ask them if they had anything to say in their own defense. I had my hand on my .45, and they were scared to death and told everything they knew. Actually, they were fighting each other to tell off on Mr. Pollard.

The crowd heard how Mr. Pollard planned the assassination and, according to them, forced them to go along with him. He threatened their jobs and threatened them personally. Mr. Pollard, according to them, was evil and lower than whale shit. He led them astray, and they were as much victims as I had been."

"I listened to them as long as I could stand it, then declared them guilty of complicity in the assassination. I spared their families, but I banished them. Once they realized they would not be killed, they were happy to be banished. I did tell them that if we ever saw them again they would be shot on sight. I guess they haven't realized that banishment is the same as a death sentence. Let the saber tooth cats and wolves deal out their punishment. The Marines escorted them to the front gate and unceremoniously dumped them outside."

"I guess Katy will have to find several new supervisors."

Katy nodded at that statement and said, "Yes, I will have to choose better this time."

I said, "Katy, there is no fault here. You had no way of knowing, and he was doing a good job. We just didn't know what was going on in his head. He was just for himself and not the good of the colony."

General, what was the reaction from the crowd when I shot him?

The general said, "I sensed only understanding. After all, most of them saw him shoot you, and you only did to him what he did to you. There was no sympathy for Mr. Pollard or the others for that matter. I can tell you this, though. I don't think anyone else will try to assassinate you. They saw you dead and in their minds you came back to life. They don't understand it, but they certainly accept it, especially the villagers. After this they believe you are Zeus, and they will never be convinced otherwise."

"I don't think it should be explained how. Your rebirth needs to remain a mystery."

Genesis Prime Log: 07 Jan 0003

On this cycle I called for a meeting with the Sheree and Chaplin Calvin Kline. It was not a closed meeting so several others were present and welcome, especially the general. I figured it was time to offer some explanation on how I had survived the assassination, especially to the Sheree. I was pretty sure that Chaplin Kline knew, but I wanted to ensure that secret would remain secret.

When they had gathered, I said, "Cdr. Rumbee I wanted to explain myself to you and the other Sheree. I am not a god. I did not heal myself. As you already know, I think, I exist and live within this dome. My essence exists within my brain enclosed within and through extension into a much larger brain that extends into every part of this ship and some parts outside. The body you have grown to know as Admiral Johns is a clone of my original body. My mind in the dome telepathically controls the body. By itself it has no conscious. I transmit my conscious and essence into the body and live through it, but I am here." I pointed to the chrome dome.

279

"I'm not sure you knew this about me, but it is necessary for you to understand what happened and how I am still alive. During the voyage Dr. Rossen cloned a second body. I have transferred back and forth between these bodies. We eventually put one of my bodies into cryogenics. When my body was assassinated Doc thawed out my other body, which I am living through now."

"Most among my staff were awake during the voyage and knows this about me, but most do not. I want to keep it that way, because I don't have another spare body to transfer into if this one is killed or dies. Both of my bodies had been modified with the Immortality Gene, and I might have survived if the killing shot hadn't been through my brain. My body would have healed itself. You might as well know the whole truth. Myself, my staff and a select few others have modified DNA with the Immortality Gene. This means we also do not grow old. We remain this age for time immortal. Rumbee, you speak of long lived, well we are truly long lived."

Doc injected before I could continue saying, "What you said about the brain shot killing you may not be completely true. I put your injured body on life support. If your mind had actually been in your body's brain your body would have been brain dead, but since it is not, the Immortality Gene will grow your brain back. Once it has been restored, you should be able to transmit to it again."

I said, "I hadn't thought about that. That's good news. Thanks Doc,"

I detected Renee communicating with the other Sheree. I think he had realized what was happening with me and he was giving one of those "I told you so" message to the others. None of the Sheree had anything to say. It seemed they understood completely and instantly accepted what I said.

Chaplin Kline said, "Yes, I knew what had happened, and I did keep your secret, but how the devil am I supposed to compete with Zeus the immortal? The villagers and even many of our own colonist are believing you have been resurrected from the dead and that you are the Olympian god Zeus. What am I supposed to tell them?"

I said, "Well, I don't want them thinking I am a god. So, tell them I believe in the God, and I will attend one of your services. The rest is up to you. You know I don't believe in organized religion, and the roof didn't fall in on me when I went to your church, but I died just the same."

CHAPTER 14
(The French Connection)

Genesis Prime Log: 20 Jan 0003

At this staff meeting I took the podium first. Akiko had got us all thinking about saving other humans, but I had stalled further discussion. I wanted to think things through thoroughly, which I have done.

I said, "Akiko, I have been considering your desire to save others from Earth, and I have a possible objective." Everyone set up in rapt attention. "Since you mentioned the Japanese Hope Project in the last discussion, it got me thinking about the other failed projects on Earth. Those projects would be the most prepared and equipped concentration of prepared humans, like us. Their plans and preparation would be geared toward survival in space and colonization on another planet. Now, of the German, Chinese and French failed projects, only the French project stood a chance of success. Unfortunately, the French were ready to launch when they were destroyed. I'm thinking that we could drop back in time and snatch their entire vessel and project before they are destroyed and teleport them here to Genesis Prime."

"We will have to discuss whether we want them here in our colony or elsewhere. I say this because their personnel obviously have not been properly screened, since they were destroyed, probably from within. That would be hard to do without saboteurs, since their spaceport and project are located on French Guiana.

We know that the French project was destroyed by radical Islamic terrorist, and there is not a significant population of those on French Guiana. The native population there is sparse and predominantly Roman Catholic. The engineers, professionals and workers at the spaceport, however, come from France and all over Europe, since the European Space Agency is also a partner there. The spaceport is located on the Northern cost of South America, protected by sea on the East and dense unpopulated land all around, making it naturally protected from rogue armies. So, based on these facts, we must assume the attack on their project comes from within."

"Actually, the French project is the only one of the projects I consider safe to try to save. We could easily be considered hostile and attacked by military defenses over Europe or China. They are just too dangerous to attempt, where French Guiana seems relatively safe."

Akiko secretly transmitted, "I knew you would eventually respond to me. You always do. Thanks my love. I will show you how much later."

Katy, now attuned to our telepathy, and I chuckled at her transmission, because Rumbee and the other Sheree looked at Akiko when she mentally spoke. I transmitted back, "You're welcome my love, but remember that our secret communications are not so secret anymore." At that Akiko visibly blushed, and the Sheree flashed a knowing grin.

The general said, "If we expect sabotage and embedded terrorist we should keep them separated for a while to give them a chance to find the sabotage and rout the terrorist out. Besides, they might not find them all, and there could be explosions. We want to keep those away from us. Wait, I assume they were not destroyed by an atomic detonation."

I said, "No, it was not an atomic detonation, but it was a significant conventional explosion. Still, what you suggest is a good idea, general. Does anyone have a suggestion where we should land the French?"

Rumbee said, "You could land them on our side of the mountain outside our wall. Once they have been cleared of bombs and terrorist, we can build them a wall. We just love to build walls."

At that statement, the Control Room exploded in laughter. None were expecting humor coming from the Sheree, and it magnified the reaction from the group. I knew the Sheree had a sense of humor, but few others knew. They kept it low key, but with their increased ease of our group they were beginning to let it out. This obvious in-your-face joke was the first time it had been displayed for all to see, and showed their trust of us. It was also funny.

I said, "I think we are all in agreement to attempt this rescue, but let's all consider the options. If we have no objections we will launch in five days."

Genesis Prime Log: 25 Jan 0003

Kim, Linda and Rumbee had calculated the precise time and location over French Guiana's

284

spaceport, and we materialized over the French saucer. When Kim told me, I had been somewhat surprised that the French had built a saucer, but then it was the smart thing to do. The French obviously had been successful in obtaining the formula for Wonder Metal and the gravity technology. The saucer was far easier to encompass within our gravity shield than a standard rocket propulsion craft.

It didn't take us long. Our Plasma Bubble deployed and we winked out. To the casual viewer at the spaceport they might have missed us. We reappeared outside the Sheree wall, withdrew the Plasma Bubble, then lifted off again, leaving everything from the spaceport deposited there, including some of the outside equipment and workers that had been stationed around it. It was a clean transfer and quite surprising to those within.

Once we resettled in our landing site, we began transmitting to the French saucer. It took a few moments to find the right frequency and for them to respond. They responded in French, so I spoke to them in French. Actually, my entire staff and I had taken a session on the META unit to learn French before we embarked.

I said, "This will be hard for you to understand, so it might take a while. We mean you no harm. In truth we have just saved you. We desire to meet with your upper command staff. Please disembark your vessel and you will be led to our control facilities for a full explanation of what just happened. For your own safety, please comply immediately."

Our transmission was met with only silence for a full ten minutes, but they finally responded, "We will comply."

I watched through a camera as five people exited their bottom ramp to meet a team of Marines. They were quickly searched and led out of my sight into the Sheree complex and tunnel leading toward us.

While we waited we began to laugh at the French workers that had been caught outside. They were running around trying to figure out what the hell just happened. I'm sure it was traumatic for them, but their antics of running one way then the other and finally just setting down on the ground to wait seemed so comical to us.

In about fifteen minutes the wide-eyed French group was led into the Control Room and were directed to seats vacated for them.

I said, "I'm sorry but there is no time for introductions. We can do all that later. I will give you a very brief analysis of your situation so you can begin your search immediately, but let me assure you that you are safe from us and our alien friends, the Sheree. We too were an escape vessel from Earth, two actually."

"Your vessel has been transported approximately 186 light years from Earth and 138 years into the future, and you are here to stay. Just accept these facts, and when you notice two suns outside, that fact may help you believe."

"We intervened in order to save you, because your vessel and all its personnel will be destroyed by internal sabotage in 48 hours from now. By us snatching you out of your timeline, we are giving you the ability to stop the sabotage and find the perpetrators before it occurs. Our historical records indicate that you were destroyed on the ground by radical Islamic terrorist just days before you planned to launch. That fact may help."

"If you provide a computer link to us we can assist in finding potential terrorist. I would suggest that you evacuate all personnel from your ship and commence a search by trusted personnel immediately. If you wish we can assist you with your inspection. Once you have found and cleared the explosives, we assume your destruction was from explosives, and identified and dealt with the terrorist, come back and we will answer all your questions."

During my quick speech, the French group lost their glazed look and seemed to transform into angry and serious warriors.

One stood and said, "Of course this is a lot to take in so quickly, but I do believe you and that your intentions are good. We will return to our ship immediately and try to solve our internal problems. I will have the computer link up and operating within the hour, but I must decline your offer to help with the inspection. We know our ship very well and what to look for, and you do not. You would just be in the way. I look forward to being able to ask several thousand questions."

Genesis Prime Log: 26 Jan 0003

The apparent leader of the French Project was true to his word, and established communication and computer link with the Genesis within an hour.

We also witnessed the evacuation of personnel from their saucer. All those disembarking were burdened with gear, which probably supported an extended stay outside. I also noticed that they moved far away from their saucer in case of an explosion. They should be fine for a while, but soon we would have to temporarily bring them behind the Sheree wall for their protection.

It didn't take me long to plunge into the computer and its programming, data and personnel files. It also didn't take me long to find suspicious and probably dangerous member of the crew. As I discovered, Iran was a heavy contributor of funds for the French Project, but even though the money came from Iran, the French government insisted on French credentials in the form of the ship's name. They called it the Charles de Gaulle. I thought that was fitting.

The fact that funding came from Iran obviously influenced much of the personnel staffing. Even so, this was an escape project designed to save humans from extinction. As such it was planned to be successful, but apparently there was a strong radical blend to the staffing. It would not be easy to weed the radicalized bad ones out due to the high percentage of Muslims among the crew and colonizers. I began to harbor an element of regret for bringing the problem among our colony. I didn't regret saving them, but I might have considered moving them to another continent. I guess the important thing right and main priority now was their survival.

I did find some Trojan files, which I deleted and corrected. They were designed to prevent fire suppression and water pressure, none capable of much initial damage. Those files would, however, definitely prevent or deter putting out fires started from other sources. So, I continued my search of the personnel records and hoped the crews within could find the planted bombs.

The Charles de Gaulle was an impressive vessel and project, but it was less than half the size and capacity as the Genesis. They had cryogenic chambers capable of holding one thousand souls, but they didn't have them full. I suppose our untimely extraction was before they finished filling them or more probably all those hundreds in the meadow were eventually going to full them before they launched or soon after.

Ironically, their destination, like the Hope, had been Mars. They did use Wonder Metal in their construction of the saucer and had gravity drive but not much more in the way of advanced technology. This undoubtedly would be a source of irritation for the general against his corporation contractors. Also like the Hope, their mission had little chance of success, but they deserved an "E" for effort. With our assistance, they now had a solid chance of success, if they didn't explode from the sabotage.

As I research the personnel files I discovered a good 50% of the awake personnel were questionable, even the Europeans. In truth trying to screen out the radicals from their crew had not been much of a priority. I was, however, able to narrow the list down to about fifteen definite radical leaning and active participants in past terrorist indoctrination and activities. One of them had even come into our ship among the five department heads.

I was very surprised to find out the leader of the project was Frank Rothchild, an orthodox Jew. To discover an orthodox Jew among so many Muslims seemed highly unusual, especially as the commander, but Mr. Rothchild was highly, very highly, educated at Oxford and had been highly successful at past project which he had headed. He was not French. He was British and assigned by the European financial conglomerate as the project commander. That must have been an interesting conversation.

When I had done all I could do to help them, I sent a private communication to Mr. Rothchild relaying my suggested list of terrorists among his crew, including his astrophysics, Omar Ackerman. After that we waited.

Genesis Prime Log: 27 Jan 0003

Kim, who had been monitoring the French activity, said, "There is some activity outside the French saucer."

We all quickly began watching the monitor. We saw Frank Rothchild and what must be about ten of their security or military come out from the saucer and head toward the encampment. They were also roughly escorting whom I believe to be Omar Ackerman. When they reached the encampment five other men were pulled out from the crowd and escorted away from the crowd. Mr. Rothchild spoke to all, then the six men. We couldn't hear what he was saying, but we figured it out when they were lined up facing the armed security and summarily all shot.

At first I was shocked, as were the other in the Control Room, but I quickly realized that they had dealt with the saboteurs ... no more saboteurs, at least those saboteurs. I was beginning to like this decisive leader. It took me almost 140 years to fully learn this lesson, and he just did it on day one of his new command.

After the execution, the leader and his three remaining department heads headed directly toward us. The Marines were notified of the approaching party. This time when the group appeared on camera at our end of the tunnel they were being escorted by a group of Sheree. I'm sure this made the French group uncomfortable but probably no less shocking than anything else they have been bombarded with in the last 48 hours.

The French delegation was led into the Control Room and found seats. They seemed reserved and waited to be addressed.

I said, "Mr. Rothchild, may we assume you found the sabotage on board the Charles de Gaulle?

Mr. Rothchild stood and said, "I see you have done your homework Admiral Johns. Yes, we found four bombs planted in key strategic locations designed to explode flammables aboard our vessel. I see you found and corrected the program designed to ensure failure of our fire suppression system. Thank you. All the bombs were timed to go off five hours ago. Since we have had no explosions we must assume we found them all. We also identified the terrorist, most of them anyway. They were so blatant that they left their fingerprints and DNA on the bombs, and they were all on your list of potential terrorists."

"We want to thank you and your staff for your intervention in our imminent disaster and for transporting us here to a safe, habitable planet. Our future survival was haphazard at best on Mars. I dare say we now have a fair chance of survival."

"If I may, let me introduce our team. As you have discovered, my name is Dr. Frank Rothchild, and I am the commander of our team. Dr. Paul Lafayette is head of security, Dr. James Lacroix is head of engineering, and Dr. Aimee LaSalle is head of life support. Dr. Omar Ackerman was our astrophysicist, but as it turned out, he was also leader of the saboteurs and is no longer with us."

I noticed from Dr. Rothchild's short speech that he too had done his homework. He called me by name and probably knew a great deal about us. Also from his introduction I was quick to pick up the PhDs of his department heads. They would be highly educated and probably the top list of those available, like my whiz kids. He had not found it necessary to point out that he had executed the terrorists, knowing that we had watched the execution. There was also a message to me in this action. He was letting me know that he controlled his crew and would do whatever was necessary for success. I liked that, because he did not shirk away from a hard decision.

Dr. Rothchild continued, "We make the assumption that since you transported and saved us, you are offering us an invitation to join your colony. If so, we gladly accept your invitation. We do, however, have many questions we would love to ask you."

I said, "I'm sure you do have many questions, but we have an easy way to answer many of those questions. I suggest you hold those questions until after you have been exposed to our META unit. Even this will be explained during the process. Doc, can you and Homer take our new friends and recruits to the clinic and hook them up? Oh, and Doc, don't forget to teach them English and Sheree in the process."

Doc gave me a knowing smile and said, "We will teach them many things."

I said, "This will probably take the rest of this cycle. We don't use "day" in our vocabulary, because humans from Earth relate to a day as being 24 hours, and a cycle on this planet is 29 hours. We found that confusing. Due to this learning time I suggest we meet again tomorrow for your follow-up questions."

"One additional suggestion I might offer you. Being outside the walls can be dangerous for numerous reasons. You will soon understand. I suggest you move your outside people within the Sheree's wall or vessel until you choose a permanent location, at least set guards to ensure their safety."

They were confused and didn't know what was about to happen, but they followed Doc and Homer out. Homer had used the META downloads more than any other human, so I chose him to help them feel comfortable and take charge of the other crew members.

Tomorrow should be interesting indeed.

The group was back early and anxious, and the Sheree came with them again. Rumbee seemed extremely interested, but then that could also be because he found me interesting or didn't want to miss anything.

When I and the other staff members came into the Control Room for our coffee the French delegation of four jumped to their feet.

I waved them informally back to their seats and said, "How was your session with the META units? I think you now understand why we didn't try to explain how it works. It would have taken far too long, and you wouldn't have understood it anyway until you personally experience it."

Dr. Rothchild spoke in English and said, "The META unit was incredible, probably one of the most enjoyable and satisfying experience I have ever had in my life. It was rewarding beyond belief. I must say, experiencing others thoughts and emotions is something I thought I would never live, and that is exactly what I felt that I did, live other's lives. As amazing as that was, the vast knowledge and information transferred cannot be compared. Not only did we gain a vast amount of data in the blink of an eye, but we now feel like we truly experienced your history and participated in your challenges and achievements."

"I might say it was very unnerving experiencing the news and reports of our French Project's destruction, even though now it never happened. The paradox of time travel in reality is complex and confusing."

"We certainly appreciate the downloads you provided us, but it does seem that we have joined you in a hostile world. The Gaters and Markee humans represent a serious threat, not to mention the potential threat of the Moors."

I said, "We saved you, but our motivation was in saving other humans. You are not obligated to join us. We can transport your entire project anywhere on this planet or even to a second planet in this system. You are free to choose."

Dr. Rothchild said, "I have total control and authority to speak for our group, but we have discussed that option and elect to stay with your group. We would not have survived any of the attacks you have fought off. In addition, your technology and medical advancements far exceed our capabilities. No, our odds are far better aligning with you, and we just might be able to add to your arsenal and army. We also have a thousand highly educated trade and professional personnel in hibernation that can join the workforce here."

"We realize that we will be required to accept your leadership. I do, however, strongly suggest that we keep the Charles de Gaulle operational and under my command as a war ship."

"Very well." I said, "We will have to discuss the deployment and housing of your personnel. Cdr. Clark will analyze your supplies, needs and how best to use your inventory of personnel. We already have infrastructure to support a colony, and it doesn't make a lot of sense to recreate them.

In the weeks that quickly passed much had been accomplished with the French team.

With Mr. Pollard being gone, Katy had taken over many of his duties he had been doing, minus the politics. The colony was pleased to gain the French. There were multitudes of vacant positions, due to the lack of personnel, and the colony wanted the expertise the French brought. The colony convinced Katy to recommend that the French be allowed to share their facilities on this side of the mountain. I allowed the move, since the Sheree weren't overly enthusiastic about sharing their facilities. They were willing for the sake of the whole colony but pleased to see them move.

The Sheree didn't get out of building the wall, however. They had committed, but they built the wall across the complex, making their wall the internal defensive wall inside the complex. Now we had multiple defensive walls 25 feet tall, so a breach anywhere on the outside wall would still have a secondary defensive wall, and in some cases, three walls. Additionally, the internal area behind the second wall was now compartmentalized. The colony complex was impressive. The Sheree also added a wall around both vessels and the laser and power generator, baring access when the gates were closed.

Quarters had not been built for all the French personnel coming out of hibernation, but they inherited the tent city the Genesis and villagers had used before their quarters had been completed. The city below was filling in, but we still had plenty of room for expansion when required.

Homer had taken his task seriously and had cycled most of the French personnel through the Learning Center. Doc made sure they got a good dose of history from our timeline in the META download, which they now belonged to. The French were all now fluent in English and several other languages and fully indoctrinated.

Linda had been insistent that the French vessel be given a spot on top of Mount Olympus fairly close to the location of the Genesis. She said their military armament could be better utilized at that location. Again I allowed that, because the argument made sense. Any armament positioned on the top of the mountain could protect either side, which also pleased both the Sheree and colony.

It seemed ironic that Linda would be the one concerned with weapons of war, since in her capacity as engineer and designing the Genesis Project, she had hardly considered weaponizing the Genesis at all. Her Berkley passiveness had clouded her thinking. I was the one that finally equipped the Genesis with the high powered lasers, otherwise we wouldn't have had any defenses at all. It's amazing how a pacifist can change their thinking under the personal threat of annihilation, and without the lasers and the Sheree's weapon technology, we would have been dead long ago. I would bet Linda wishes she could go back and weaponize the Genesis. Now she had the opportunity to utilize the weapons the French had brought, and apparently the French weren't plagued by pacifists.

The general was very supportive of Linda's desire to build a platform for the Charles de Gaulle. He hadn't commented on the French weapon arsenal, but I could tell he was impressed. It must be good to impress the general. I decided to wait and be surprised, but this cycle was the time, and I was looking forward to this staff meeting.

As everyone settled in for the meeting, I took the podium and said, "Well, I'm anxious to hear about the weapon arsenal. Everyone seem excited about it, so let's get started.

A smiling general replaced me and said, "Our colony gained many new weapons and weapon systems when the French joined us. Most would be considered conventional, although all are advanced weaponry, and many are experimental and previously believed nonexistent. There are two weapons that top the list. The most impressive is the long range E M Rail Gun. If you haven't heard of it I'm not surprised. It's not supposed to exist. It's an Electromagnetic Projectile Launcher that very accurately launches a non-explosive projectile at a velocity of seven times the speed of sound (almost 8,000 ft/sec) for 125 miles. No warhead is required; it simply explodes what it hits, and this included Wonder Metal."

The original plans I saw at the Pentagon of this weapon detailed a large weapon, but our French associates were able to commandeer prototypes of a reduced size version, three actually. One of these is being retrofitted on the Genesis as we speak and the other is being installed adjacent to our mountain laser."

"What makes the Rail Gun especially beneficial is that the projectile is not an energy beam, so it can fire through our energy shield, which is also being installed on the Charles de Gaulle."

The next impressive weapon is the Dread Silent Weapon System. It is also very impressive for a shorter range weapon, and I do mean impressive. It also launches projectiles at a rate of 120,000 per minute, also at a velocity of up to 8,000 projectiles per second. It has no gunpowder, no recoil, no sound, and no heat signature. It destroys its target the same way the Rail Gun does. The weapon is extremely accurate and small, only 28 lbs. The Charles de Gaulle has two mounted under the saucer's lip, and yes, we have installed two on the Genesis and others on our internal walls and the Sheree's wall. This Dread weapon is also the perfect weapon for our saucers. Thankfully, the French brought along a large number of them."

"Some of the other weapons worth mentioning are the XM25 Smart Grenade Launchers, The Taser Shockwave, the Soviet 9K32 Strela (SA-7 Grail) shoulder fired surface to air missiles, and more."

I jokingly said, "Damn, Dr. Rothchild, were you going to colonize Mars or destroy it? Don't get me wrong though. We certainly are thankful that you brought so many advanced weapons, but it just seems like overkill for a colonization mission."

Dr. Rothchild laughed and said, "Well, I did say our vessel could serve as a war ship. We brought anything we could makes holes within the rocks on Mars. We expected to have to live in caves for a long while, besides, we didn't know what to expect. Yes, we came prepared for any situation, and I'm glad we did with so many enemies to deal with."

Genesis Prime Log: 10 April 0003

Kim called this emergency staff meeting, and I partially knew the reason. I had seen an invasion landing on one of the remote continents. This time it was captured on one of the satellites and recorded, and Kim had been analyzing the footage. He must have discovered something really important to have called this emergency, not that another invasion wasn't important. I could read Kim's reactions and realized he was far more agitated with this action than he had been with passed invasions. Seeing this I was becoming agitated also and anxious to discover the source.

Kim said, "I have the sad duty to inform you of another invasion. An army of Makee humans have been deposited on a remote portion of the farthest most southern continent. This fact is not as disturbing as what we discovered about it."

"After the last invasion I worked with Linda and Doc to create a new program to immediately identify the appearance of another Plasma Bubble through satellite surveillance. Once one was detected the program was designed to focus in on the Plasma Bubble and record whatever was going on. Ultimately the goal was to try and capture the Plasma Bubble and operator."

"As we suspected, however, the Plasma Bubble did not remain long, but the activity for a brief few moments was captured on video. I'll play this video and allow you to interpret what you see."

Kim started the recording on the large monitors. The screen was immediately filled with the Plasma Bubble. Within the bubble could be seen thousands of human warriors, then the bubble disappeared, leaving the army standing on the open ground. The picture zoomed in toward the middle where a flash of reflected light shown off of the bright Plasma Bubble Generator. As the picture continued to zoom in everyone could clearly see a Sheree standing at the controls, but standing beside him looking on were several Gators and several others of something else most of us did not recognize. We didn't, but our Sheree did. There was a sudden jumble of clashing telepathic communications coming from the Sheree and several loud gasps. I didn't understand the communication, and I'm quite sure they didn't either. We all looked toward them to see a combination of fear, surprise, and outrage.

I quickly said, "What's wrong, Rumbee?"

Rumbee said, "Can you zoom in on the Sheree?"

Kim quickly did as Rumbee requested. The image of the Sheree focused and filled the screen. Rumbee was instantly bellowing fury toward the monitor and visibly shaking with barely controlled rage. All the Sheree present demonstrated the same rage, as if they could go berserk at any second. I had never seen a Sheree angry, and I'm not anxious to ever see it again.

I said, "Please, Rumbee, help us to understand what we are seeing."

After a few calming moments Rumbee said, "We recognize the Sheree in the video. He is

Ambassador Percee, and we thought him dead. If he is alive then he has been in control all along and caused the demise of the Sheree Race and the enslavement of those scientist you rescued from Markee. He is smart, but he is not excessively technical. To function and utilize Sheree technology he would need the help of the Sheree scientists."

"He has been using us all this time. We thought the leader among the humans was another smarter human, but it was the traitor Ambassador Percee. With us gone he apparently has learned much about the technology. Certainly, he can read the instruction manuals. It has been him launching the attacks against us. Ambassador Percee wants his scientists back and me and all of you dead, and he is apparently willing to collaborate with other hostile and dangerous races to accomplish this."

"Rumbee turned to Renee and Spee for a quick exchange of thoughts then continued, "Ambassador Percee is mentally flawed, like the Respected Leader Sheen, whom you met. I believe you call them psychopaths"

Yes, I certainly remembered that asshole I killed. If this ambassador was like him I could understand Rumbee's anger, especially after destroying the entire Sheree Race.

I said, "I understand. What else can you tell us about what you saw?"

Rumbee said, "Well, as we observed, the ambassador has obviously made alliances with both the Gaters and Moors. The other entities you saw were Moors. Just how he made contact with the Moors, I have no idea. Possibly he has been searching the route through space, anticipating their approach. If he was in control on Markee, which he obviously was, after the fall of my government he might have learned of the landing of the Moors here. The ambassador's mind is flawed, but he is not stupid. To the contrary, he is a brilliant diplomat and tactician. He may have come to the same conclusion as we have about the Moor's pending landing. Apparently he found them and aided them in their travels with the Plasma Bubble. That's my guess anyway."

"As far as the Gaters are concerned, he dealt with them on Markee and knows their language. These Gaters may very well know him. At any rate, we must conclude that they will attempt a joint attack upon us here, and we better be prepared."

Linda asked, "Does the ambassador know the time travel technology?"

Rumbee said, "No, the scientists kept it a secret and didn't put it in any manuals. That is another reason he wants to recapture the Sheree here."

CHAPTER 15
(The Battle)

As the staff settled in for this cycle's meeting I said, "We've all had a couple of days to digest the information gleaned from Kim's research and Rumbee's analysis. I would like to hear your thoughts and recommendations on how we should respond to this latest threat."

I was somewhat surprised when Paul Lafayette, the French head of security, went to the podium. This would be the first time I heard anyone speak from the French group other than Dr. Rothchild, who seemed to do most of their talking.

Dr. Lafayette said, "Admiral Johns, I appreciate the opportunity to voice my thoughts on the situation, but in all honesty, I didn't have much choice. I have spent much time with Major General McCullah analyzing this data, and it was strongly suggested that I present our joint analysis and recommendations. As he so tactfully put it, 'Let everyone know you have a voice and not just a pretty face.'" At that the room burst out in laughter.

"At any rate, we must assume Ambassador Percee has a master plan. He would have learned our defense strategies and offensive capabilities by now from his previous attacks and those of the Gaters. We shouldn't expect him to try those same failed attempts again. We must expect a new and unexpected attempt. He will come at us this time with new strategies. We have the advantage, however, since he cannot know we are aware of him and his alliances."

"The renewed invasion is identical to the last. There must be a reason. We believe he is testing us with a new defense strategy or offensive weapon to try. More likely it is both. By now he knows we will attack the invading army to protect the villages, and the general and myself agree that we must not reveal our new weapons in this engagement. Those weapons must remain a surprise until he has committed his joint armies in an all-out attack on the colony, or we discover where he is hiding."

"We also agree that it is far better to take the war to them rather than waiting on them to come to us, but until we know where they are we can't attack. Cdr. Kim has been monitoring Genesis Prime via satellite, and Cdr. Clark has been sending out scouting voyages to Genesis Two and Markee, but so far we have not found them. So, we must wait and strengthen our defenses."

"Assuming we have time, we have assigned our French personnel to Sgt. Major Gomez's militia training boot camp. Hopefully, they will be ready to help when the time comes. The general has already dispatched the ore carrier to pick up the villagers. Those too will join the boot camp. Additionally, we have other surprise weapons we can bring against any attack, but we are under no illusion that this will be an easy battle. We will be vastly outnumbered and the raw volume and sudden flood of attackers could be impossible to defend against. We are also making contingency plans for evacuation of our complex, just in case."

I said, "Thank you Dr. Lafayette for that report. Apparently, you are more than just a pretty face." Again the laughter rang out. "Are there others that wish to address this group?"

Doc stood and said, "Is it worth considering using time travel to go back and alter the Markee history and take out this Ambassador Percee? We might eliminate him before he causes all this trouble."

Rumbee said, "I have considered this option, but in all probability it would alter your timeline as well. There are many paradoxes that might create, some horrible to consider. I think we have already seen how difficult it can be to alter history. No, I don't recommend that action."

"One option I did consider was going slightly back in time to before the ambassador appeared, since we know where he will appear, and plant a bomb. We could kill the lousy bastard when he does appear and destroy the Plasma Bubble. The problem is that the plan he devised is already in the works, and we wouldn't change anything. We would in fact be in worse shape. We need him to deliver the armies to the battlefield from where they are hiding so we know where they are. If we can't engage them we will always wonder when and where they will show up. I think we need to end this conflict once and for all and get on with our lives."

I said, "I hadn't thought of the idea of setting a bomb, but I agree with your assessment. We need to have this war and get it over with. Damn, I wish we knew where they are hiding so we could take it to them."

"Still, I like the idea of planting explosives in the battlefield. We can detonate them when the battle is engaged. What do you think General?"

A grinning Mac said, "Yes, yes, I like it. We will plan the charges and set them within the next couple of days."

It surprised everyone when Renee said, "We might also consider looking ahead in time to spot the locations of the appearance of our targets. We could even capture the ambassador for interrogations."

I felt the tension explode out, no not tension, rage radiate out from Rumbee. It was an intense serge of mental energy, and Renee cringed from its strength. I'm sure Akiko felt it too, but I doubt if any of the others did. This was very uncharacteristic of Rumbee, to show such strong emotions.

Rumbee bellowed, "No! The bastard needs to be quickly destroyed."

I had never seen Rumbee angry like this before, and I had never known Renee to speak out while Rumbee was present. My mental alarms went off. Was Renee trying to tell me something? He used the word "interrogate". Could it be the ambassador knew things that I should know? If so, why would Rumbee not want me to know. Something was wrong, and I vowed to find out what.

I chose to ignore Rumbee's outburst and said, "I like the idea of looking forward just enough to identify the locations. Linda, I know looking into the future could be as scary and confusing as looking back into the past. It could also be dangerous. But, you might consider that option, and if you feel comfortable, do so? At least we will know when."

I motioned for Linda and the general to stay after the meeting, so they delayed leaving. Once everyone left I called them closer so no one else could hear.

I said, "Linda, if you feel comfortable looking into the future and decide to risk it, I want only you and maybe the general to know what you find. Report back only to me."

The general gave me a puzzled look and said, "Okay Nick. What's up?"

I said, "Maybe nothing, but Rumbee obviously doesn't want us to talk to the ambassador, so that is exactly what I want to do. That's why I want you to keep it strictly between us, for right now anyway."

Genesis Prime Log: 15 April 0003

The ore ship was back with the villagers, and Homer had taken them under his wing, cycling them through the META Center. As soon as they came out Katy was assigning them duties, although most of the men joined Sgt Maj Gomez's training sessions. We would need as many warriors as possible, since we believed the major portion of the coming battle would be defense against a massive flood of charging soldiers. The general told us that this strategy against us had almost worked twice in the past, and there would be a lot more warriors charging this time. He was afraid they could be successful this time, so he had devised elaborate signals for several stages of retreat and finally evacuation into the Sheree tunnel if necessary.

Linda and the general also came to me in private and reported that they successfully went ahead in time and knew the exact date of the alien attack and their strategy of attack, and more importantly, the exact locations of the appearance of the ambassador's plasma bubble. This was all good news, because I had some surprises planned for them.

Linda, Rumbee, and the new French engineer, Dr. Lacroix, had completed the installation of the Dread weapons on the saucers and Disrupter shields and adjusted them to also reflect lasers. With this task complete we were ready to attack the Markee army.

We knew we were just going through the motions of attacking, playing a game with the ambassador. We were expected to be beaten back by their defenses and offensive weapons, and that is exactly what we would do. There was no way we would show our new weapons until the main attack, when the Moor fleet presented itself.

We lifted off with only the Genesis and quickly reached an attack altitude high above the marching army. We could see no difference, but we knew the defenses were there. We activated our laser and began firing the focused bursts down upon the army. As we suspected, the army was protected by an energy shield, and our laser bursts reflected off the shield scorching the ground all around. From the scorched ground and the resulting fires we could easily identify the location of the shield, which protected the entirety of the army. I wasn't about to take any major risk for the Genesis against any offensive weapons, so our altitude remained high and we were somewhat protected. They fired many disrupter bursts at us, which were stopped by our shield, but they sent no lasers blasts. I'm sure they wanted to leave the surprise of lasers for when the Moors attacked.

The result of the engagement was status quo for both sides. No damage was done to either side, and they would now be satisfied that their shield would protect them. We verified that we could identify the location of the shield generators, and we had given them the confidence they needed to launch an all-out attack, so we retreated back to Mount Olympus to ready for the main attack.

Genesis Prime Log: 20 April 0003

We still didn't know where the ambassador was hiding with the armies, but we felt confident that he would commit his armies. Actually, we knew more, a lot more. Thanks to Linda's search into the future we knew when and where they would attack, and we were ready.

I called an early staff meeting for this cycle, but I believe everyone knew why, due to the general's preparations. He had mobilized our defenses and ordered the non-combating women and children into the inner security of the caves and the Sheree noncombatants into their internal shelter in the tunnel. He had even gone to the extreme of closing the outside security doors to the caves.

When all were present I said, "I guess you all know by now, this cycle the battle begins. All outward signs indicate life as normal, so they can't know their secret has been discovered. Our security forces are positioned and ready, and we have some ... many surprises in store for them. Remember, however, we can't fire our new French brought weapons until all the enemy armies have been deployed. This means we must be prepared to fight a hard battle to repel the invaders from our walls. We can't let them inside our walls before we are able to fire the rail gun."

"Thanks to Linda, we have the advantage of knowing when they will attack and also that they will attack both this side and the Sheree side simultaneously. This is why we have split our security force. Unless anyone has something to add, deploy and be ready."

***

The alarms began to sound seconds after the first Markee army appeared on the battlefield. Our Energy Shields deployed immediately, so Plasma Bubbles filled with armies could not deploy within our shields inside the walls. One Plasma Bubble was repelled by our shields and had to move to the field, so it was extremely fortunate that our shields deployed immediately. Gunfire began soon after to repel the Gators storming out of the river.

The first of our surprises met the charging Gators. The general had stationed the Sheree weapons we had nicknamed "The Freezer" along the riverfront. The Sheree technology, now weapon, froze the water in the river and drastically slowed the flood of Gaters. The reduced flow was easily handled by the Security forces, and many of the Gaters were caught in the freezing rays and turned into hunks of ice. Most didn't even make it to the wall.

Armies of Moor warriors appeared and merged with the Markee armies. They fared much better, due to the shielding, since we couldn't fire our lasers. The armies on the Sheree side did not have the river to contend with, so they were reaching the wall faster, but the enemy on the river side were also using "The Freezer" technology to build ice bridges for the charging warriors. They weren't far behind.

As they reached the walls they discovered some of our next surprises. Unfortunately, the French didn't bring many of the various conventional, although advanced, weapons, but there were enough to make a lasting impression on our enemy. At various locations the attackers charged into a Taser Shockwave and were instantly electrocuted.

In other locations they were hit with blasts from The Active Denial System. What an impressive weapon that is. The blast caused pain so intense they simply lost their will to fight and ran away, at which point their own armies killed them for acting cowardly.

Also spattered throughout the wall perimeter were PHASR Rifles, which caused blindness. They began to run into others, falling and clawing at their eyes until our Marines shot them.

Our defenses worked fantastically, but the enemy numbered in the tens of thousands and they kept coming in Plasma Bubbles, while we waited for the Moor fleet to make its showing. We were holding off our main defenses until all the enemy forces were exposed.

Kim announced, "I have located the Moor fleet. They are launching from the southern continent. They must have materialized there to offload their warriors for further transfer to our location in the Plasma Bubble, but now the fleet is launching again, five massive war ships. They are exposed now and will be here in fifteen minutes, maybe."

That was our queue to attack. Our plan called for the Genesis to launch and engage the Moor fleet in the air, while the Charles de Gaulle remained to aid in the attack on the ground forces. I liked this timing, because we could now isolate some of the Moor armies on the southern continent to be dealt with later. I knew positively that there would be no more Plasma Bubble. Those armies would be waiting a long time to be picked up. They would find us instead.

The Genesis soared high to gain a line of sight on the Moor fleet, and once we had a focus on one of the Moor warships we fired. It instantly exploded from the 8000 ft. p/s projectile. It never even knew it was under attack. We focused in on the second ship and fired again. The Moor fleet was still 150 miles from us, but we could easily see the second ship vaporize.

The last three war ships quickly turned around and sped off in retreat. Wisely they took off in different directions, making us commit to following only one. The Genesis raced after the one in the center and focused on it. The third ship vaporized. We then turned and raced after the fourth, but it had gotten a sizable lead and was beyond range of our Rail Gun. The Genesis was gaining on the craft, but we could see it launching its attack craft.

As we gained upon the craft I ordered the launch of our saucers. Once we reached the maximum firing distance of the Rail Gun, we fired. The fourth ship burst into dust and flames, but we could see at least fifteen small attack craft had survived and were heading directly for us. Our gallant saucer formation charged them, while we wheeled around to search for the last war ship. In the distance the sky was filled with laser blasts directed toward the saucers, but, thanks to the Sheree shields, we could see the laser streaks reflecting off the shields at various angles.

The saucers equipped with the Dread Silent Weapon System, as advertised, were silent and provided no heat signature or flash of gunpowder. As a result, we could not see the saucers firing, but we could certainly see the Moor attack craft vaporizing. That air battle was short-lived and a decisive victory for our saucer fleet. We got to witness most of the battle, while we sped away, leaving the saucers to find their way back to Atlantis and the ongoing battle there.

During all the excitement Kim had lost the last Moor war ship. It simply vanished, and we could not find it, so I decided to take us back to Atlantis, also.

When we returned to the airspace over Mount Olympus we observed the battle still heavily in progress, but much had changed. None of the enemy's energy shields were active, and large, deep holes were visible on the battlefield, evidence of the Rail Gun projectiles. To say using the Rail Gun on the shield projectors was overkill would be a gross understatement. It would take us weeks to repair the ground damage. With the Rail Gun projectile velocity at seven times the speed of sound, the projectile concussion alone would have been devastating to the enemy warriors at that close proximity. This was abundantly evident by the large number of dead warriors along the trajectory of the Rain Gun projectile. I hadn't considered this fact, and it was fortunate that the Charles de Gaulle was stationed high on the mountain and overshot our own complex.

Our forces had other options for taking out the shield generators, such as the French brought XM25 Smart Grenade Launchers. This weapon could launch and detonate grenades at programmable distances up to a half mile, and it was obvious that the general had ordered their use and shut down the Rail Gun, because of its damaging effect to the ground and possibly injury to our own troops.

We took the situation in quickly as we approached. We were winning the battle, maybe, but they were still coming. The dead were piling up against the outside walls in the main area, forming a ramp of sorts the charging solders were using to reach the top and begin breaching. Even as we settled in and began firing our laser, we could see that the general had ordered a general retreat back behind the second wall. Our defenders were flooding through the second gate and repositioning on the wall. On the Sheree side the walls were higher and encompassed area smaller and easier to defend, so they were still managing the defenses well.

With the destruction of the enemy's shields, Linda's mountain laser was currently firing on the

Sheree side, so we concentrated on the river side. We began a swath of burning flesh just outside the wall, melting down the pile of dead enemy and those live ones daring to get close. We stopped the breach and began sweeping an ever widening swath.

At one point I bellowed to the two Dread operators, "Fire at the Freezer weapons so they can't make more ice bridges!" Hell, they could already be destroyed. It would take a long time for them to melt. I suddenly realized what I had said and I blurted, "Kim, take manual control and fire a solid laser beam at the ice bridges. Melt them! No bridges ... no more crossing."

The returning saucers saw what we were doing and began sweeping back and forth along the riverbanks on the other side taking out the solders on the banks that might have a Freezer and pounding the ice with their high velocity projectiles. The combined effect of both weapons assaulting the ice bridges began to work, and large chunks were breaking loose in the strong current and flowing down stream.

With the reduction of enemy warriors crossing the river and being forced to bunch up on the bank, the Genesis reverted back to the computer controlled laser targeting and firing program. The rhythm of quick short burst of the firing began, reminding me of the rhythm of a sewing machine. The efficiency of the computer targeting program began doling out death through the enemy ranks. Slowly the battlefield began to clear of live warriors from the riverbank and reach farther out, as the swath of death continued its sweeping deadly scythe. The efficiency of this grim reaper's scythe of death was horrifying to watch.

The tide of battle turned swiftly on both the Sheree side and human colony side, but still the sheer numbers of the enemy took hours to empty from the battlefield. Finally the rat-tat-tat of the laser slowed and eventually stopped all together.

The victory of the cycle was long and hard coming, but it finally ended. There was no attempt to begin the clean-up due to the exhaustion of the combatants. The defense forces continued to maintain a vigilant watch, but they organized in shifts to eat and rest. Work would start again with the next cycle.

Genesis Prime Log: 21 April 0003

The cleanup began in earnest early this cycle. Doc was concerned with diseases from all the rotting corpses. He wanted to get them buried, burned or safely disposed of. Many, of course, floated out to sea with the melting ice, and many others had been reduced to dust from the laser fire. Suffice to say the number of dead was beyond count.

It was the general that came up with the idea of bulldozing the carcasses into the holes left by the Rail Gun. They were deep, and needed to be filled in anyway.

We had all been very lucky, lucky that we returned in time to join the battle. Even then, we almost lost the battle on the colony side. Surprisingly, however, we had lost very few on our side. The general reported five in the defense force had been killed by rocks from those damn Gaters. Their projectiles of rocks were extremely lethal and accurate, as we had learned from the first engagement. The battle was all weaponry, assuming you counted the damn rocks. Throughout the engagement it never reached the level of hand-to-hand combat.

The enemy had been devastated. Well, some of the Gaters might have swam away, but the Moors and Markee army were wiped out, except for some that might have retreated and hid in the forest. Marines were out now canvassing the woods for any stragglers.

We still had a couple of Moor armies to deal with and a missing warship to find, so we lifted off of Mount Olympus and headed toward the southern continent. Kim said the armies were still there, but he hadn't seen the warship anywhere. There was one sure battle we could engage in, so we went there. I was thankful that the warship hadn't picked them up and hidden them away. I didn't want to have to deal with them later.

The Genesis established a high altitude and began our attack. They didn't have a chance, and they were stranded there. They could run, but they had nowhere to go. It took us several hours to wipe them out."

At one point Chaplin Kline came to me and said, "Admiral, do we have to destroy them. They are sentient beings and helpless, and we are killing them without any thought, like stepping on ants. Can't we just leave them be?"

I said, "Well, Chaplin Kline, I'm not enjoying this either, but you saw the battle we just had.

Remember that they attacked us, would have destroyed us, and would try again if they had a chance. No, we really don't have much of a choice."

When we finally finished, I asked, "Kim, do you have any idea where that last Moor warship could be hiding? Without a Plasma Bubble they can't have left the planet. They have to be here somewhere."

Kim said, "Admiral, I scanned every continent for them through the satellites, and I've even had, and still do, the computer systematically scouring every foot of ground on this planet. It hasn't found anything either."

I said, "You said you checked all the ground, but what if they are hiding in the ocean? Could they be underwater?"

I knew I embarrassed him, because he was bent over a monitor, and the bald spot on the back of his head turned red. Kim then stiffened and set up in his chair, obviously in thought.

Kim said, "Oh, horse shit. I know where they are!" He began adjusting controls and staring at the monitor. After a few moments he turned to me with a big smile and said, "Do you remember that I once reported to you and the staff that there was a large underwater structure in the ocean? I have always wanted to investigate it, but we have just been too damn busy. Well, I'm now thinking that it is the central complex of the Gaters, and guess what is setting underwater docked next to it? When you mentioned the warship could be underwater, I remembered the structure, and sure enough it is there."

I said, "Great! We got em. Let's go get them."

Not only had we found the last Moor warship, but we had found the headquarters of the Gaters. Hopefully we would end this war for good and be able to get on with our lives.

As we approached from our altitude, we could easily see the warship under the water. The Gater complex was not as easily seen, due to moss and native colors of the surrounding water and underwater plant life, but the structure could be seen, mainly because of straight walls and corners of the structure.

The structure wasn't going anywhere, so we concentrated on the warship and aimed the Rail Gun directly down to avoid any deflection from firing into water. We fired the Rail Gun and the water and warship erupted into steaming tentacles of water, bubbles and debris shooting in all directions. The ocean colored in mud, and we could no longer see the structure, but we knew where it was and fired again. Shockwaves radiated out from our targets, sending large wave crashing over the surface. There was no doubt that both targets had been utterly destroyed.

Having completed our mission, we returned to Mount Olympus.

Genesis Prime Log: 22 April 0003

I held my surprise as long as I could, but my curiosity was getting the best of me. I did wait until all the staff had arrived before I nodded at the general. The general returned my nod and motioned for the Marines to enter. The Marines entered dragging a very reluctant Sheree in handcuffs between them.

I announced, "Ladies and gentlemen let me introduce Ambassador Percee, our enemy leader."

Silence fell heavily in the Control Room and shock was on all faces of the staff, all but one. Cdr. Rumbee's face was contorted in pure hate. He was visibly shaking with barely controlled rage, but he held his silence with obvious considerable effort.

It was my Katy that broke the silence when she said, "How in the world did you capture him and when?"

I said, "We can thank Linda and the general. During Linda's brief venture into the future she identified the perfect time and location, and she prepared a surprise for him. Lt. Boland was hidden in a concealed trench with his own Plasma Bubble generator, and when the Ambassador materialized with one of the armies, Lt. Boland snatched him and his generator up and transported himself, the Ambassador, and his generator inside our walls. The general had Marines waiting to capture him. He has been locked up until now, since we didn't have time to deal with him earlier."

"The capture of his Plasma Bubble at the time when chose prevented more armies from joining the battle. Those armies we dealt with last cycle. I wish we could have captured it earlier, but we had to wait until the Moor fleet was located. As you now know, all five Moor warships have been destroyed, along with their stranded armies and what we believe was the main complex of the Gaters. The Gaters may not be destroyed, but they have certainly been drastically reduced. As far as the Markee human armies, without the Ambassador and his Plasma Bubble they no longer represent a threat to us."

"We can take our time dealing with the Ambassador. Maybe we can learn more about the war he has wages against us and why."

Surprisingly, it was Taka that spoke first. Taka spoke in Sheree and said, "Well, I for one would like to know why the Ambassador is so pissed at us. What did we ever do to him?"

The Ambassador came alive at hearing Taka speak in the Sheree language. He must have realized suddenly that we understood or could be made to understand his language.

Ambassador Percee said in Sheree, "Thankfully you can understand me. You have misunderstood my intentions. We were not against you humans; we were trying to save you!"

The general blurted, "You tried to save us by killing us?"

The Ambassador responded, "We were trying to get to the Supreme Sheree Leader, but you protected him. The Supreme Leader has unimaginable mental powers, and we believed him in control of you humans. Our goal was to kill the Supreme Leader, which would release you from his control. Does he not control you?"

I said, "No one controls us! We control our own destiny."

Rumbee regained his composure and bellowed at me, "You should not have captured him. I told you to kill him. You will be sorry for disobeying my order. The Ambassador is dangerous. He spews lies and falsehoods. He will poison your mind."

The Ambassador screamed back, "You are the liar. You enslaved the entire human race on Markee and would have feasted upon them until they were all gone had I not intervened. Most Sheree did not agree with you, and thankfully enough of the Sheree had compassion for the humans to help me. What was their reward? You had them killed by your brainwashed and controlled human robots."

Rumbee began to quiver with rage and stiffened. His eyes were intensely focused upon the Ambassador. The Ambassador also stiffened, but his eyes seemed to roll back into his head. It was immediately obvious to me that Rumbee was transmitting some form of mental energy.

I yelled out, "Stop Rumbee!"

Doc seemed to understand what was happening and he quickly ran toward Rumbee and slapped him hard across the face, which broke Rumbee's concentration. Rumbee seemed to slump, as if his legs were made of rubber, but he was caught by two of the Marines. I'm not sure what the Marines planned to do at my instruction, but they continued to hold him.

The ambassador quickly recovered and said, "As I said, some of the Sheree, like the Supreme Leader, have strong mental powers. You just saw what he can do. He can do that much easier on humans. Watch out!"

The warning came too late for most in the room. Rumbee began again with the intense concentration and the humans in the Control Room stiffened and froze ... all but me. That was

323

Rumbee's mistake, since my mind is protected in the dome, I was not affected as the other humans, but I remained still. I wanted to see Rumbee's intentions.

As if talking to himself, a smiling Rumbee said, "Admiral, you have served me well and saved and protected me, but the war is over now, and I have won. I don't need you now and will now take command. You and your kind will continue to serve me, and I will feast on your children. You, Ambassador Percee, will now die."

This had gone on long enough. Rumbee had fooled us all. I now remember the fear Renee showed and how he had once pleaded with me to show respect to Rumbee. I also remember the warning he had obviously tried to convey to me about the ambassador. Even now Renee was cowered with the other Sheree against the wall.

I calmly said, "Well, well, Rumbee. I don't think I will allow you to take command."

To say that Rumbee was surprised would be a major understatement. It startled him so bad that the trance he was projecting dissolved, and the other humans in the Control Room began blinking, as if awaking from sleep.

I said, "I'm pleased that you like to talk to yourself, because I now know exactly who and what you are. You had me and the others completely fooled, but no longer. Before you attempt to repeat that action I want you to take a look at these two visual centers." I pointed them out on the bulkhead. "You will notice two laser units aimed directly at your head. If you give me the slightest excuse I will blow your head apart. Do you understand me?"

For emphasis I continued, "All those in the line of fire please move aside."

Rumbee looked totally defeated and simply said, "Yes, Admiral, I fully understand."

I said, "Good. General, have your Marines guard these other Sheree until we get a better understanding of what just happened."

"For the others in the room, I'm afraid you missed what Rumbee just did and said. Of course I recorded it for you." I then began the playback. It was so short, I even played it back a couple of times to make sure none missed it. The reaction was instant hostility. The general even pulled his .45 and aimed it at Rumbee.

I continued, "Renee, I think I still trust you, because I believe you tried to warn me. Additionally, on Genesis Two you broke with past Sheree policy and freed the humans ages ago. I would like you to address us, and I recommend that you not hold anything back"

A very frightened Renee stepped to the podium, but I detected mental communications of encouragement from most of the other Sheree. He obviously didn't want to be there. I could see the internal struggle, but he seemed to make a decision. When he spoke, he spoke in the Sheree language out of respect for the ambassador, or at least to make sure the ambassador understood what was being said.

Renee said, "Yes, I did take a major chance by trying to warn you, and we are still in danger." When he said that he looked toward Rumbee, "Will you protect us?"

I said, "I will let no harm come to you or the other Sheree for telling the truth."

Renee said, "Thank you, Admiral. I have known Ambassador Percee in the past, and I have always shared his compassion for humans. I had no power to change Sheree policy until we were stranded on Genesis Two, as you call it. Before that time our policy toward humans was dictated by the ruling administrators such as the Respected Leader on Genesis Prime, whom you met, and his brother, Rumbee, the Supreme Leader on Markee. Their family line has ruled the Sheree race for thousands of years. Once we were isolated from them, and this condition seemed permanent, I freed the humans,"

Rumbee and the Respected Leader, whatever the hell his name was, were brothers? I despised that arrogant bastard, and if they were brothers, it gave me another reason to mistrust and despise Rumbee.

"I and the other Sheree were pleased when you saved us and reunited the remaining Sheree here. We welcomed the opportunity to be part of this colony. We still do and wish to remain with you as part of your command. When you brought Rumbee into the Control Room that cycle, we were totally shocked and afraid he would destroy what we believed was a good relationship. When he appeared to be willing to accept a lessor position and follow your direction and be reasonable, we thought he may have changed and our relationship with the colony might survive."

"As Rumbee told you at the start, his captivity had humbled him and made him subject to change.

326

Also, since you evidently saved him from captivity, we thought he owed you and accepted his role and changed. Of late, however, since we discovered the existence of Ambassador Percee, Rumbee's hidden true self has emerged. We don't support him, most Sheree never did, but he is powerful and does have hidden powers we are defenseless against. He can force us to support him, like he has done for hundreds of years and his father and grandfather before him and so on."

"You are preceptive, and I knew you would detect my subtle warning. I also knew that once warned, you would capture the ambassador, which is what I was hoping for. We wanted you all to know the truth, and the ambassador's capture presented the opportunity to do so. We also know the ambassador has done some terrible things, things of which he can't be forgiven, but he has done what we could not have done, reveal the secret and truth."

"Admiral, we like it here, and we want to stay and raise our children. We have a purpose here beyond simply survival."

I said, "Thank you, Renee. We have taken in much information and have a lot to consider and discuss. I think we need to take some time. In the meantime, we will keep Rumbee and the ambassador in detention, separate areas, general."

I turned to Rumbee and pointed for emphasis and continued, "I will remind you that your mental tricks do not work on me, and I will be watching you. Yes, I have visual centers in the detention area, and if you attempt any of your mental tricks I

will exercise my threat to sizzle your brain.   I
might add that you really disappoint me, Rumbee."

"Let's adjourn for now and consider our
options."

CHAPTER 16
(Aftermath)

Genesis Prime Log: 15 April 0003

I waited two cycles, thinking. I assume the others did also. On the third day I called for another meeting. For me the time had been spent in reflection with also some speculation into the future. I don't mind saying that the colony's wars looked like they were over, and the safety and security of the colony now seemed assured. Still, if my long life had taught me anything, humans would never be satisfied. Greed and vanity would eventually corrupt the peaceful existence of our colony. We had seen that on Earth many times. We had seen it on Markee. We had seen it onboard the Genesis during the voyage, and we had seen it here on Genesis Prime. Hell, we had even seen it among the Sheree now, and I was very tired of seeing it.

The president must have laughed when he had extracted my promise to save the human race. At the time I didn't know it was impossible, and that the human race would not allow itself to be saved. The human race would eventually destroy itself again, no matter how hard I tried. The only thing the human race loved more than self-destruction was war and destroying others.

Maybe it was time to just leave and start over somewhere else. Don't I deserve some rest from an impossible task? Haven't I paid my dues? How many times must I save the human race? How many times should I allow the human race to try to kill me? Yes, I was reaching my limit of tolerance. Maybe the human race was not worthy of being saved or surviving.

I'm thinking this last episode with Rumbee had really depressed me. I mean, how could I have been so fooled about him? How had he been able to hide his true self from me for so long? Hell, I had trusted him completely; I even liked him and considered him a friend. I think what unsettled me the most was wondering how many others I consider friends have a secret psychopathic center core hidden from me. How can I make sound decisions without being able to trust my own judgment?

I put all these unbidden self-doubts away when I heard the general speak. I think he guessed the nature of my thoughts.

The general had come in early and said, "Nick, we can't always know the hidden agendas of a person, especially if they are good about concealing them. You think logical and well, and I have learned to trust you and your decisions. You are one of the very few that has won me over in this regard. Don't begin to doubt yourself. Just move on and do what you think is right. I trust you."

That made me feel much better, and I said, "Thank you, Mac. I appreciate that more than you can imagine. Alright then, bring everyone in and let's get this started."

I had kept watch on Rumbee as promised, and he had not attempted another mind blast. In fact, he seemed mentally defeated. All he did was mope around in his detention cell with his head lowered,

330

but after seeing his true self exposed, there was no way I could believe this was anything but an act, which he apparently excelled at. Rumbee had kept up his act now for many months, and in all honesty, had he not exposed himself so openly, I would probably have given him the benefit of the doubt.

The Marines led both the ambassador and Rumbee into the Control Room and seated them in the front row but with sufficient distance between them. I chuckled to myself when I noticed that the others were keeping my line of fire open. They knew I could and might kill either or both of them.

I sat in the captain's chair, having rearranged the configuration of the podium.

I spoke in Sheree and said, "The first thing on the agenda is to decide what we are going to do with Rumbee. Would anyone like to comment?"

The general was the first to speak, "He needs a death sentence! We can never trust him among us, and we sure don't want him free. I say death."

Captain Rothchild said, "He deserves no less than death. We couldn't trust my terrorist, and we exercised a death sentence upon them. Rumbee deserves no less. I say death."

I said, "Renee, the Sheree have a vote in this. What do the Sheree recommend?"

I detected a burst of telepathic communications among the Sheree, but instead of Renee, it was Spee that jumped up.

Spee screamed, "We don't want him! We never wanted him! We ally with this group. Kill the arrogant bastard!"

Rumbee jumped up and bellowed, "I will kil ......"

I knew that would set Rumbee off, and I'm sure Spee knew it also. I think he did it intentionally to force action. As soon as Rumbee stood and began his rant, I blasted a laser hole completely through his head. Rumbee dropped instantly back to his seat, then tumbled on to the floor...dead as a side of beef.

I said to the Marines, "Please hall this piece of shit out to the dump."

The Marines grinned hugely, followed immediately by the general.

Once Rumbee was out, I said, "Ambassador Percee, we haven't heard much from you. Actually, we didn't give you much of a chance. Would you address this group and kindly tell us what we should do with you and why we shouldn't condemn you to death for your war crimes?"

Ambassador Percee slowly stood so he could be heard and not be shot in the process and said, "I understand your questions and concerns, and I certainly understand how you may think badly of me. From your viewpoint I might be wondering the same thing, but I need you to see things from my point of view also. I want you to understand the pure evil you had brought within your protection."

"I and the humans of Markee have been at war with the Supreme Leader and his minions for hundreds of years. He and his followers enslaved the humans, reduced them to animals, fed upon them, and brutalized them and those that tried to support them. I began organizing the humans and fought back. It took us hundreds of years to finally win the war. Many died in the process, including the majority of the Sheree. Once the humans tasted revenge and lust for battle, they got out of control and killed Sheree indiscriminately, good and bad. I survived just barely, and I was able to save the Sheree scientists, as you know."

"I was just regaining control of the humans when you come along and liberated our arch enemy, Rumbee. You then attacked us and rescued the remaining Sheree scientists and liberated most of the Sheree technology. I naturally believed you were under Rumbee's control, and with the Sheree technology you possessed, Rumbee would be able to wage a renewed war with us. Under those conditions you could win, and Rumbee would be restored to power. He would wipe out all the humans on Markee."

"I had to fight back, and to do that I recruited the Gaters and Moors. Both of these races have experienced the cruelty of the Supreme Leader. The Gaters owed me, because my group freed them from the Sheree and transported them here. The Gaters were nothing more than food for the Sheree leadership. The Gaters are sentient beings and remembered what I did for them and willingly joined me. The Moors didn't need much of an excuse, since they live for war. All I had to do was offer them technology."

"Yes, we fought against you, but we were after Rumbee to break his control of you. We hoped to save you. We could have won, too, but you surprised me, and you captured me and the last of my Plasma Bubbles. So here we are now, both of us thinking we were in the right. Sadly, we were both wrong, but we had a common enemy."

"I want to thank you for allowing Renee to visit with me. He has revealed much to me, and I stand in awe of your group. I am especially thankful for your group's help to save the Sheree race and help us reproduce. Without your help our race would soon die out."

"Renee and the other Sheree say they give you their allegiance freely and that none of you, especially you, Admiral, were under Rumbee's control. I was wrong about that and came to the wrong conclusion, but you do have to admit that your actions appeared to be in support of Supreme Leader, Rumbee. Rumbee was quite capable of influencing his will upon humans, even forcing his will. He may very well have subtly influenced your actions, but it appears that you were supporting him for your own purposes. He would have welcomed that, and it would have been unnecessary to force his will. For this misunderstanding on my part I am truly sorry, but I hope you understand why I came to that conclusion."

"Renee tells me that my armies have been totally decimated, and that I am the only one left. You fight well, and I totally underestimated your abilities. I lost the battle, and I regret the loss of my solders and allies. Well, I don't necessarily regret the loss of the Moors. I would have had to fight them eventually. Still, I won the war if it prevented Rumbee from regaining control of all of us."

"I guess that is all I have to say. Renee also tells me you are a fair and just commander, so I willingly accept your judgment."

The general said, "You speak well, ambassador. I can see how you became an ambassador, and much you say is believable, except one thing. One of your armies attacked a helpless village and brutally killed all its inhabitants. You are responsible for all those deaths. You knew Rumbee wasn't in that village. Explain that."

The ambassador said, "That was unfortunate. That was not my intentions, but once I transported the Markee army I had little control of them. Remember, they have been brutalized and starved. Those humans are virtual animals because of the way they were treated. They have absolutely no education or morals and live in a primitive environment. There is no social structure. My control over them was at best very limited. They followed me because I identified the enemy for them and gave them a focus for their hate."

"Remember also that in every instance where I transported an army I located them far from villagers to give them a chance to escape. Sadly, that didn't work in this case."

"After this war my plans were to try to educate and civilize the Markee humans, but that would take centuries. Before I could start that I had to win the war. So, yes, they fought for me, but only to the extent that I could point them in the direction of the enemy and let them go. I couldn't control them."

I said, "Who wants a death sentence for Ambassador Percee?" I waited for a while, but no one spoke up. I certainly had mixed emotions about him. Part of me believed him or maybe wanted to believe him, but he had caused us a great deal of problems. We had survived all the challenges, and we were certainly stronger because of it. Because of him we had discovered the deceit of Rumbee and potential betrayal and threat of him. Without the ambassador we probably wouldn't have known until it was too late. We owed the ambassador for exposing the threat, and everyone knew this. This is probably why none called for his death.

It was Renee that broke the silence and said, "Admiral, we Sheree believe him. Those of us Sheree stationed on these remote worlds were aware of the unrest on Markee and the start of the war before our isolation. Ambassador Percee even visited us on Genesis Two to solicit our help, but he received a hostile welcome from the Respected Leader here on Genesis Prime. What he has said sounds true, and we would know if he was full of deceit. We would allow him to join with our Sheree community if you allowed. I can promise you this: if we find that he has lied or tries to undermine our security or our relationship with you, I will execute him myself."

That revelation was somewhat startling, coming from the Sheree, and I knew Renee was not just speaking for himself. They shared a common bond of agreement.

I said, "I'm inclined to go along with Renee's proposal, within limits, and I think most of you here are as well. Still, I would like to hear any disagreements." I waited. "Very well. Ambassador Percee, it looks like you will be allowed to live, but I caution you that you will be watched closely."

The ambassador said, "Renee was correct. You and your group are fair, and you will not regret your decision."

Over the last two months the colony has prospered and grown. Food production was at an all-time high, the ore refinery was producing a high volume of Wonder Metal, and most important, we were safe, except for an isolated snakebite death or run in with a saber tooth cat. We maintained guards, but there was no real danger. In short, I was getting bored.

The only challenge I had received was the ambassador's offhanded comment about trying to introduce education among the Markee humans. To make that a reality we sent the saucer to Markee on several occasions and captured several isolated groups of humans on Markee and force fed education through the META unit. They truly were animals and were dragged in kicking and screaming, like Homer had, and were redeposited on Markee with an abundance of knowledge, hopefully with enough to begin a cultural change on their home world. Once that project was complete, life got boring again.

Akiko, Katy, and myself had begun to discuss other options for ourselves. We were immortal and our lives together would be extremely long, and if they were uneventful, our lives would seem far too long. We knew we had to excite our lives and find ways to introduce new challenges, or we would die of boredom.

It wasn't just the three of us. In various conversations with others of my key staff, I heard much of the same concerns. It was with these thought in mind that I called for a staff meeting.

When they were all assembled I said, "Akiko, Katy, and I have been talking. We want to explore the Galaxy." I just let that settle on all in the room.

Doc said, "You're not going without Linda and I."

Taka said, "I echo that feeling."

"Me either." added Kim.

Homer said, "You're not going without Naomi and I."

The general said, "Margret and I are going, too, and all the original Marines will want to go, the immortal Marines."

Renee blurted, "The Sheree want to go, too.

Calvin Kline joined in, "I have to go with you. It might take forever to win some of you over to Jesus."

I said, "I was hoping all the immortals would want to go. I think it would be best if we immortals stick together, and allow the colony to grow without us forever leading. I'm thinking we can find a new Mount Olympus and start a new colony of immortals somewhere else, while we search for new adventures.

I said, "Dr. Rothchild, your French team was leaving Earth to face a major challenge in survival. I dare say you and your crew missed and skipped over about 150 years of that struggle, but we are going to thrust you back into that fight. When we leave you will be in charge of this colony. We have seen that you are capable of making the hard decisions necessary for survival. But, and this is a big but, just so you don't get overzealous, we will remain in control and return from time to time to check on you."